THE LEGACY SOARS!

The Legacy Soars!

CHERYL DEVENNEY

A lot happened in America during the nearly four years of World War II. With the bombing of Pearl Harbor in 1941, the country went from a nation which had finally emerged from a devastating depression to a world superpower of citizens hell-bent on fighting the Nazi and Japanese regimes. Building a strong military force was essential to retain our freedom at all costs, but ultimately not the only tool in winning the war.

Uniting the civilian population for the common cause of defeating Hitler, Mussolini, and Hirohito was essential. As a result, the U.S. government set out to mobilize civilians from all walks of life to "do their part for the war effort." *THE LEGACY SOARS!* is about one family's contribution to fighting the war on the Homefront.

PRESENT DAY

San Diego, California

Carly sighed as she and her friend Alexis walked out of their classroom on the campus of the West Coast School of Design in San Diego. "I love my classes," she said, "but I'm ready for this long Thanksgiving weekend. I really should use the time to work on my semester project, though. December 17th is getting awfully close."

"I know what you mean," Alexis said. "I'll be pulling a lot of all-nighters to finish mine on time. But I need a break, so Tyler and I are going club crawling on Friday night."

Carly ran her fingers through her long blond hair. "God, I haven't done that for a while."

"Hey,"—Alexis stopped— "why don't you come with us?"

"I don't know—I wish Dylan were here to go with me. You know how close we've gotten since we met last summer."

"But he's in New York State. Besides, it's only one night. You've been working hard, and you need to unwind a little." As Carly got into her car, Alexis continued to plead. "Oh, come on, Carly. We'll have a blast."

"Well," Carly said as she pondered the idea, "I do have a new dress I just finished—"

"Good. We'll pick you up about 9:30."

———

Carly, the only child of a single mom, had traveled to Kingsburg, in Central New York State, the previous summer to meet the family of her recently deceased father, whom she'd never known. She had great memories of getting to know her cousin Brooke. They had been slow to warm up to each other but soon became good friends.

Brooke had introduced her to Dylan Moran, a tall, dark-haired guy with blue eyes and a quick wit. In between visiting with her newly discovered grandmother and other family members, she and Dylan had gone out a couple of times. Unlike the guys she usually dated, Dylan had manners and treated her like she was special. When she returned home, they began a long-distance relationship via texting, social media, and phone calls. Through their correspondence, she found a soulmate who could relate to her life experience, having come from a broken home himself.

On Thanksgiving morning Carly pictured her New York relatives sitting around Aunt Sandra's dining room table, but she couldn't quite imagine what their celebration would be like. She picked up her phone and called Brooke.

"Hey, Brooke," she joked, after wishing her a happy holiday, "do your mom and grandma make Italian food along with the turkey on Thanksgiving Day?"

"How did you guess that?" Brooke said with a laugh. "It wouldn't be Thanksgiving without some manicotti on the side."

"Sounds delicious. Oh, it's so good to talk to you. I can't wait until you come visit over spring break," Carly said.

"Me, either. I want to spend every day at the beach!"

Carly reminded Brooke that her mom, Amanda, had promised if Carly's grades were good, she would be able to visit her father's family in Kingsburg the following summer.

Carly was especially looking forward to seeing Grandma again. She had told Carly fascinating stories about her own parents, Tina and Tommy Capello, during the 1930s. What an amazing surprise it had been to see a photo of Tina and discover how much Carly resembled her great-grandmother.

———

On Friday night, Alexis, Tyler, and Tyler's buddy Jared picked up Carly and drove to a local park. There they pulled out a bottle of whiskey and passed it around. They each had a few drinks and, headed for the Gaslamp District in San Diego. The historic strip of restaurants and clubs was a popular spot for drinking and dancing. Though Carly had been reluctant to go out, once they flashed their fake IDs at a crowded club, she wasted no time slipping into the vibe of the room. The energy surrounding her drew her in, and before she knew it, she was dancing with Jared.

After hitting three clubs, Jared hooked up with another girl. That didn't stop Carly from talking to and dancing with other people. When she'd had enough, she needed some relief from the stuffy room, so she slipped outside.

"Well, hello," said a voice in the dark.

She turned to see a guy appear out of the shadows and approach her.

He grinned. "Much cooler out here, isn't it?"

Carly blotted her forehead with a tissue. "Oh yeah."

"I noticed you on the dance floor. Are you here with a date?"

"I'm with some friends," she said.

"Feel like dancing with a new friend?"

Always a sucker for straight blond hair and a cute smile, she said, "Sure."

He grabbed her hand and walked her back inside to the dance floor. "By the way, I'm Zack."

"I'm Carly."

Leaning in, he murmured in her ear, "What do you do when you're not here?"

"I'm studying fashion design."

"No kidding," he said. "Did you make that dress?"

"Yeah. Like it?"

He stepped back, looked her up and down, and winked with approval.

"Are you in school?" she asked.

"No way. I race stock cars."

"Really?" she said with surprise. "That's cool. I've never known a race car driver."

"Ever been to a professional race?"

"No."

"We've got to change that."

"I'd love to."

At that moment, Alexis ran over to them. "Hey, kids, we're going to Tyler's loft. Meet you outside."

Carly looked at Zack for his reaction.

He grinned. "Sure, I'm game. Lead the way."

During the ride to Tyler's, Carly remembered Dylan and had second thoughts. *It's no big deal,* she told herself.

The group continued their partying at the loft, with music, booze, and Ecstasy. By four o'clock they had paired off into different rooms.

Zack threw himself onto the mattress on the floor in the living room. "Come on, Carly." He patted it. "Plenty of room for two here."

A woozy Carly flashed on Dylan's face, but the aphrodisiac she'd taken proved stronger than the memory, and she joined Zack on the bed. His kisses were warm and wet as they fondled each other. It took a while for him to acquire an erection and finally penetrate her. When he did, she welcomed him inside her and enjoyed the intimacy.

He climaxed, then slid onto the mattress beside her.

"Wow, you're terrific," he murmured as he took her into his arms. Carly snuggled against him and drifted off to sleep.

The next morning Carly tried to open her eyes but only managed to squint from the sunlight streaming into the unfamiliar room. She struggled to focus, and when she finally did, she was confused by her surroundings. Head pounding, she sat up and spotted a snoring Zack lying next to her. It took her a minute to remember how she'd gotten there.

"Zack," she mumbled.

Zack stirred, turning a bewildered face toward her. "Oh, hey, good mornin'." He pulled her against him. "Great night, wasn't it? I slept like a baby. How about you?"

"Oh yeah." She curled up in his arms.

"I'm not good with steady relationships." He pushed her hair out of her eyes. "But can I give you a call sometime?"

"Sure. I'm pretty busy with school, though."

He brushed her lips with his. "We'll just have to make time."

On the way home, she mumbled silently to herself. *Damn it, I should've stayed home and worked on my project. All I wanted to do was relax a little, not end up in bed with a stranger. And why do I feel so guilty? I've only seen Dylan a couple of times. Well, hopefully I'll never hear from Zack again.*

———

Two weeks later, when that night was a distant memory, she heard from Zack. He invited her to his racing competition the following weekend. He was a nice guy and she'd never dated a race car driver, so she accepted. It might be fun.

She found the race exciting and Zack attentive. He introduced her to his friends, and they all went out to celebrate his win.

Finally, alone in the car, he took her into his arms and kissed her.

"My place isn't too far from here. Want to see it?"

She knew what he really meant. He was happy and high on his win and wanted her to help him celebrate in bed.

Would that really be so bad? she asked herself. But Dylan's face appeared before her, and she hesitated.

"I'm sorry, Zack," she finally said. "I've got to get home."

Later that night in her own bed, she thought about Dylan. When they had met the year before, they were just acquaintances. Through their long-distance relationship they discovered their similar family circumstances, and they become good friends. But did that mean that her hanging out with someone else was betraying their friendship? With him so far away, she didn't see how it could possibly matter. Maybe she should have gone with Zack after all.

———

As if he'd sensed her thoughts, Dylan Face Timed her the following week. "Hey, Carly," he said after they exchanged greetings. "I'd like to come out there to visit you during winter break. Would that be good for you?"

She hadn't seen that one coming. "Really?" she said. "Do you think you could actually do that?"

"I've got some savings from my summer job, and I think seeing you is the best way I can spend it."

He sounded so excited, that she replied, "That would be so great," she said. "I can't wait to show you around the San Diego area. I know you'll love it."

"Sure, but not as much as I'll love seeing you," he said.

Over the following days, though Carly and Dylan began to plan for his visit, she kept their arrangements quiet for over a month. Finally, she told Zack that an old friend would be visiting for the next couple of weeks and not to expect to see her. Luckily, Zack seemed to take it in his stride.

She had yet to tell her mother. She needed the time to be sure that Dylan was coming and get up the courage to tell her. When she did break the news, she made light of it, saying that a guy she'd met in New York was coming out to visit, and she looked forward to seeing him.

"He'll be here from December 27th until January10th."

"But you'll be back in school on the 5th."

"I know, but that's a Thursday, and we'll have the weekend before he leaves."

"And the other days?"

"He can drop me at school and hang out at the beach."

Amanda sighed and scratched her head. "You're not planning on having him stay here, are you? I don't even know the boy."

"I figured you'd say that," Carly said, "so I found a local hostel and booked him in there."

"Good idea. That'll be much cheaper for him than a hotel."

———

When Dylan arrived, she found their encounter at the San Diego airport a little surreal. They hadn't actually spent much in-person time together, and she didn't know how to greet him.

Should we kiss? Awkwardly, she stood on her tiptoes and kissed his cheek.

He leaned over and gave her a quick hug. Grabbing his hand, she led him to the baggage claim area. While they waited for his bags to arrive and then walked to her car, they made small talk.

"Ah, this weather is great," Dylan said as he peeled his jacket off. "I left below-zero temperatures and huge snowbanks at home. Is it always like this here?"

"Pretty much. We get some rain occasionally. Oh, here's my baby." She pointed her key fob at her red Mustang.

Dylan grinned. "Nice."

When they walked into the house, Amanda met them at the door.

"So glad to finally get to meet you." She offered Dylan her hand. "I've heard so much about you."

"Thank you, uh—

"Oh, you can call me Amanda." She gestured Carly and Dylan to the couch in the living room. "I'll get us some soft drinks."

Carly breathed a sigh of relief. *So far, so good.*

After a few days of sightseeing, Carly introduced Dylan to some of her friends, who joined them clubbing a couple of times. To ensure that she and Dylan wouldn't run into Zack, she made sure she and Dylan steered clear of the clubs and other haunts that she and Zack had frequented.

Still, Zack texted her often, telling her he missed her and looked forward to seeing her soon. She responded with cute emojis and said she missed him, too.

While she and Dylan spent their days tooling around the local beaches and attractions in her Mustang, they became reacquainted.

"You know, I've spent many a day this past six months, thinking about being with you again," Dylan said.

"Me, too," she said, a smile lighting her face. "But I thought it would be next summer in Kingsburg, not here in Encinitas."

Before long, she remembered all the things about Dylan that had attracted her when she'd met him in Kingsburg. He was different than most of the guys she'd dated, including Zack. His restraint was a novelty for her after knowing so many aggressive guys.

It took a few days, but it soon became normal for them to brush up against each other at every opportunity. Dylan eventually grabbed her hand or put his arm around her often throughout the day. It seemed like the thing to do, and she liked the way his hand locked into hers so naturally.

One night when Dylan was out of earshot, Amanda said, "Carly, I see the way Dylan looks at you. Does he know about Zack?"

"No. And Zack doesn't know anything about him, either."

Amanda shook her head and grinned. "I have to say, it's going to be fun watching you juggle these guys."

Carly stuck her tongue out at her mother in jest.

Amanda chuckled. "Just remember, it could blow up on you if these guys get wise to what you're doing."

Carly took her mother's warning with a grain of salt. Dylan was a sweet guy, and she wished he lived close by, but a long-distance relationship was hard to maintain. She liked Zack and wanted to keep him in her life after Dylan left Encinitas.

———

One day, with her mother at work, Carly and Dylan took advantage of the empty house and explored their physical relationship. Kissing, fondling, and unsure of how far the other would go, they hesitated before taking the next step. Dylan was a wonderful kisser, though Carly couldn't help but compare his tentative lovemaking with Zack's self-confident manner.

Preoccupied, they barely heard the pounding at the front door.

"Carly, what's that noise?"

"What?" She listened, heard the knocking, and went to the door with Dylan right behind her.

"Zack!" she said as she opened the door.

Zack barged in, took one look at Dylan, and grabbed a handful of his t-shirt. "So. This is your visiting friend!"

Carly peered into Zack's eyes and could see he was high on something. "Zack, this is Dylan."

Zack ignored her and hurled a punch at Dylan's face, but he was off balance and his punch barely connected.

"Listen," Carly said, "Dylan's just a friend."

Zack sneered at her. "You mean like I was just a friend that night in the loft?"

"No, I—"

Zack threw another punch, but Dylan, who stood about six inches taller, had heard enough. He grabbed Zack and locked his arms down.

"Zack," Carly said, "please go home. I'll call you tomorrow."

Zack jerked himself out of Dylan's grasp and slammed the door on his way out.

Dylan dropped down onto the sofa. "So, I'm just a friend, huh? I wish I'd known that before I spent all my savings to see you."

Carly edged into a chair, her gaze directed to the floor.

"I'm going back to my room and book a flight on the next plane to New York. I'm sure when Zack hears I'm gone, he'll be back."

"No, Dylan, don't leave. I feel like we're just really getting to know each other, and I want to give us chance."

"It's not that simple. I can't hang around just being your buddy, until you figure out who you want."

"But I thought we were good friends."

"Carly, that's not enough for me. From your emails, I thought you felt the same way."

She joined him on the couch and wrapped her arms around him. "Can we start over?"

He answered by giving her a long sensual kiss.

"Mm," she murmured.

They sprawled out on the couch, and he took her into his arms. When he kissed her softly, she responded with a deeper kiss, took his hand, and led him upstairs to her bedroom. Taking her cue, he pulled her onto the bed where he made his way down her body with his lips, stopping to gather her breasts in his hands. He alternated sucking each nipple until she moaned for more.

Continuing down her torso with his tongue, he passed her hips and found the precise spot, where he lingered until she cried out as she climaxed. After allowing Carly a few moments to recover, Dylan eased his body over hers and slipped inside of her. He swayed gently before making several thrusts, until she came again as he exploded inside of her.

That's when Carly learned the difference between satisfying a boy's sexual needs and being with a man who made love to *her*. He had touched her the way no one had ever done and put her emotional and physical needs above his own. She felt closer to him than she had ever dreamed she could be with anyone.

———

The next day, as they cuddled on the couch and she faced the thought of him leaving, she blurted out, "I wish you went to school here. Then we could be together like this all the time."

"Me, too," he said and kissed her forehead. "I don't want to leave you."

They talked about him attending a Los Angeles college the following year. He could complete his third year at his New York college at home and continue at a four-year school in the LA area. That way, Carly would finish her two-year fashion design program at the same time he graduated. He and Carly spent the last days of their time together checking out college options and choosing his favorites from among the available possibilities.

For a couple of weeks after Dylan left, Carly threw herself back into her schoolwork, but on the weekends she moped around the house. Amanda saw her lying on the couch watching reruns of her favorite shows once too often.

"Carly, you haven't gone out with your friends since Dylan left. Why don't you call them?"

"Uh, I don't feel like it."

"I've never seen a boy stop you from seeing your friends."

Carly shrugged.

"You like him a lot, don't you?"

"Yes. If you must know"—she sat up—"I've never liked any boy as much as I like him. I think he's *the* one."

"So, I guess Zack is out of the picture now."

"Yeah."

"What changed your mind?"

Carly didn't know how to tell her that Dylan was a fantastic lover.

Her mother smiled. "I understand. He's a very nice guy, and . . . he's great in bed."

Carly, embarrassed, pulled her knees together and up to her chin.

"But you're so young, and you have school to think about."

"I know. That's why he's going to apply to a school in LA. So, he'll be close when I'm at the LA campus next year."

Amanda's eyes widened. "Wow. You've got this all planned out. Are you sure that's a good idea?"

"Sure, why not?"

"What about your design career?"

"What about it?"

"How can you concentrate on that while you're pre-occupied with seeing Dylan?"

"I'll manage."

Her mother started to disagree but seemed to have second thoughts.

"OK," she said, and left the room.

———◆———

As she often did, Carly called her grandmother in Kingsburg to share her progress toward her fashion degree.

After bringing Grandma up to date, she said, "Mom has promised me another vacation in Kingsburg and I'm getting so excited about visiting you this summer.

"Oh, that's wonderful," Grandma said. "We'll have a great time. I'll show you more pictures of Tina and Tommy. And Tina saved some interesting things from the war years that I think you'll like."

"I'd love to see all of them. Now that I'm actually studying fashion design, I feel closer than ever to Tina."

Carly heard the front door open and close as her mother came home from work. "OK, Grandma. I'm looking forward to that. Love you." She ended the call as her mother entered the room.

"Who were you talking to, Carly?"

"Grandma in New York. She said to say hi to you."

Amanda sighed. "That's nice. But didn't you just talk to her last week?"

———◆———

As the semester progressed Carly immersed herself in classes and projects and received kudos from her design instructors. She continued to stay in touch with her cousin Brooke in Kingsburg and looked forward to Brooke's visit to San Diego during spring break. But a few weeks before the date, Brooke called to cancel her trip.

"I'm so sorry, Carly," she said, sounding anything but sorry. "I've got the chance to attend a seminar the navy is offering, and I just couldn't turn it down."

"I don't understand."

"Well, if I join the service—"

"You? Join the service?"

"Yes. I'm thinking about it. They will pay for me to finish my education. Plus, having the opportunity to travel with the navy and get a great education at the same time has been at the back of my mind for a long time. I have to give it a try."

Carly didn't really understand Brooke's desire to be a sailor, but she couldn't argue with someone pursuing her dream. "Then you have to do it."

Nevertheless, for the next two days, Carly sulked. "Spring break won't be any fun at all," she complained to her mother over dinner. "There's nothing to look forward to, now that Brooke has something 'more important' to do."

"Don't be so sure," her mom said, reaching into her briefcase and retrieving an envelope. Her eyes twinkled in anticipation as Carly opened it.

"Whaaaat?! A week in Hawaii?!" Carly waved the airline tickets wildly and grabbed her mom in a bear hug.

Eyes shining, her mom hugged her back.

That hug made Carly realize how long it had been since she had spent any real time with her mom or had had a heart-to-heart talk the way they used to. She'd been so focused on Dylan, her summer plans, and her New York relatives that she'd shut her mom out of her life. She made up her mind to change that during this vacation together.

As Carly and her mom soaked up the sun on the beach at Waikiki, Dylan's name came up, although Carly had attempted to avoid the subject ever since they arrived.

"I'm sure you've noticed how many cute boys have given you the eye," her mom said. "Just since we've been out here today."

Carly smiled. "I saw a couple. It's been good for my ego."

"Don't you feel a slight bit tempted?"

"I haven't seen anyone that's looked better than Dylan."

"What is it about Dylan that is so much better than the guys here or at home?"

"He's just different. So many guys only think about themselves. He's more concerned about me, and I like that."

On a day in early May, Carly's phone rang. With heart racing, she checked the caller ID, and saw it was Dylan.

"Dylan!" she said. "Oh, it's great to hear from you." She hesitated, then asked the question that had been on her mind for weeks. "Any news about an LA school?"

He chuckled in that cute way of his. "Well—" he said, drawing out the word for suspense —"I just got an acceptance letter from the private university."

All of a sudden Carly's world brightened.

When she told her mom the news, she sensed that Amanda didn't welcome it. Carly suspected that Amanda had secretly hoped that Dylan would not be accepted to a California school. *Well,* Carly thought, *I'll just have to show her that I can have Dylan and my own career, too.*

———◆———

The first week in July had finally arrived, and Carly was packing her suitcases for her three-week visit. This was a day she'd been longing for since visiting Kingsburg last summer, but even more so since Dylan had spent winter break with her. As she packed, she couldn't help but remember doing the same thing last year, and how she had dreaded having to go. What a remarkable difference a year made. She could never have imagined that meeting her father's family would change her life so much.

Brooke and Grandma met Carly at the airport with hugs and kisses. They couldn't stop talking all the way home as they passed the same trees, rolling hills, and green fields that Carly remembered from the previous summer. But unlike last year, Carly now saw them as the promise of an exciting vacation ahead with her extended family.

They drove to Brooke's house, where they were greeted with kisses and hugs by Carly's Aunt Sandra and Uncle John, Brooke's parents. Later that day, the rest of the family joined them for dinner to celebrate Carly's return. Carly greeted them at the door with hugs and kisses. Her grandma's sister, Aunt Maria, and her husband, Joey, on whose farm Carly had stayed last year, came with their daughter Charlotte and her husband Walter. Their daughter, Christina, a recent MBA graduate came too.

The group reminisced about meeting Carly last year, and how she had redesigned Brooke's teen beauty contest dress at the last minute.

"I'm still convinced that I wouldn't have even won second place if Carly hadn't altered that goofy dress Mom picked out into such a cool one," Brooke said, causing a pleased Carly to blush in embarrassment.

This time she would be staying at her Aunt Sandra's house and share Brooke's room. The two cousins were inseparable for the first couple of days as they caught up on each other's lives. She enjoyed her time with Brooke, but soon, all Carly could think about was being with Dylan again.

The next day, as the girls shared their favorite TikTok videos, Aunt Sandra called up the stairs, "Carly, you have a visitor, and he's pretty cute."

Carly flew out of the bedroom and down the stairs. "Oh my God," she cried, "Dylan! I thought you said you had to work today."

He grabbed her off the last step and spun her around. "I did, but I called in sick."

Putting her down, he kissed her long and hard, until she nuzzled her face against his chest. "Oh my God, I missed you," she said.

"I was counting on that. I missed you, too."

Dylan joined the family for dinner, and she and Dylan made small talk until they could excuse themselves, saying that they were going to a movie.

Brooke smirked, and with a perceptive look, told them to enjoy themselves.

Carly mouthed, "Thank you," and pulled Dylan through the door.

———◆———

Later that week, Carly and Dylan saw each other on his two days off. Unlike a lot of Southern California, the area didn't have freeways that took them from town to town. They drove the backroads lined with trees and fields that went for miles. Driving off the road, they looked for remote spots, hidden from passing traffic, to climb in the cargo area of his SUV.

That still left plenty of opportunity for her to enjoy what the family called their summer camp on Liberty Lake. Four days after Carly arrived, she, Grandma, Aunt Sandra, and Brooke drove the familiar road to the lake.

"The house looks beautiful," Carly said as she walked into the lake home and noticed the redecorating the family had done to the already charming house. With plenty of luxurious bedrooms and baths and a gourmet kitchen, it was much more than a *camp*. They had even refurbished some of the already lovely rooms of the house over spring break, keeping it up to date with current trends.

"Well, Mom had a hand in that," Brooke said, winking at her mother. "She loves to redecorate."

The four of them spent two weeks at the lake house. Carly loved seeing the lake again. If anything, it seemed more beautiful than ever. The crystal-clear water beckoned them. Dylan and Brooke's dad arrived for the weekend, and Carly spent it waterskiing and boating during the day and cuddling with Dylan around the campfire at night.

The second weekend of Carly's visit. Aunt Maria, Uncle Joey, her cousin Christina, and her boyfriend, Phil, joined the family Saturday for a small reunion. They all seemed to really like Dylan, and that pleased Carly. She couldn't imagine a better way to spend her summer vacation.

Dylan and Brooke's parents left on Sunday night. Aunt Sandra left her car and drove home with Brooke's dad, but Carly, Brooke, and Grandma stayed on a couple of more days to tidy up the camp. As they worked, Carly remembered having had to clean the lake house for Brooke's graduation party the past summer.

"You don't know how much I resented you, Brooke, for having to clean this place for your party last year."

"And you did such a great job!" Brooke said with joking sarcasm.

Carly threw a pillow at her and mouthed "bitch" in jest, so that Grandma wouldn't hear her.

When they finished their work, they plopped down on the sofa and admired their job.

Soon, Grandma excused herself, and when she came back, she had two photo albums in her arms.

"Girls, I spent the better part of last year searching for and organizing all the family photos and mementos that I could find. Then I had copies made of them and created these albums for each of you. They are like a story of our family in pictures. Would you like me to go through them with you?"

"Oh, cool," Carly said. "I loved hearing about Tina last summer. When I'm working on my own designs, I always think of her, and how strong and wonderful she was to achieve what she did during the Great Depression. She's a real inspiration for me to keep going when I get discouraged."

Grandma nodded. "A big part of these albums is from World War Two. When the war came along, everything got harder for her and the whole family."

"Even harder than the Depression?" Carly asked with surprise.

"Yes, in many ways it was."

"Grandma," Brooke chimed in, "Mom always told me that I'm headstrong, just like Tina's sister, Eva."

"Oh, you're right. She had a mind of her own, and she didn't worry about what others thought of her. She did something very impressive during the war."

"Oh, Grandma, tell us. We'd love to hear it. Right, Carly?"

"Absolutely."

"But wait," Brooke said as she got up from the couch. She went to the kitchen, and in a moment, she returned with soft drinks for everyone.

Then she settled into her chair. "OK," she said. "Now."

PRELUDE TO WAR

(Kingsburg, New York—1937)

Inside Irene's Dress Shop, Tina's best friend Rosie sat across the table from Tina and her sister Eva. Rosie and Eva were helping Tina decide on her wedding gown and bridesmaid dresses.

"Whew!" Irene said as she joined them. "I finally could put the CLOSED sign in the window." Irene was an old friend of the Benedetti family who had stepped in as a surrogate mother to Tina, Eva, Angelo, and Carmen after their mother's death five years before. Tina had begun her career as a fashion designer while working at Irene's shop and later became half owner.

"You sure are more enthusiastic about planning this wedding than your last one," Rosie said with a mischievous wink.

"Yeah, I can't imagine why," Eva teased.

"Well, that's how it should be," Irene said. "I didn't say anything at the time, but I really worried that you barely had the time for Eddie until practically the last minute. I knew that something wasn't right."

Tina and Tommy had announced their engagement to a roomful of citizens at the school building dedication two weeks before, and they had wasted no time before choosing June 26 as their wedding date. Unlike last time, Tina made most of the plans. It would be a small affair compared to the wedding that restaurant owner Eddie Pecora had arranged for Tina and himself the previous year.

———◆———

Church bells rang out promptly at nine o'clock in the morning on June 26th, announcing High Mass inside the south side's St. Paul's Catholic Church. Tina and Tommy had belonged to this parish in the Italian section of town since childhood. The officiating priest, Father Milano, was a family friend.

Standing beneath the familiar stained-glass window, Constantina Benedetti and Battista Tommaso Capello took their long-awaited vows before God and their loved ones. After the wedding breakfast and a sitting with the out-of-town photographer, Tina and Tommy dashed home to change for their trip to a honeymoon retreat in the Catskill Mountains. Friends and family hugged them and wished them well as they left for their three-hour ride in Tommy's work truck with a JUST MARRIED sign hanging from the back.

———◆———

Tina opened her eyes in the sunny honeymoon suite and smiled down at her new husband, snoring next to her. She leaned over and quieted him with a passionate kiss until he woke and responded.

"Good morning," she said, then turned to get out of bed. "Come on, get up. I can't wait to see this place and the grounds. It was too dark to see anything when we got here last night."

He grabbed the back of her negligee. "Whoa. You can't kiss me like that and take off. Come back here."

She turned to him, smiling.

"I like the view from right here," he said, and pulled her into his arms.

———◆———

The three-day honeymoon flew by as they swam, canoed, and explored the sprawling grounds.

On their last night, Tina rested her head on Tommy's shoulder as they swayed to "Moonglow" in the resort ballroom.

"This really has been like a dream," she said. "I'm afraid I'm going to wake up in my bed at Pa's house to spend another day without you."

He placed his finger beneath her chin and tilted her face so he could see her eyes. "And I thought I'd lost you when you got engaged to that lying cheat, Eddie. If no one had discovered he sabotaged my work on the school building—Well, I don't know how I would've handled seeing you two married." He placed his cheek on hers and held her tighter. "I love you so much, honey."

"Oh, Tommy," she said, her voice tender, "I never thought I could be so happy."

The next evening, Tina and Tommy had an early dinner so that they would arrive home well before dusk. As they approached their house, they passed by kids still playing out in their street. Then the truck tires crunched their way onto their makeshift driveway. Tommy turned off the engine and leaned over to give her a soft kiss on the cheek.

"Well, here we are, honey. Home sweet home."

Tina looked across the lawn to what had once been a shabby cottage, now transformed by Tommy into a cute white dollhouse with a kitchen, living room, three bedrooms, and a bathroom—including a shiny white tub. "It's beautiful." She snuggled into his chest, resting there for a moment.

Then she jolted up, smiling, grabbed the car door handle, and said, "Last one in has to carry in the suitcases!"

A week after their honeymoon, Tina and Tommy invited the Benedetti family for Sunday dinner. Tina's father, Dominic, a foreman on the railroad, brought Irene with him. The two had been very close since acknowledging their love for each other the previous year. Tina's brothers, Angelo, 19, and Carmen, 11, arrived together.

"Oh, Tina, I love the pretty, bright colors you've chosen for the walls and furniture," Irene gushed. "Don't you, Dom?"

"Oh, uh, yes," he said, and eyed Tommy. "You're a pretty good builder, son." He pounded the wall to test its strength.

Tommy beamed. "Thanks, uh, Pa. That means a lot coming from you."

While they waited for Eva to arrive, Tina and Tommy showed everyone around their cozy home, pointing out the tiny touches that Tommy had added to make it inviting.

As they returned to the dining room, Tina asked, "Shall we keep waiting for Eva?"

"Nah," Carmen said. "We've waited plenty long enough."

Everyone seemed to agree, so they took their places around the table.

Tina took the minestrone from the stove. She'd prepared it in same pot their mother had used. The family agreed it was almost as good as her mother's, so by the time Eva got there the soup was almost gone.

"Sorry I'm late," she said as she took her place at the table, "but the night waitress didn't show, and the boss had to call someone else in."

"Well, your loss. You missed Mama's minestrone," Angelo said.

Baked lasagna and salad followed the minestrone, topped off with a homemade rum cake.

"Great meal, sis," Angelo said to Tina as he pushed away from the table.

"Yeah," said Carmen, "I miss your cooking." He looked over at Eva and pinched his nose. "Now you're married, we're stuck with Eva's cooking."

Eva stuck her tongue out and threw her napkin at him.

Their banter melted Tina's heart, because she often experienced the pangs of homesickness since she'd moved out of her father's house.

In the next couple of months, the town showed Tommy their confidence in him as a general contractor. Capello Building was doing well. In fact, he had barely trained several new workers before he needed to hire more. His late hours didn't bother Tina. She loved seeing him finally able to enjoy his work and gain the respect of his customers.

And Tina found married life didn't significantly affect the time she could spend on her design work. With Tommy so busy, she even had time for occasional outings with Rosie and her year-old daughter. She and her best friend stayed close, even though their plans often included little Elena. Of course, things would probably change with Rosie expecting her second baby any day.

———◆———

In August of 1937, Tina peeked into Rosie's hospital maternity room and saw her dozing. She tiptoed to her bedside and placed the bouquet of flowers on the table.

Rosie stirred and squinted. "Tina, have you been here long?" She rubbed her eyes and sat up in the bed.

"Just walked in. How are you?

"I'm OK, but pretty sore. He was a big boy. Have you seen him?"

"Yes. He's so beautiful with all that black hair. So, his name is Francis, after Frankie?"

"Yes, and John as a middle name, for my father."

"That's sweet. Frankie sounded so excited and happy when he stopped by our house last night. I think Tommy is jealous."

"It'll happen for you guys."

"Not soon enough for Tommy," Tina said as she sat down on the chair next to the bed.

"What about you?"

"I like having this time to ourselves and for my work. That is, as long as I know that it will happen someday. I just worry that we might have a problem."

"Oh, that's silly. You've only been married a few months."

"That's true," Tina said. But Rosie didn't know that she and Tommy had been intimate with no protection at the cabin on the lake two years ago and during their two-month engagement.

———◆———

With no baby expected on the horizon and Tommy working so many hours, Tina took advantage of her freedom to further her design business. She picked up another design contract with a local manufacturer and traveled to NYC to meet with a manufacturer she'd worked with while living there.

As she got out of the cab at her Times Square hotel, the distinctive clamor and scent of the city reminded her that it had once held the promise of her dream to be a major fashion designer. Though her career had taken a different turn, the frenetic pace of the surroundings energized her and brought out the confidence she needed to promote her designs to the dress company.

Later, as she boarded the train for home, she experienced the familiar sense of loss that she'd had two years before upon leaving. But by the time the train arrived in Kingsburg, she had reconciled her feelings with the hefty check the company paid her for the line of women's suits that included mix-and-match skirts, blouses, jackets, and trousers—all of which would have her initialed logo, *CB*, on the tag. Who'd have guessed that she could have both Tommy and a design career, too?

———◆———

At the end of December 1937, twenty-three-year-old Eva broke her engagement to a high school friend she had resigned herself to marrying.

For the umpteenth time, her father said, "So, Eva, now that you broke up with Carl, what are you gonna do? You're not getting any younger, and you need to settle down with a nice boy."

"Thanks for reminding me, Pa," she said without hiding the sarcasm.

"Heh, it's true."

"Believe me, Pa, I'd like to find somebody, but I don't want to settle down, especially in Kingsburg, and certainly not with a townie with no plans to go anywhere else."

"What's-a matter with Kingsburg? Look at your sister. She thought she wanted to go to New York City, but she's happy now, right here, with her sewing."

"My sister has the design career that she always wanted and is lucky that the love of her life lives here. But me? I think dressmaking is boring. I'd rather wear pretty clothes than make them!"

"Well," her father said, "I don't know what's going to happen to you, and I worry."

She leaned over and gave him a peck on his check. "Don't worry, Pa. I'll be all right."

———

March of 1938, Eva first took the job at the train station diner, it was fun because she enjoyed talking to travelers coming and going from other places. But she soon learned that most of her customers were the same locals, commuting to and from nearby towns every day.

On this quiet Friday, as Eva joked around with one of them, she heard an unfamiliar voice from behind her at the other side of the counter.

"Uh, miss, can I interrupt your little party to bother you for a piece of apple pie and a cup of coffee?"

Eva twirled around and spotted a mustachioed man in a business suit. "No problem. So sorry I didn't see you there."

"I can't imagine why not," he snapped. "Can I get that pie now?"

"Yes. Coming right up." She glanced back at the previous customer with a smirk, rolled her eyes, and then fetched the rude man's pie and coffee.

She put the food down in front of him. "Here you are, sir," she cajoled. "Hope it sweetens your day."

Eva turned around and noticed that another customer had hopped up onto a stool. The man looked to be about thirty.

"What a jerk," he said to her.

She smiled, nodded, and said with sarcasm, "The customer is always right." She regained her friendly tone. "Now what can I get for you?"

She knew she hadn't seen him here before, or she would've remembered his blond waves, sunburnt nose, and cute grin.

"Oh, make it a ham-and-cheese sandwich and a lemonade."

"You got it. Be back in a minute." She went off to prepare the sandwich and drink.

When she placed the order in front of him, she had to ask, "You're not from around here, are you?"

"How can you tell?"

She shrugged. "I've never seen you, and we get our share of out-of-towners through here."

"As a matter of fact, I'm not. I'm from Albany, but I'm a cargo pilot out of Kingsburg airfield."

"No kidding? I heard that they've opened that up recently, now that businesses are starting to come back to town. So, you actually fly the planes?"

"Yeah, it's my job."

"I thought most goods went by train."

"That's starting to change. Some companies have high-priority cargo that needs to get there faster, and the planes are getting more reliable."

"Wow, that must be exciting. But isn't it dangerous?"

"Not if you know what you're doing up there."

She grinned. "And you do, huh?"

"I've been flying since I was a teenager. My uncle flew with the Lafayette Escadrille in France during the Great War and taught me everything he knew."

Eva flashed a smile. "So, Mr. Flier, what brings you to the train station today?"

"One of the other pilots is going home to Massachusetts for the weekend, and he needed a ride to and from the station." He sipped his drink. "Hey," he said with a charming grin, "since I'm grounded here till he gets back, how about we take in dinner and a movie tomorrow night? And maybe you can show me around town."

Eva didn't hesitate. "Sure," she said, then called over her shoulder into the kitchen, "Irma, if you cover my Saturday night shift, I'll return the favor next week."

She couldn't pass up the chance to go out with pilot Glenn Peterson. She'd dated a few out-of-towners in the past, hoping the dates might lead to more than a night out. But she found out the hard way that the men only wanted a certain kind of girl for a quick one-night stand. Even though the chances were good that her date with Glenn would follow the pattern, she didn't care. The fact that he was a pilot intrigued her. She'd never met anyone who had flown in an airplane, let alone piloted one.

———◆———

Saturday night came quickly for Eva. She carefully dressed in her best outfit and walked to Glenn's hotel, where they had dinner in the dining room. Conversation came easily, and Eva was charmed. As she and Glenn strolled toward the movie theater afterward, the March breeze caused her to button her coat. She listened wide-eyed to the stories of his escapades in the air. Neither of them noticed when they walked right past the theater. But that didn't matter. No fiction film could top his real-life adventures amid the clouds.

"But aren't you ever scared up there?" she asked.

"I've had my moments, but I'm an excellent pilot."

She smiled. "You've got a pretty big ego, haven't you?"

"I guess so, but you have to reach a point where you have confidence in yourself up there, or you're doomed. The fact is, there are far more car accidents, and yet lots of people still drive cars."

"That's true," she said. "I'm never afraid when I drive a car. I don't know about a plane though."

"What d'ya say I take you for a spin up there sometime?"

"Oh, would you? When?"

He grinned. "How about tomorrow?"

Eva tossed and turned in bed that night. Glenn intrigued her. Never in a million years could she have imagined meeting someone like him in Kingsburg, a man with such a spirit of adventure. She worried that she couldn't compete with other, more worldly girls from bigger cities. And what if she hated flying—or worse, got airsick? She'd heard that some people did. She fretted over these things until nearly dawn and barely got up in enough time to make eight o'clock mass. She had arranged to meet Glenn at the bus stop at ten o'clock for a ride to the airfield.

When they arrived this quiet Sunday, Eva followed Glenn around the airport. She stood in awe as he pointed out the different planes lined up on the tarmac. Their massive size dwarfed her, but instead of feeling intimidated by them, she saw them as symbols of liberation. She couldn't wait to climb aboard and find out how it would feel to be carried into the sky.

He helped her into the two-seater cockpit and buckled her into her seat.

"So, are you ready to find out what it's like to fly?"

When she nodded, he flipped switches and twisted dials until the engine came alive with a roar, lifting her off her seat. As the plane began to move, she gripped the strap hanging next to her and gulped back her fear.

Speeding down the runway excited her, but as the plane rose, her stomach turned over, and she feared she might lose her breakfast. That sensation passed, and another took over, as her body resisted the climb that pulled her back into the seat.

"Try to relax and go with the feeling. Don't fight it," he said. "Take some deep breaths."

Eva tried her best to obey, but she couldn't calm down until the plane leveled off.

"That was fun," she said and looked out the window.

He smiled. "You get used to the takeoff, and then you'll love it. Take my word for it."

She hoped so, because she loved being up there, looking down on everything and everyone else. She couldn't imagine never experiencing this feeling again.

Eva found herself daydreaming about flying while filling salt and pepper shakers at work and while washing dishes at home. She looked forward to the times that Glenn came to town. They enjoyed each other's company, and never had a dull moment. They explored the countryside surrounding Kingsburg, went to dances, movies, and dinners.

But the thing she liked the most was when he took her up in his plane. He had been right. She soon got over her takeoff jitters and learned to love ascending gradually into the clouds. After a few months, he had taught her everything he knew about flying and even let her take the wheel sometimes.

In the late spring, she heard of an opening for a waitress in the airport coffee shop. She applied and got the job. She still had to sling food and deal with testy customers, but before her shift and during slow times at the coffee shop, she visited the flight line.

In only a few weeks, she became friendly with the ground crew and the other pilots. Despite their obvious attraction to her as a potential date, they finally realized that she had been bitten by the flying bug. They gave up asking her out and seemed to enjoy passing along everything they knew about flying airplanes. She gleaned so many things about aviation, planes, and pilots that it opened her world.

The more time she spent with them, the more she knew that being a passenger wasn't enough for her. She told them that she wanted to become a licensed pilot. A couple of the guys tried to discourage her, but before long, two of them were allowing her to co-pilot and later pilot their planes, and they began to document every hour she flew them.

She continued to date Glenn on the weekends once a month or so, but then his delivery route changed, and he didn't get to Kingsburg as often. When they were together, the subject of her flying always came up.

"So, I'm curious," he said one evening over dinner, "does your family know that you're flying planes?"

"Tina does, but I wouldn't dare tell my father. He'd have a fit. Besides, I'd rather break the news after I get my license. Then he'll know that I'm really serious about flying."

Glenn shrugged. "Well, I guess you know him better than I do."

She changed the subject. "What about you? I miss seeing you all the time. I thought we were pretty good friends—"

"That hasn't changed. I just figured that you didn't need me anymore now that the other pilots are taking you up."

"But that doesn't mean I don't want to spend time with you," she said.

"Well, this new company I'm working for keeps me pretty busy, and I'd hate for you to count on seeing me, and then I don't show."

"Still friends, though, right?" she asked.

"You bet." He leaned in and kissed her. "The best kind."

———

The more Eva talked to Tina about flying, the surer Tina became that Eva's main interest was to snag a handsome pilot.

"Those pilots are vagabonds," Tina told her one day as they sat visiting in Tina's kitchen over coffee and a slice of Tina's pizza fritte, sprinkled with sugar. "You shouldn't get too attached to them. They just want to show off so you'll go out with them. You may not remember—you were little then—but other flyboys have come to town in the past. They called themselves barnstormers, and they made a living performing aerial tricks and selling rides to the kids."

"Tina, just go up in a plane with me. Then you'll know what I'm talking about. Please."

Tina shook her head. "No thanks."

"Oh, come on, Tina. You're just being a chicken."

Tina didn't like being backed against a wall. She couldn't admit to Eva that the thought of flying frightened her. Though she had had the nerve to venture on the train to New York City on her own, she didn't understand what held planes up in the air, and she didn't really care. She always figured cars, trains, and boats were made for travel, and that's all she needed.

"Oh, all right. I'll go with you next Saturday," Tina lied, simply to change the subject. "So you'll stop annoying me."

———◆———

As the new year began, Tina worked either at Irene's shop or at home, depending on the task. She came to the shop to see customers for measurements and fittings or when her assignment called for a special tool or machine that she didn't have at home. One of her three bedrooms had become her workroom, and she loved the quiet and being able to spend time in her beautiful new house.

Some days when Tommy was out of town on a job, it could get lonely in the house. Those days, she would go to her father's house to help with the boys and cook meals for them. She found that she missed Carmen's ready laugh and Angelo's funny stories about the customers at his job. The two had become a little more self-sufficient out of necessity. Without her contribution to the family income, her father and Eva were working more, and the boys were forced to take on more household chores. She couldn't help but feel guilty about that, even though she had known that it would happen when she married.

Angelo still worked at Sarducci's Groceries, but he had been promoted to clerk and had worked full-time since graduating from high school. When not working or helping around the house, he split his time between dating girls and hanging out with his buddies. Carmen, though he wouldn't admit it, still needed supervision. That's when Irene filled the gap by cooking and helping him with his homework.

———

Tina and Tommy continued to try their best to get pregnant. The doctor had suggested they use a birth control technique that relied on her basal body temperature. She would take her temperature each morning before rising to see if she was fertile. When her temperature elevated during her cycle's ovulation time (usually a couple of weeks before her menstrual period), that was the best time to have sex to get pregnant.

She hated having to reduce the beautiful act of making love to something so calculating, but she really needed to find out if hers and Tommy's love could create a child.

Though she tried to focus on her work, the thought of having a baby dominated her thoughts. It had become an obsession. She began to think that since God had already blessed her with design talent and Tommy, having a baby might be asking too much.

———

One morning in April, she re-checked the chart she had made of her cycle. It told her that her period was late.

Now stay calm down, she told herself. *You know your periods are often erratic.* But she had to know, so she stopped at Dr. Channing's on her way to work to take a pregnancy test.

More than a week dragged on while she waited to hear. She decided to go to her father's house and busy herself with cooking and cleaning. That helped, but on her way home, she stopped at the doctor's office.

"Well, let me see," the nurse said as she thumbed through a stack of papers on her desk.

Tina bit her lip and shifted from one foot to another. *Oh, be there. I can't take waiting another day.*

"Ah, here's today's reports. I don't know how they got to the bottom of the stack. Uh, let me see."

Tina cleared her throat. *Oh, please God. Make it positive.*

"Well, Tina. Congratulations are in order. You're expecting."

The nurse scheduled an appointment for her to see the doctor the following week. Tina took the card without looking at it. At the moment, her mind was flitting from the thought of Tommy's face when she told him the news, to trying to comprehend what the news entailed. She had thought about the possibilities of it many times, but a jolt of panic hit her. *Oh my God. Can I do this?*

She had assumed that upon hearing the news, she would run to Rosie and tell her. Instead, she walked to the park, where she sat in silence before going home. She stroked her stomach with the realization of a life inside. It made her appreciate that talking about having a child and actually having one were two different things.

She had helped raise Carmen because her mother's poor health often prevented her from taking care of her son. When her mother died, Tina became his primary caregiver, so she was sure she knew how to raise a child. But she had never felt the full weight of that because she knew the biggest responsibility remained with her father. This would be different. The baby would be part of her and Tommy.

The awareness of that brought a smile back to her lips, and she hurried toward home to tell Tommy the good news.

On the way, Tina stopped by the grocery store to pick up the ingredients of Tommy's favorite supper. She would make baked eggplant parmesan, ziti macaroni, and braciole. She stopped by the bakery to pick up two pasticciotti for dessert. Luckily, Tommy was working close to home that day and would be coming home on time. She set the table with candles, changed into a new dress, and waited with anticipation.

He took one look at her and the table and turned to her with a grin.

"What's the special occasion?" he said, with hope in his voice.

She beamed, grabbed his hand, and placed it on her stomach. "Feel our baby?"

He looked into her eyes. "Really?"

She nodded, and he wrapped his arms around her. "When?"

"Around the first of January."

"I knew we could do it," he said, kissing her. "You're the best thing that ever happened to me."

———

With Tina needing to slow down as her pregnancy progressed, Irene began spending most late afternoons and early evenings at the Benedetti house, to be there for Dominic and the boys. Every week, Irene and Dominic would make Sunday dinner for the whole family. It became a way for everyone to catch up on each other's lives. Even Eva made a point of attending when her work and social life permitted.

On a Sunday at the end of June, Dominic stood and raised his wine glass.

"Please, let's toast to a special lady." He faced Irene. "She has done me the honor of accepting my proposal of marriage."

Carmen screamed as each one in the group voiced their approval of their father's announcement.

"It's about time," Angelo shouted.

Everyone agreed, and Eva asked when the wedding would be.
"We hope the church will have a free Saturday in July," Irene said.
"Yay," Carmen yelled.
"Oh my gosh." Tina said. "We've got to start planning right away."

It turned out that the plans would be simple with only the immediate family gathering in the church rectory on a sunny July morning. Irene carried a small bouquet of white baby roses and looked lovely and years younger in the light blue dress she had made. Dominic looked distinguished in his dark blue suit and silver hair while pacing around waiting for the priest to take his place.

Angelo, acting as best man, tugged on his own collar, while trying to adjust a squirming Carmen's bow tie. Tina, Irene's matron of honor, arrived on Tommy's arm, glowing, and looking stunning in a summer maternity dress.

But once the ceremony began, Tina couldn't hold back her emotion while listening to the priest's words, uniting her father and godmother as husband and wife.

Not surprisingly, tears moistened her eyes for the long-awaited union of the couple. But when she pictured her father speaking those same words to her mother many years ago, the tears began to puddle in her eyes and stream down her cheeks. She thought she might have to excuse herself, but she looked over at Carmen with a huge grin on his face, and it warmed her heart. She took a deep breath, brushed away her tears with one of her mother's hankies, and knew that Mama was smiling down on the family.

———

During the month of November, Tina spent most of her time at home at the sewing machine. She had arranged to have all her design orders finished by the end of the month in order to devote the whole month of December to preparing for the baby's arrival. She and Tommy had the nursery ready after the first week. That left her the rest of the month to concentrate on sewing baby clothing and blankets, which she had begun designing as soon as she found out she was pregnant.

Tommy made sure that he didn't schedule any out-of-town jobs for December and January. He had promised Tina that he would be there for her and the baby the first month. By the middle of December, they knew they would be dealing with snowstorms and freezing temperatures, so Tommy scheduled one-day-only jobs, mostly in the valley.

But mid-December's weather surprised them all. The characteristic high snowbanks did not materialize because the temperature went no lower than forty degrees at night. A week before Christmas, the typically elusive sun brought daytime temperatures up to the seventies and people outside in their shirt sleeves. So, when Tommy received an emergency call from a former customer whose pipes had burst from an underground explosion, he didn't hesitate. He jumped into his truck and took off for the town fifteen miles west of Kingsburg.

The short December day ended, and darkness set in while he worked underground. When he went back up to call Tina to let her know when he'd be home, he looked out the window and saw the ground blanketed in snow that sparkled in the moonlight. He smiled with surprise and placed the call. When it didn't go through, he decided to go outside and find another phone.

As he stepped out, his legs sank into the snow, buried up to the knees. Around him, the snow had covered the streets, sidewalks, and cars. Traffic lights blinked, and horns honked as drivers called for help from the police officers and firefighters attempting to rescue them from their prospective tombs.

Tommy's only choice was to go back inside, finish his job, and hope to God that the snowplows would clear the streets enough for him to get home. In the meantime, he continued trying to reach Tina. She had to be worried, and that wouldn't be good for her and the baby right now.

———

At home, Tina had finished sewing a baby bunting: a cute, quilted long jacket closed at the bottom and zipped up the front. She had chosen a pale-green fabric with a tiny baby-rattle print. It could be good for either a girl or boy and would be perfect to bring baby home in on a chilly winter day.

She looked out the window and saw it snowing. *Maybe we'll have a white Christmas after all.* As darkness began to fall, she still hadn't heard from Tommy. She had figured that fixing burst pipes would be a big job, but surely she would've heard from him by this time.

Before going into the kitchen to start dinner, she went to the door and pulled it open. Snow drifts dropped from above the door jamb as she tried to stick her head outside, causing her to jump back to avoid them. When she did step out, she saw that snow had coated the street and buried the vehicles.

"Oh, this doesn't look good," she said to the empty house as she ducked back in and shut the door. "Tommy will be driving home on the icy roads. Damn it. Why did he have to take that job so far away today? He'll be lucky to get home at all tonight, let alone for dinner."

As the evening wore on, he still had not called or come home. She got into bed, but sleep eluded her for what seemed like hours. Picture after picture of reasons why Tommy hadn't made it home marched through her head. Finally, she drifted into an exhausted sleep.

She awoke to a jolt of pain. She changed positions and tried to go back to sleep. The pain continued, and that worried her. *It can't be the baby. It's too early.*

After a couple of hours, the pains were still coming and going. She telephoned Irene, hoping not to alarm the whole family, but Angelo answered. He had just gotten off the night shift at Sarducci's.

"Angie, I think it's the baby. I need Irene."

The streets were not drivable, so Angelo and Irene walked the two blocks to Tina's. After Irene assessed Tina's situation, she told Angelo to go get Dr. Channing.

"Oh, Irene. I'm scared. It's too soon."

"Not according to the baby," Irene said with a smile. "He or she is the boss now."

Tina giggled, then sobered. "But Tommy isn't here. He has to be here."

"Your father called a friend from the railroad who runs the snow-plow and told him to go get Tommy at his job."

"Can he do that?"

Irene nodded. "Dominic has worked with Jim for over twenty years. He'll do it for him."

<hr>

When Dr. Channing arrived, he examined Tina and told her it would be a few hours before the baby arrived. Irene made the doctor a cup of coffee while he waited. In the meantime, Tina prayed that Tommy would get there. She needed him to hold her and assure her that everything would be OK. In between pains, she thought of all the baby clothes she still had to sew and the supplies she still needed to buy for the baby.

None of that matters, she told herself. *The only thing that matters is that the baby is healthy. Oh, Blessed Mother, pray for us.*

Tommy arrived while Tina was in the throes of labor. He insisted on seeing her, despite the doctor telling him he should wait outside her room.

"Are you worried about her or me, Doc?"

"Both. She might get too emotional, and you might not be able to watch her in such pain."

Tommy stuck his head in the bedroom door. "Tina, honey, I'm here. Can I come in? The doc says I shouldn't."

"Oh yes, Tommy. I need you!"

Pushing past the doctor, Tommy rushed to her and grabbed her hand. He kissed it and her sweaty forehead. "I'm here, baby. Everything's going to be all right." He sat down on the edge of the bed. "We started this thing together. We're going to finish it together."

———

At six forty-five a.m. on December 21, 1938, six-pound eight-ounce, Battista Tommaso Capello, Jr. arrived, boasting a full head of hair. He was immediately declared the cutest baby that had ever lived by his parents and their families. As Tommy had done when he was a gambler and a small-time hood, he strutted around with a breast pocket full of cigars, giving one to every man he saw. Now, this was a real reason to be proud!

Tina still couldn't believe that she and Tommy had made this beautiful child. With her nose and Tommy's wavy black hair, he was the perfect combination of them. Admiring him together, they both agreed that with having each other, their successful businesses, and now Tommy. Jr., they had it all.

———

While the United State continued to work its way out of the Depression, a European conflict began on September 1st, 1939, when fascist Germany, led by Adolph Hitler, invaded Poland. Over the next year, England and France tried to push Hitler back, but by the summer of 1940, France had fallen to Germany and England was being subjected to a murderous aerial assault.

As reports of Hitler's takeover in Europe grew, talk of a possible US intervention in the war sparked many conversations and speeches from activists, including the famous aviator, Charles Lindberg, who spoke forcefully against US involvement. Still, most of the people in towns like Kingsburg gave the war in Europe no more than a passing thought as they went about their everyday lives.

Time flew by as Tina and Tommy learned the joys and woes of parenthood. Tommy Jr. was a happy baby who turned into an inquisitive toddler. He began talking early to everyone's delight.

In February of 1941, Tina and Tommy's second son, Peter, arrived right on time. Tina couldn't believe how different the two babies were. Peter was colicky, and she despaired of ever making him comfortable. Exhausted by sleepless nights, she cried along with him as she paced the floor. Eventually, the colic subsided, and the family caught up on their sleep.

Besides the colic, the boys differed in development. Whereas Junior talked early, took longer naps, and had a more serious nature, Peter slept less and spoke later, but his easy-going personality, sense of humor, and contagious smile made everyone want to hug him. Having the children had curtailed some of Tina's design contracts. Irene and Mary, Tommy's sister-in-law, helped out with babysitting often, but Tina hated the times she couldn't be with her children.

Tommy's business had been granted a government contract to help build the new airbase, thirty-five miles away. Getting that contract legitimized him as a businessman, and the income from the project would be more than enough to make up for her lighter workload

———◆———

On a Sunday in early December of 1941, Tommy, Tina, and their two boys had just enjoyed a noontime dinner at his parents' house. They and Tommy's brothers' families took turns each week at their parents' dinner table. It gave each family time with the parents.

"That was a great meal, Ma," Tommy said as he rose from the dinner table and planted a kiss on his mother's cheek.

"Thank you," she said, smiling. "It's easy, because I know what you like."

With dinner finished, Tina wiped the boys' hands and got them out of their chairs. The men went off to the parlor to smoke cigars, drink wine, and listen to a football game on the radio between the New York Giants and Brooklyn Dodgers. Tommy Junior climbed up on his grandpa's lap, and Tina put Peter in a playpen. With them occupied, she began clearing the table.

"Tommy is making good money now," Tommy's mother said as Tina piled some dishes on the kitchen table. "Is it not hard for you to work on your designs and take care of the family, too?"

"It can be, but I'm afraid if I don't continue, I might lose contact with the buyers and my customers. I worked too hard to let that happen. I love my work."

"I guess I don't understand. I never wanted to do anything but be a wife and mother."

"I have friends that feel the same way, and that's fine, but I—" Tommy's voice, bellowing from the parlor, interrupted her.

"Holy cow! Tina, Ma," he yelled from in front of the radio speaker, "come here quick. Listen to this!"

Tommy's mother grabbed a dish towel to wipe her soapy hands and followed Tina into the parlor.

The Mutual Broadcasting System had preempted the game for a news bulletin from the Hawaiian Islands at two twenty-six p.m. Eastern Time.

"Japanese planes are bombing our battleships in Pearl Harbor," said Tommy's father, as Tommy, Jr. tried to distract him with a toy in his face.

"Oh my God, that's terrible," his mother said. "I never heard of that place. Why do we have our ships there?"

Tina only heard a few words of the report before Peter started crying from the playpen, demanding attention. "It's OK, sweetheart," she said and pulled him up into her arms. "Mama won't let those bad guys hurt you."

People stayed glued to their radios that day and the next. The continuing updates and commentary caused confusion and panic throughout the valley. What did it all mean, and might there be an attack on the mainland, particularly on the West Coast, and possibly on the East

Coast? Would this attack be the impetus for the US to take up arms along with Europe? The Benedetti's and Capello's couldn't help wondering how this would change their lives.

CALL TO ARMS

After President Roosevelt's declaration of war speech on December 8, some in Kingsburg wasted no time volunteering for the armed forces. Angelo and his friends fell within the twenty-one to thirty-five age range to be drafted, and a few of them jumped at the chance to broaden their small-town horizons.

Twenty-three-year-old Angelo was not one of them. Mr. Sarducci had just promoted him to produce manager, and when that happened, Angelo proposed to Annie Rosetti, the lovely twenty-year-old cashier at Sarducci's. They had set a July date for the wedding, and Angelo had no desire to leave her, or his job, for the service—war or no war.

Soon after, Tina learned she was pregnant again. Baby number three would join them the following September. *This is my chance to have a little girl,* she thought. Then fretted that having a baby during these uncertain times, might not be a good thing. But like Angelo, she would not allow it to make her feel guilty for bringing a new life into the world.

Soon after the war started, Eva's passion for flying convinced her to get her pilot's license as soon as possible. She asked Glenn to prepare her for the written part of the flying test, and they met as often as he could arrange to be in Kingsburg. But money was still an issue.

"Irene, I've taken a job at the arms factory."

"Really? I know a lot of women are doing that, but I thought you loved working at the airport."

"I do. I love being around the planes and flying them. That's why I want to get my pilot's license, but it costs a lot of money."

"I've heard the factories pay good."

"Well, I won't be earning as much as the man I'll be replacing, but a lot more than the coffee shop."

Eva stopped going to the movies every week and buying drinks with friends at the local bar-and-grills to save money. She also cut back on nonessential clothing and make-up. Even though she volunteered to work overtime as much as possible at the factory, she still needed more money to be able to take the pilot's flying test. It was hard to maintain her diligent schedule, and sometimes she longed to go out on weekends with her friends from work.

Sally nudged her one Friday night. "Come on, Eva," she said, "you're wasting this whole war by not partying as much as you can."

"Yeah, come with us to the USO dance tonight. It'll be a gas," said Margaret.

"Sure," Rita said with a wink. "It's our patriotic duty to show the soldiers a good time."

"Well—," Eva started.

"Oh, Eva. You know you want to go. You haven't been out with us in weeks."

Eva hesitated. *They're right. I could use a night of relaxation.* She opened her mouth to say yes, but she pictured herself sitting in the cockpit, high above the clouds. No amount of partying ever gave her that sensation, and she wouldn't trade it for the world.

"I'd love to, girls, but no, thanks. I just can't."

In February of 1942, two months after Japan's attack on Pearl Harbor, President Roosevelt had signed an executive order permitting the government to take "every possible protection against espionage and against sabotage."

Tina and Tommy gave it no thought. They couldn't imagine anyone doing such an evil thing here in Kingsburg. That is, until one evening in late March as Tina readied the boys for bed.

"Tina," Tommy yelled out to her from the living room, "come here and listen to this report."

As she sat down beside him on the couch, the radio news continued. "This out of San Francisco. Fifteen hundred Japanese Americans are being rounded up by authorities in California. Now considered potential spies for the enemy, the government has deemed them a security threat to the country. Forced to leave their homes and property, they are being sent to hastily constructed government facilities called relocation centers for the duration of the war.

The government is said to have also set their sights on German and Italian aliens who might be sympathetic to their native countries."

Tommy shook his head in disbelief. "Germans and Italians represent at least half of the population of Kingsburg. But I can't imagine anybody around here being a fascist sympathizer."

A week later, as Tina washed up the dinner dishes and Tommy roughhoused on the living room floor with the boys, Tommy's mother suddenly opened the front door and stepped in.

"Tommy," she called out over the noise. "I knocked, but no one answered."

"Oh, hi, Ma." He looked at the boys with pride. "These little guys were making too much noise." He looked behind her. "Where's Pa?"

She bent over and kissed each boy on his forehead, then turned to her son. "Oh, Tommy," she said with fear in her voice, "I need to talk to you."

"Sure, Ma, come on in the bedroom." He put his arm around her shoulder and called into the kitchen. "Tina, would you watch the kids for a minute?"

He closed the bedroom door and squeezed her hand as they sat down on the bed. "Is it Pa?"

She gulped and then blurted, "They took him away."

"What? Who took him?"

"They were from the government and kept talking about Mussolini. They barged into the house and started going through our things. They found an old picture of Mussolini in one of our bureau drawers. I thought he threw that away, but—"

Tommy panicked. He knew his father had at one time considered Mussolini a great man. But things changed when Italian patriots like Federico found themselves destitute under the dictator's regime. He and others fled to the United States and switched their loyalty to their new country.

"Where did they take him, Ma?"

"I don't know. They gave me this, but I was too upset to read it." She handed him a card, and he recognized the address of the local National Guard Armory. He directed his mother into the kitchen and left her with the boys while he took Tina aside to tell her that he had to go find his father and why.

"Try to calm Ma down, will you? She's a nervous wreck. I'm going to the armory."

"I will. You be careful and watch your temper. You're pretty excited, yourself."

He kissed her. "All right, I promise."

Tommy tried to calm down, but he boiled with anger. Why his father? Why suspect him as an enemy alien? Occasionally, after drinking a little too much wine he would talk about the old days in Italy. Had he said things he shouldn't have to the wrong person?

At the armory, Tommy learned little from the closed-lipped authorities. Just that they had been told to detain Federico Capello while they continued their investigation.

No one got much sleep in the Capello house that evening. Tommy tossed and turned all night, keeping Tina awake, and their boys cried out more than usual. The next morning, the youngsters seemed to sense their parents' distraction and reacted by fussing and misbehaving. Tommy left earlier than usual with plans to visit his uncles and aunt, hoping to hear confirmation from them that his father was innocent of the charges against him. Tina gathered the kids and went to her father's house to talk to him and Irene. Luckily, it was Saturday, and they would both be there.

The boys made themselves at home after giving Dominic and Irene their requisite hugs and kisses. Tina wasted no time explaining her early morning visit.

"Oh, Tina. That's terrible," Irene said while hugging her.

Dominic's face went white. "Did they charge him?"

"No. They say they're just holding him while they investigate."

"This is not good," he said while shaking his head. "And it's just the beginning. They won't stop with him."

Irene said, "Oh, Dominic, you worry too much. You've done nothing wrong."

"You think that matters to them? All they need is to find a connection to the fascists."

"Oh, Pa. Irene's right. They—"

"You don't know what can happen. Suspicion is all they need before they ruin your life." He shook his head. "You don't know what it was like years ago. They trusted none of us from the old country." Under his breath, he mumbled, "I knew that family would bring trouble."

"Pa! You're talking about my husband. The father of your grandsons."

Dominic gulped. "I know that, but you changed Tommaso, and he made something of himself. And I would die for my grandsons.

But not for the old man and his brothers. They always want something for nothing, no matter how they have to get it."

Tina understood what he meant. She had felt the same way about Tommy when she first met him, a man who made his money by breaking the law. In fact, she would have never gone out with a guy like him, let alone marry him.

"I know, Pa. But what am I going to do?" she said, on the verge of tears. "It's Tommy's family. Don't make me choose."

On Monday, at Irene's shop, the two women agreed that the situation with Tommy's father had been a low blow to both families.

Tina sighed deeply. "I'm just afraid that this ridiculous charge is going to tear our family apart."

"I know," Irene said. "The babies have brought both our families closer. Your father had started to accept the Capello's, and things have been getting better. "We just have to work to keep things this way. It will be up to you and me, you know."

—◆—

That became almost impossible after an article hit the local newspaper the next day with the headline, "LOCAL IMMIGRANT SUSPECTED OF BEING ENEMY ALIEN!" The article listed few details but went on to name Federico Capello as having been taken into custody for having allegiance to and giving financial support to Mussolini's Italy. The statement set off a firestorm of rumors within the small town.

Irene found herself on the front line of them in her shop soon after the story came out.

"You know, Irene," said Edna, a north side customer, "if our friendship didn't go way back, I might not be able to overlook the gossip about the Capello family."

"I appreciate that, Edna, but there's really no proof of it, and I should think you would want to wait to hear whether or not it's true."

"Maybe, but I've heard lots of stories about those people. I never could see what Tina saw in Tommy Capello. She's such a nice girl, and so talented. I always thought she was too good for him."

———

In the meantime, the country had gotten busy mobilizing not only the military but civilians to come together for one common goal: to beat the Axis countries of Europe and Asia, being led by Adolph Hitler and Benito Mussolini. Citizens feared that their influence threatened to take over American democracy with their fascist ideas and prejudices.

Soon, the entire population was called upon to do their part. Since rubber-producing regions in Asia had been taken over by Japan by March of 1942, tires became rationed in the United States. Not long after, automobiles followed, as auto manufacturers were forced to shut down production of new cars so they could fulfill military orders for jeeps, tanks, and ambulances.

———

Tommy's aunt, uncles, and cousins had told him that they knew nothing about any direct connection between his father and Mussolini. As for financing the fascist government, they only knew that Federico had sent money back to his aged parents while they were still alive.

Time seemed to stand still for Tommy while he waited to hear from the authorities and what they had found out. When he finally did get a call, two weeks after his father was taken away, all he was told was that his father had been transferred to a facility outside of town while the investigation continued. They gave Tommy the address of the place, and a phone number, saying that he might be able to visit his father there.

Tommy wasted no time making an appointment to see his father. His mother had been inconsolable until she heard that she would be seeing Federico in a few days. She spent those days gathering some of his personal items and cooking his favorite foods to take to him. When they arrived at the internment camp, the guards checked the items she had brought and told Tommy and his mother that they had to take turns seeing Federico, thirty minutes each.

Tommy insisted that he go in first. He needed a few minutes alone with his father to hear his side of the story.

"Pa, do you know any more about who reported you, and what they said?"

"No, the officers said nothing." He sat down on his cot and sighed. "Uh, sometimes I shoot off my mouth about the old country, but you know me, son. I love this country for taking us in. We were starving over there."

Tommy rested his hand on his father's shoulder. "I know, Pa. I'm gonna get you outta here."

As Tommy drove his mother home, he cringed, thinking about what he had just promised his father. How the hell was he going to get him out? He hadn't felt this helpless since the former mayor had beaten him down, years ago. and thrown him out of town.

When Tina met Tommy at their door, despite his usual kiss to her and hugs and tickles for the kids, Tina could tell something was wrong.

"How did it go today, hon?" she said as he went to the sink to wash his hands.

"It was good to see the old man, but I didn't know what to say to him. I don't know how I'm going to get him out of there."

"What about your brothers? Can't they help?" She handed him a bottle of beer and said with a hint of anger, "Why does it always have to be you?"

A week later, Tina, who tired easily from the pregnancy, had reached her last nerve dealing with her boys. They had been especially rambunctious throughout the day. Now, she grabbed Peter off the floor to prevent a glass baby bottle from falling off a table and onto his head. As she pulled him to her, she felt a burst of liquid in her panties, and her heart sank. *This can't be good.*

Tommy was working out of town that day, so she called Irene to drive her and the boys to Dr. Channing's office.

Irene stayed in the waiting room with the boys while Tina shook with fear in the examination room, waiting for the doctor.

When he arrived, she told him what she had experienced.

"Let's take a look," he said, and went to work.

After a few minutes of silence, he said, "I'm afraid you've lost the baby, Tina. It will take a few minutes for me to clean you up."

Tina's eyes welled with tears. "I knew something was very wrong. I never had anything like that happen the first two times."

When he had finished his disagreeable task, she sat up and asked. "Is it something I did?"

"Probably not. These things happen for lots of reasons. Many of them are out of your control. Sometimes the baby is just not strong enough to survive."

She took a deep breath and nodded.

"However," he continued "the war has put a strain on all of us right now, and I've heard that your family has been going through a very bad time lately. There's always a chance that the pressure you've been under could've contributed to it."

She bit her lip.

"But, as both a doctor and a religious man, I believe that this baby was just not meant to be."

She shrugged, not quite convinced.

He smiled. "You have two healthy boys and a husband who loves you. There's plenty of time for more children."

———

Tommy drove home that night with a lot on his mind. Up until now, he had been able to keep his father's incarceration away from his bosses at the airbase construction site. Tommy and the project manager, Hank, had hit it off from the beginning and respected each other's work. So, when the guy had approached him that day saying he'd heard about his father's trouble, Tommy wasn't sure what to say.

"Oh, it's some bullshit investigation based on a rumor," Tommy said dismissively. "There's nothing to it."

"I know you Italians take a lot of shit from some people. I grew up in a neighborhood with a bunch of Italian guys. They were all pretty decent and just trying to get by like the rest of us. As far as I'm concerned, what's happened to your old man has nothing to do with your work here."

Tommy breathed a sigh of relief. After losing some of his other customers, he needed this job more than ever. Besides that, he knew that having a government project could raise his standing up there with the big companies in the construction business.

Still, he feared that his father just being a "person of interest" might be all it would take for the government to drop him from this airbase project. But he wouldn't tell Tina about his talk with Hank. She didn't need any more aggravation in her life than she already had.

———

He walked into the house grinning from ear to ear, ready to greet his sons and the usual pandemonium. Instead, he saw and heard nothing. He walked into the kitchen to check on dinner and found no sign of it. He assumed the family had gone to the Benedetti's to eat, so he went into the bedroom to change out of his work clothes before joining them and planned to go over there, too.

Instead, he found Tina asleep on the bed, gripping a handkerchief. He sat down beside her, and she stirred. When she opened her eyes and saw his face, she threw her arms around his neck and pulled him to her.

"What's wrong, honey? Where are the kids?"

"They're at Pa and Irene's."

"Why? What's going on?"

Tina drew back to face him. "Oh, Tommy, we lost the baby!"

The news hit him like a boxer's punch he didn't see coming. "No! What happened?"

Her swollen eyes brimmed with tears as she related the events of the afternoon.

"But why, how—?"

"I don't know. Dr. Channing said it just happens sometimes."

"But your other pregnancies— It never occurred to me that this could even happen."

"I know—" Her voice melted into sobs.

He gulped. "Are you all right. Did it hurt?"

"I'm crampy. Kind of like having my period."

He patted her stomach gently.

"Oh, Tommy, I'm sure it was a girl. I lost my baby girl," she whimpered.

"Did the doctor say it was a girl?"

"No. It wasn't big enough for him to tell."

He hated to see the pain in her expression. "So you don't know for sure." He squeezed her hand. "It might've been another boy." He gave her a gentle smile and said, " If it was, you'd have had three little bruisers to take care of instead of two."

His smile made her smile, and he pulled her to him and caressed her face with his lips.

"We should go get the boys," she said, wiping her eyes.

"That can wait. We've got to eat," he said. "Come on. I'm taking you to the diner for their juiciest hamburger and biggest piece of blueberry pie."

———

When Eva heard about Tina's miscarriage, she went by Tina's house that evening. Tommy opened the door and let her inside.

"I heard about the baby. I'm sorry," she said as she gave him a hug. "How is she?"

"She's better now and sleeping. She was pretty upset this afternoon."

Before Eva could respond, Junior and Peter showed up at the door.

"Hi, Aunt Eva," Junior yelled as he pushed Peter out of the way, before grabbing her hand. " Come look at the building I made with my blocks."

Before she could get to his creation, Peter swept by and knocked it over, causing Junior to tackle his brother to the floor. Peter screamed as they wrestled around, "Get off of me." But Junior wouldn't let him up. Finally, Peter freed himself, and jumped on top of Junior. To which, Junior yelled, "I'll get you!"

Eva looked up at Tommy with an understanding smile, and shook her head. "Give her a kiss for me, will ya? I'll see her tomorrow."

———◆———

Eva had finally saved enough money to file papers to get her license. The flying exam consisted of a written and a flying test, and again she turned to her tutor, Glenn.

"Well, do you think I'm ready?" she asked him with hope in her voice after he quizzed her.

"You had me fooled with your flirty personality when we first met," he replied. "I have to admit I didn't think you could handle any part of piloting a plane. There's so much math and technical jargon to learn, but you've got it down."

"I don't admit this to everyone," she said with a coy smile. "I did very well in math and calculus in high school. It just always came easy to me, but that never attracted the boys. Being a silly flirt got me more dates."

He grinned and shook his head. "Well, it helped you become a good pilot, and you're ready to ace the test."

She leaned over and gave him a smacking kiss. "I have you to thank. I would've never even tried it if it weren't for you, and I couldn't have had a better teacher."

———◆———

Early in the morning two days later, Eva took a seat, ready to begin the written part of the exam. Her stomach was in knots. What if she failed? All her hard work, all her flying hours would have counted for nothing. But she needn't have doubted herself, because after so much preparation, the answers came easily. Her emotions fared better during the flying session, due mainly to the self-confidence and joy in flying she had acquired over the past year. All the work had paid off on the day she received her passing test results and held her brand-new pilot's license in her hand.

Irene, who had supported Eva's flying from the beginning, hosted a party for her at their house. No one was more surprised about Eva's accomplishment than her father and Angelo.

Neither of them had shown much interest in her passion for flying and wrote it off as another excuse to hang out with the pilots.

"Jeez," Angelo said to her with a laugh, "my buddies will never believe that my sister drives airplanes. Ya did good, sis."

Eva smirked at him.

"So what was wrong with getting married and having babies?" Dominic shook his head. "No, you gotta fly with the birds."

Tina gave her a bear hug. "I'm so proud of you," she said. "I know how hard it is to work for your dream, and how thrilling it is to finally have it come true." She smiled. "I might even go up in a plane with you one of these days."

"I'm not holding my breath for that," Eva teased.

Unfortunately, the rumors of the elder Capello's incarceration were still alive and well in Kingsburg and had spread to Tommy's local customers.

"Hey, Carl," he said as he put down his toolbox, "I'm here to flush out that system for you. Sorry I'm late, but I've been spending most of my time at the airbase site, supervising my crew, and I—"

"Uh, look, Capello," Carl said with an uncomfortable shrug, "I had somebody else take care of that. I figured you were busy with your old man and his problems with the government. And besides, I wouldn't want anybody, you know, umm, associating my business with—"

"You, too, Carl?" Tommy said. "We grew up on the same street."

Carl lifted his palms and shrugged.

Tommy went to his truck, cursing out loud at Carl, his father, and God. He figured he'd better stop for a beer at his favorite bar and grill so he wouldn't take his rotten mood home to Tina and the kids. He sat at the bar, downed a couple of beers, then got up to leave. He had only gone a few feet when two tipsy guys blocked his way.

"How's your old man holding up in jail, Capello?" the shorter stranger asked.

"Who wants to know?"

The taller guy stepped forward. "We do."

Tommy, knowing where this was going and wanting no part of it, tried to step around them. "Look fellas, I'm late getting home to my wife and kids."

The taller guy grabbed Tommy's arm and pushed him toward a nearby booth. "We heard your old man's cozying up to the enemy fascists. I figure we got to fight them, wherever we see them."

Tommy's nostrils flared, and planting his feet in a wide stance, he raised himself to his full height. "Well, you better find yourself another guy, 'cuz I ain't a fascist. Now get out of my way and go home and sleep it off." Tommy pushed through the crowd that had gathered, darted out to his truck, and drove as fast as he could to Tina's arms.

———◆———

In June, and now licensed, Eva hoped to get a job as a cargo pilot. She had always envied Glenn and the other pilots she had worked with and pictured herself flying from city to city like them. She loved the idea of seeing new places and meeting new people.

Glenn had told her who to contact for a job, and she wasted no time reaching out to them. With only a good word from Glenn, Eva got her first job. Although some of her first flights were only short hops to nearby cities, and were far and few between, they made perfect on-the-job training for her. She'd never admit it to her customers, but she loved flying so much, she'd do it for nothing.

———◆———

After losing the baby, Tina had thrown herself into her design work. She tried her best to complete the designs for her current contracts but found she wasn't nearly finished by her deadlines.

"I don't know, Irene. I set out every day to work but end up thinking about the baby and even tearing up sometimes."

"Don't be so hard on yourself. It will take time to get over it."

"Tommy is no help. He was comforting when it first happened, but now he's gone a lot and doesn't like when I bring up the subject while he's home."

———◆———

Tommy would never admit it to Tina, but he faced a struggle every day to keep his company afloat. So, losing the baby, in fact, lessened the strain on him. He knew it was a sin to think that way, and that tore him up inside, too.

Damn you, Pa! He loved his father, but his father's cockiness had caused damage to his family for as long as Tommy could remember. It just never occurred to him that it would someday be devastating to Tina and the boys. On top of that, his luck finally ran out at the airbase job.

"I'm sorry, Capello," Hank told him at the end of a workday near the last part of June. "They found out about your father and said they had no choice but to put your contract on hold while they looked into his case."

"Shit." Tommy shook his head. "I was hoping Pa would be cleared before the brass found out. What am I gonna tell my guys? They figured they were set for a while."

Tommy couldn't tell Tina about the suspension. She was still raw from losing the baby. So, he acted like nothing had happened, leaving home each day as if he were going to the airbase.

After one of those days, he shuffled into the house and heard Peter wailing. He found Tina in the living room, sitting in the rocking chair and jiggling him in her arms. He went to the radio and turned off "The Adventures of Ozzie and Harriet," a weekly radio comedy.

"Hey, hey, what's all the noise about?" He bent over, kissed her on the lips, and took Peter from her.

"I don't know what's wrong with him," she went to the kitchen and picked up a dish of food on the floor. "He just won't go down."

"Where's Junior?"

"I finally had to put him to bed and let him cry himself to sleep. I tried that with Peter, but he wouldn't go for it." She pushed her hair out of her eyes. "Where have you been? You couldn't call me?"

"I, uh, got tied up on a job and didn't realize the time. Sorry."

She licked her lips and sneered. "But somehow you found time to stop for a drink."

Tommy pretended not to hear her remark and took Peter into the bedroom.

When he came out of the bedroom, he helped Tina clean up the kitchen. "Bad day, huh?"

She shrugged.

"I know the kids can run you ragged. You need some fun. Why don't you call the sitter, and we'll go to a movie or something?"

"It's not just them. It's my work. I can't seem to focus on it." She opened a cupboard door to put up the plates, then turned back to him, with watery eyes. "And I missed my deadline for Grossman's. They dropped me, Tommy. Irene says I'm still grieving for the baby, but I swear I'm over it."

"Are you, honey? I know how much you wanted a girl."

"I did. I do, but it's not just that. The manufacturers are not accepting any more fashion designs." She hung up the dish towel. "We can't get new material for the dress shop because the factories are making army field and aviator jackets and tents now. The government is telling us to repair or alter old clothes to conserve. The war has taken over everything!"

Tommy knew how right she was. If it hadn't been for the war, the government wouldn't be trying to crucify his father for being an enemy alien, and they wouldn't have suspended his contract at the airbase.

With no new design contracts, Tina had no choice but to fall back on her part ownership of Irene's shop. Fortunately, business had picked up after the government suggested that, in lieu of buying ready-made clothes, ladies should sew their own new clothes or mend or alter old dresses. Such repurposed clothes were patriotically referred to as "victory fashions." Although many women complied, some had neither the time, talent, nor inclination to do so. With the draft snatching men out of factories, many women had left their homes to fill the vacant jobs.

One Sunday morning in July, Tina and Tommy had just come out of church with the boys, who were dressed in matching outfits. Almost everyone commented on how adorable they looked, but a neighbor pulled her aside.

"Tina," she said. "I can't wear skirts to work in, but I don't own enough slacks to last the whole week. If I go to Irene's Shop on Friday afternoon, can you measure me for some?"

"Of course, Betty."

"Oh, good. I'll tell the other girls. They need some, too."

Tina and Irene spent the following week inventorying their bolts and pieces of fabrics. Luckily, Irene had received a large shipment just before December 7th.

"This is a good amount," Irene said. "But it won't last long if we keep getting more orders for pants."

"The War Production Board suggests that everyone rummage through their closets and drawers for material to repurpose their old clothing," Tina said.

"I hate to have to tell our customers to do that," Irene said. "They're just coming out of the Depression when they had so little. It's hard to tell people that they can't spend their hard-earned money how they want to."

"Well, if we're going to stay in business, we've got to get really creative with what we have, and what's available."

———

Eva had tried to maintain her factory job while accepting cargo pilot assignments. It worked for a few months, but with more and more of the male pilots flying for the US Army Air Forces, her cargo jobs picked up and she quit the factory.

Her now erratic schedule caused problems at home with her father and Irene, so she arranged to move into an apartment with one of the out-of-town women she had met at the factory. Eva shared the news of her new arrangement one night as the family gathered around the dinner table. But instead of being pleased, her father threw his napkin down, shoved his chair back from the table, and stood up.

"It's bad enough I got to worry about you flying with the clouds. Now you won't come home at night to sleep in your own bed. *Puttana itinerante.*"

Eva gasped, cheeks flaming. "That's a rotten thing to say."

"That's what the neighbors are gonna say," Dominic bellowed.

"Dom, you know it's not true," Irene said.

"*I* know it's not, but will *they?*"

Eva's chair crashed over backward as she shot to her feet. "I've never cared what the people in this town thought of me. I'm not going to start now," she shouted and stormed out of the room.

Irene looked up at Dominic and shook her head. "Sit down and finish your dinner."

———————

In May of 1942, the government began limiting the amount of gasoline people could buy. As it happened, most Kingsburg residents who lived inside the city limits were within walking distance of stores, schools, and churches and didn't need to drive their cars. Luckily for Tommy, he still had the gas rationing "B" designation sticker given to workers in the military industry. It allowed him eight gallons a month (twice has much as for nonmilitary drivers) and made it possible for him to drive to Syracuse, a city near the airbase, to pick up jobs from people and businesses who didn't know his family name.

Before long, the war crept into their kitchens. The word came from Washington that sugar would have to be rationed. At that time, the government set up ration boards in towns and cities across the country. One of the Benedetti's' neighbors, Mr. Golicki, volunteered to work in the local office to help regulate the amount of food each family could receive and report to officials.

When Irene saw him in his yard, she asked him how they determined a family's share.

"It depends on the number of members in the household, and the availability of each item. I assure you, all Americans are under this rationing program."

Regardless of the need, Irene always hated having to tell Carmen that he couldn't have his favorite dessert.

FOOTHOLD IN WAR

In early June 1942, during the Battle of Midway, near the Hawaiian Islands, America achieved its first decisive victory. The Japanese had planned to lure the American battleships into a trap. But the Americans were able to determine the date and location of the planned attack so that the US Navy could prepare its own ambush.

After hearing that, Angelo made up his mind that if called to serve, he would join the navy, but until then, he remained determined to follow the path he had set for himself to work hard and rise above the obstacles that had been established for him as a boy.

He and Annie had just about everything set for a late July wedding. But their plans fell through when Angelo received a draft notice to report on July 20th. Determined to marry before Angelo left, the couple asked the church to squeeze them into Saturday morning, June 27, at eight a.m. Eastern War Time, ahead of another wedding set to begin nine a.m. Happily, Tina had finished making Annie's dress.

With the families and friends of the couple looking on with anticipation, the ceremony began with the traditional wedding song . A radiant Annie walked down the church aisle toward Angelo, who beamed and shifted from foot to foot until she reached him. Then they turned to face the priest.

Tina watched the ceremony with tears in her eyes. Despite Angelo's twenty-four years, she saw a fifteen-year-old boy. She remembered the trying times of those years when she worried he would be lost to the prejudice and drawbacks of being the son of a poor Italian immigrant trying to make his way on the wrong side of the tracks. Looking at him now, she knew that despite all that, he had turned into an honorable young man with a work ethic that insured he would reach his potential. But now, he had to leave it all to serve his country, God knew where. And she again feared that he might be lost.

The newlyweds spent a long weekend in Niagara Falls, after which they stayed in an auto court outside of town until he had to report. The night before, Dominic and Irene cooked an Italian feast for the whole family, knowing that Angelo wouldn't get anything close to it in the service. The next day, Tina and Irene comforted Annie at the train station as a nervous Angelo prepared to board. Tina teared up as she watched the sensitive young boy who couldn't even kill a chicken for supper wave goodbye, and she prayed to God and to her mother to watch over him from heaven.

———

Kingsburg cheered with the rest of the country when the battle on the island of Guadalcanal in the South Pacific Theater, starting in August of 1942, became the first offensive victory achieved by the US in the Pacific Theater of the war. Ultimately American troops lost only sixteen hundred men, but over four thousand were wounded and several thousand more died from disease, compared to the twenty-four thousand Japanese soldiers killed. Unfortunately, the numbers turned into more than statistics when the Benedettis learned that their nineteen-year-old neighbor, Walter, had died during the six-month-long battle.

The gold star in the Savage's window, four doors down, served as a constant reminder that Angelo could be next. He had been inducted into the navy, as he wished, and had been sent to boot camp in Chicago. Though he still had weeks of basic training left, his vocational test score had indicated a strength in the skills needed for radio operator, and he would receive his training at the Keystone Radio School in Bedford Springs, Pennsylvania, at the end of basic training.

———

In the meantime, sixteen-year-old Carmen and his friends spent the summer of 1942 collecting scrap metal, wood, rags, and rubber for the war effort. The government had made it known that recycling these materials could be essential for winning the war. Towns across the country started scrap drives to turn the materials into much needed weapons and other necessities of battle.

Carmen, an affable sort, found it easy to talk his friends' parents and his neighbors.

"You don't want America to end up run by fascists, like Italy and Poland, do you?" he asked each of them.

They responded by shaking their heads and declaring, "No, no, never!"

"Well, rationing and turning in your scraps is the best way you can keep that from happening."

Within weeks he and his buddies, working their way around the neighborhoods and scouring the dump, had collected donations from most of the south side of town. The group used a section of the Benedetti's backyard to store the items, planning to turn everything into the city at one time.

That is, until Dominic answered a knock at the front door.

The uniformed policeman tipped his cap. "Good evening, sir. I'd like to speak to your son Carmen."

Dominic's back went up. "Why? He's a good boy. He doesn't cause no trouble."

"Well, we got a report of him stashing stolen goods in your backyard. I have to assume you know about this, and that makes you liable for arrest, too."

Dominic opened the door, and the officer stepped inside. "He doesn't steal that stuff. People give it to him."

"And why do they do that?"

"For the war. To win the war against the fascists."

"Then why do you have it all in your yard?"

"He doesn't have a way to get it to the rationing people yet. He's waiting to borrow our neighbor's truck when he gets enough money for gas."

The officer sighed. "Can't someone else do that? Why does it have to be him?"

"He's in charge of collecting it on the south side."

"And who put him in charge?"

"Uh, he did. He got his buddies to go to all over the neighborhoods to tell them to give for the war. Isn't that what Mr. Roosevelt wanted us to do?"

The officer lifted his hat and scratched his balding head. "Well, yes, sir, he did."

"Maybe someone can come with a truck and pick it up," Dominic said. "I'd like to get it out of my yard. It's taking up too much room."

The officer smiled, extended his hand, and shook Dominic's. "I think that can be arranged, sir. And I want you to know that I think it's terrible that some of your friends are in trouble, just for being from Italy. This country is lucky to have you on our side."

—◆—

As Tommy drove down the road after having only one job all day, and that one over in the next county, his truck began to shake and shimmy under him. He pulled over and discovered that his left rear balloon tire had picked up a nail. He'd be lucky to make it to his cousin Joe's tire and auto shop outside of Kingsburg. Having worked at the local quarry for a few years, Joe had wanted to be his own boss, so he saved his money and started the business.

The truck limped into the shop, and Tommy honked the horn and waited for Joe to appear.

"Hey, Tom. What's up?"

Tommy got out of the truck. "This tire is shot. I need a new one."

Joe shook his head and spread his hands. "No more new ones. Sold the last one three days ago. Uncle Sam says we can't get any more. He needs the rubber to win the war."

"Shit. Now what am I going to do?"

"I have a used one that'll work."

Tommy sat on a wooden crate while Joe raised the car on the rack.

"I'm all for winning the war," Joe said, "but this rationing is killing my business. I can only repair so many tires. And I'm running out of used ones. Hell, some people have put their cars on blocks for the duration 'cuz they can't drive with no tires or gas."

"Yeah," Tommy said, "guess we're all in the same boat."

Joe smiled as he pulled the old tire off. "At least you've got a talented wife. I imagine she's still bringing in the dough. My old lady only knows how to spend it."

Tommy jumped up with fists clenched. "I'm not living off my wife—yet!"

Joe stopped and looked his cousin in the eye. "Sorry, I know it must be tough for you."

"Forget it," Tommy said.

Joe put the good tire on the rim. "Ya know," he said as he screwed on the lug nuts, "I know a guy who can get ahold of new stock."

"You mean black market stuff?"

"I was thinking about calling him. You interested?"

"I can't." Tommy paced around the garage. "I've got enough trouble with my old man. I'm trying to get my contract back at the base."

Joe lowered the truck. "Look, Tom. You've done a lot for me over the years. I know it's bad for you now. How about you be a kinda silent partner with me? Nobody has to know if you give me a few bucks to help me get started. And I'll give you a percentage under the table. What d'ya say?"

After another day without work, Tommy gave in and called Joe. He had told himself that he'd never go back to his old ways of making an easy buck. He also thought about what Tina would think of him, but he was doing it for her. He couldn't let her carry the financial burden for the whole family. She had enough to do with the kids and working already. Still, he tossed and turned all night trying to convince himself that he was doing the right thing.

———◆———

On a day that Tommy had picked up a couple jobs, the money lifted his spirits. He brought wine home for dinner and toy trucks for the boys. After eating, he got down on the floor and played with them until they began to slow down and rub their eyes.

"Come on, fellows," he said as he took one under each arm and carried them off. "It's bedtime."

Tina got up to follow them, but Tommy looked back at her and said, "Daddy's in charge tonight. Mommy's tired and needs to go to bed early." He winked at her. "We'll give her a break."

She squinted at him until she realized his inference. "Oh yeah." She faked a yawn. "I'm so tired." She gave them each a hug and kiss and said, "Nighty night."

When Tommy entered their bedroom, he found Tina propped up on a pillow, wearing the blue negligee he'd bought her for Christmas. He gave her a kiss and went into the bathroom for a quick shower. When he returned, he dimmed the lights and stretched out next to her. After several moments of kissing and caressing, he said, "It's been a while. We should do more of this."

"There just hasn't been the time with so much going on."

"We have to make the time," he said as he lowered the straps of her gown from her shoulders and sank his face into her cleavage.

———◆———

Tina watched Tommy fall asleep next to her. Sleepy herself, she was tempted to drop off with the afterglow, but unfinished projects summoned her to the workroom to take advantage of the quiet of the night to get them done. She slipped out of bed and tiptoed out of the bedroom.

She awoke in the sewing chair in the workroom to Tommy's voice the next morning.

"Have you been here all night?" he asked.

She peered up at him through slitted eyes, nodding and shrugging. "What time is it?"

"Six-thirty."

"Where are the boys?"

"I changed their diapers and gave them their bottles in their cribs."

She smiled and said, "I'm so lucky. A great lover and a wonderful father."

"Thanks, but you've got to stop taking on so much work. You hardly have time for anything else. The boys need you—, and so do I!"

"But things are different now. We need the money."

"Why now?"

Tina lowered her gaze and her voice. "Because you lost your job at the base, and your clients in town have dropped you, too."

Tommy flopped down on a chair next to her. "How did you find out?"

"It's a small town. People talk."

"Damn them!"

"Why didn't you tell me?"

"I kept thinking they'd reinstate me. I didn't know it would go on so long."

Tina put an arm around his shoulders. "Tommy, I don't mind working more. In fact, I like it."

He shook his head and stood up. "Well, I hate it. You need to be home with the kids more, and I don't want people saying that I'm living off my wife!"

◆

Tommy continued his routine of going out of town to drum up jobs. But he simply couldn't get a foot in the door for any long-term projects, and his spirits continued to drop. At first Tina cut back on her work and tried to get through to him to improve his outlook.

He then began coming home later and later every day. When he did come home, he sulked in silence. Tina came to dread him being there. As if he realized that, he started spending more and more time out of town, even renting a room for the nights he couldn't make it home.

On a night that he did make it home for dinner, Junior hardly touched his food except to throw his carrot slices at Peter. Peter turned and poked his brother's arm with his fork.

"Ouch!" Junior cried.

"He started it," Peter whined.

"That doesn't mean he can poke me," Junior said, as he jabbed his fork into Peter's arm and made him scream.

Tommy stood up and pushed his chair back. "That's enough!" He raised his arm over Junior but then saw the shocked look on Tina's face. He dropped his arm. "Can't you get these kids to behave at dinner? And you wonder why I'm never home."

After a few more of his outbursts, Tina feared that Tommy had begun to revert to his violent past when he settled everything with his fists. She finally faced the fact that she and the kids would have to make it on their own. She'd find regular babysitters for the boys and do what she had to do: work more.

The next time Tommy came home after midnight and slipped into bed next to her, she pretended to be asleep. Yet she barely slept that night and got up at the crack of dawn the next morning. She sat at the kitchen table, nursing a cup of coffee at the kitchen table while the boys ate their breakfast.

"You're up and dressed early," he said, as he dragged into the kitchen, still in his skivvies, and slumped into a chair.

"I've got an order to fulfill today," she said, without looking up at him.

"Well, at least somebody's got a job to do."

Tina shook her head and sighed. "I can't take your miserable attitude anymore."

He looked surprised. "It's not my fault I can't find work."

"It's not our fault either. But you're taking it out on me"—she looked over at the boys—"and them."

He got up to pour himself some coffee, then sat down.

"Tommy, I've thought this over. I'd rather you not come home the next time you leave." She cleared her throat. "You're making us all miserable."

He put his coffee cup down. "Did you just tell me to get out of my own house?" he asked, his voice incredulous. "We're family."

"You'd never know it. When's the last time you spent any pleasant time with the kids, or me?"

"I'm busting my rear-end trying to find a job to support you."

"I told you we can get by on what I make until this thing blows over."

"Yeah, and the whole town knows it! I can't live like that."

She hesitated then and said under her breath, "Then you'll have to live somewhere else."

His eyes widened and he looked into her eyes. "You mean that?"

"I wouldn't have said it if I didn't," she said with regret.

Tommy stood up, teeth clenched, and ran his fingers through his hair.

"I never thought—"

"No, I guess you didn't, but I have. Every time you stay away, hardly say a civil word to us, or raise your hands to the boys."

"It's just that I—I'll get my things."

A few minutes later, he came back dressed and carrying a small bag. When he shut the door behind him, Junior said, "Where's daddy going?"

"I don't know," she cried and pulled both of her sons into her arms. "I'm so sorry."

After a few weeks, Tina began getting questions from neighbors and family. When she told Irene that Tommy was staying out of town, Irene told her that she had sensed something was wrong from the beginning.

"I didn't want to believe it was anything, so I pretended not to notice. I don't want to take sides," Irene said.

"I understand that. Tommy's hurt because he's out of work, and he resents me for making more money than him right now. It's not his fault he can't get jobs because of his father, but he was taking it out on me and the boys. I couldn't stand any more of his short temper or him shutting us out. It's best that he's by himself right now."

Tommy rented a room out of town and picked up any kind of job he could get. He worked when he could, ate, drank some, and blamed Tina while longing for her every night in bed. They made arrangements for him to see the kids every weekend, and though he enjoyed his time with them, it only made leaving them harder and harder.

This was all his father's fault. If he hadn't bragged to everyone about Mussolini, this wouldn't have happened to his family.

———

Eva, though committed to cargo flying, found out it did not lend itself to dating male pilots. After her experience with Glenn and the other guys while at the Kingsburg Airport diner, she expected to have many more opportunities for dates. Though the male cargo pilots outnumbered the female ones, not all the guys appreciated her or saw her as date bait.

While chatting about flying through bad weather with a couple of male pilots waiting for seats in the coffee shop, one looked at her and said, "You shouldn't even be up there. Wasn't working in a factory, like other women, good enough for you?"

Eva, not knowing how to take that, didn't respond.

Another guy added, "Yeah, you got to take our flying jobs, too?"

She spoke without thinking. "Well, why haven't you guys volunteered for the Army Air Forces? Too chicken? I would if I could."

She must've hit a nerve because the men said nothing, as they slithered into the nearest booth.

Eva did have opportunities to date men that she met at the many destination airports she flew to as part of her job. Some of the jobs required a layover in a town or city, and she would make the dates with good intentions. Unfortunately, a change in schedule would often prevent her from keeping the date, or it would amount to no more than a quick dinner close by the airport.

On those nights she would recall her father's remarks about sleeping in strange cities at night instead of her own bed. She could see how some women might be susceptible to taking advantage of being away from home where no one cared what they did. *But Pa needn't worry about me.* She had spent most of her teen years and beyond using her feminine wiles to entice a guy to notice her. Flying gave her the freedom to just be herself for herself, and she loved that feeling.

As the summer went on, Eva continued to rack up flying hours as the cargo business increased. She never imagined that she would be able to find work that she loved so much. She thought she couldn't be any more pleased with a job, until one day in September, while eating a tuna fish sandwich in a coffee shop, she came across a short item in the newspaper about women flying army planes across the country.

With so many pilots flying in combat overseas for the Army Air Forces, the article said, the country needed women pilots with over two hundred flying hours to deliver planes from factories to army bases for use overseas. *Oh my God,* she thought. *Could I really fly for my country?*

Eva tried to picture herself on the job and realized she didn't know much about the Women's Flying Training Detachment, known as the WFTD. She remembered that the library had out-of-town newspapers, so she strode into the public library on her next day off and looked around. She spotted a table in the back and smiled, recalling the many times she had held court with her friends surrounding her as they pretended to study. *Boy, we gave that librarian a hard time.*

She grabbed the *New York Times* from the rack, spread it out on a table, and began to thumb through it. After searching the entire paper and finding no mention of the WFTD, she turned to look for help.

A voice came from behind her. "May I help you?"

Eva spun around and came face to face with the familiar, yet now well-lined face of the woman she had tormented years ago.

"Uh, yes, ma'am. I'm looking for information about the Women's Flying Training Detachment, or WFTD. I can't find any mention of it in your latest edition of the *New York Times*."

"I'm not familiar with it, but let's check in our *Readers' Guide to Periodical Literature*. It would list any magazine or newspaper articles about them."

"Uh, OK. Anything you could find would be helpful."

That day Eva found that the women fliers organization had its roots in England in 1940. By the time 1942 came around, the country found itself immersed in a war that required every ounce of manpower for military duties, particularly combat. The new organization was headed by famous aviatrix Jacqueline Cochran and overseen by Lieutenant General Henry H. "Hap" Arnold, commanding general of the US Army Air Forces.

The WFTD started with the idea that women fliers could be used to ferry planes from the manufacturers to army airfields, thereby freeing up men for more difficult flying assignments. Well-trained women, performing a variety of stateside flying jobs, some at training facilities, could solve the pilot shortage. Thus, the Women's Flying Training Detachment would begin training recruits in Houston.

Eva thanked the librarian for all her help in locating several articles regarding the WFTD. One of the articles had explained how to apply, so Eva scribbled the information on a napkin at the table, stuck it in her pocket, and went back to work. She now had a better sense of how the group came about and understood the importance of their duties to the war effort.

Who'd have thought that she could serve her country by flying a plane? The thing she loved to do the most. She went home that night and composed a letter to ask for an interview. She wrote about her experience and willingness to use her skill for the war effort.

Chances were, she would never hear from them. But tossing the letter into the mailbox, she crossed her fingers and shrugged. She was sending the letter on something of a lark. *Surely, I can never compete with all the more-experienced fliers that have probably applied.*

Her hectic schedule in the following days gave her little time to wonder if, or when, she might get a response to her letter of application.

———◆———

A few weeks later, Eva sat down at the kitchen table, kicked her shoes off, and sorted through her mail. Sandwiched between the light bill and what she assumed was another bill, she found a letter from a friend of hers who was stationed in England. As she started tearing open the letter, she glanced down and saw an envelope with a return address from Headquarters Army Air Forces Training Command, Fort Worth, Texas.

Her mouth dropped open. "Oh my God," she said as she picked it up.

With a silent prayer, she ripped the envelope open and anxiously scanned the letter. There it was—a date and time for her interview, with Jacqueline Cochran's signature at the bottom. *The director of the Women's Flying Training Detachment actually signed the letter herself!*

The WFTD appointment would take place the third week in October. Her excitement dimmed a little as she pictured telling her father the news. She decided it best to share the news at Sunday night dinner where everyone could hear the news at once. With Angelo still in training camp, and Tommy with his parents, the only ones around the Benedetti table were Tina, her boys, Irene, Dominic, and Carmen.

"I'm so excited," she began as Irene poured the espresso. "I got an appointment for an interview with Jackie Cochran to fly military planes! Can you believe it?"

Dominic got up from the table in silence and strode into the living room, his face stoic. Eva wanted to lash out at him, but Irene patted her hand and shook her head, so Eva stayed in her chair.

"I don't believe it," Tina said. I never thought—"

"What? That they would want me? Thanks a lot."

"No. I just didn't even know you applied. That's great, sis."

"Well, I think it's nifty," Carmen said. "Some of those military planes are plenty big. I saw a story about them in a newsreel."

"I'm excited for you, Eva," Irene said. "You work really hard at flying airplanes, and I know you love it."

Eva shrugged. "Well, it's just an interview. I might not even get the job."

Given Tina's and her father's reaction to her interview invitation, Eva had trouble feeling confident that she could even sit through the interview, let alone actually get accepted to the program. Her busy schedule distracted her most of the time, but she found herself waking up in the middle of the night in a cold sweat, in anticipation of the interview. *I haven't got the vaguest idea what to say to a woman like Jackie Cochran.*

Angelo finished up his basic training but still had several weeks of radio training in Maryland before being deployed.

Although a weekend pass was practically unheard of for a new inductee, he managed to earn one by impressing his superior as an exemplary recruit. In late August, he traveled all Friday night and Saturday morning to arrive at the Kingsburg bus station at noon. Annie met him there, and they drove to a local hotel, where they spent the rest of the day and night.

The next afternoon, they went to Dominic and Irene's house for a family reunion. Tina and Eva agreed that Angelo looked well, despite his disparaging letters about navy life. They saw a difference in his demeanor. No longer an apprehensive young man, he spoke with an air of self-assurance and quiet reserve that they had never seen in him.

Annie beamed with pride as she drank in his new muscular physique. She hung on his every word, while he spoke of some of the goals he had achieved in his physical training.

"I have to admit," he said. I always thought I was pretty tough, but after a week of PT, I could hardly move. Now, I've never been in such great physical shape."

"Yeah," Carmen said with a smile as he punched Angelo's arm, "you've got some muscle there. Guess I better watch what I say to you."

The group laughed and turned the conversation to the past, citing the good ole days with fondness. Then they took their seats around the dinner table and yielded the floor to Angelo, who raised his glass for a toast.

"It's great to be here today with all of you around this table again. It gives me a chance to make an announcement. Annie and I are going to have a baby!"

————

After some time, Tina knew she had done the right thing, telling Tommy to leave the house while he worked out his issues. That didn't mean that she was happy. She hated being without him, and she knew the boys missed him terribly, too. But the last month or so before he left, things had just kept getting worse.

If anyone had ever told her that the day would come when she would tell Tommy to leave, she would've said they were crazy. She could never have imagined that even a world war would split them up. Especially when the bombs and fighting were taking place on another continent.

In her more serene moods, after the boys had been tucked in, she fell into her empty bed and replayed in her mind their early relationship when he was a gambler, and how, despite that, she grew to love him. Although she had tried, she could never stop loving him, and they eventually got married. Now, she still hadn't stopped loving him, but Tommy was a proud man whose self-respect had been taken away from him. She realized that the more love she gave him, the more inadequate he felt.

"That goddamn father of his did this to Tommy. To us!" she whispered, then fell asleep, crying into her pillow, again.

———

Tommy took his first payment from Joe's black-market operation with trepidation. He needed the money, but the moral compass he'd lived by since meeting Tina made the bills feel dirty in his hands. He decided he would save the money, and any future payouts, until he absolutely had to have them.

He continued working as much as he could. In between jobs, he worked with the lawyer that his family had hired for his father. The guy wasn't the best, but he was the cheapest they could find. Over a month had gone by with no progress in the case, leading his mother to chronic exhaustion and his father to give up hope.

Tommy stopped by his house every Sunday to see the kids and give Tina some money. But it almost made the separation worse to see them for such a short time. The boys seemed to have grown two more inches each time he saw them.

He hated missing part of their childhood. On top of that, it was all he could do each time to stop himself from taking Tina in his arms and never letting go. Sometimes he sensed that she felt the same, but he knew that until he was ready to accept her role as breadwinner or begin to make more money than she did, he had to leave his longing for her at the doorstep.

In October 1942 Eva used most of her savings for the train and bus tickets to the WFTD interview. She boarded the train for Texas with both hope and apprehension. She prayed that she would make a good impression at the interview, while scolding herself for thinking that she had the talent and guts to fly military planes. *What made me think that an Italian girl from Upstate New York could impress Jackie Cochran, the famous aviatrix, enough to choose her to fly military planes?*

She vacillated between hope and despair until the train pulled into the Toledo station some eight hours later. As she boarded the bus that would take her to the Army Air Forces Flying Training Command in Fort Worth, she decided that the ride would be tough enough without spending another thirty hours talking herself out of the job.

Eva shook with fear as she waited to be called in to meet Miss Cochran. But to her relief, the woman set her at ease by making small talk, giving her ample opportunity to relax and answer the questions. Eva hesitated to believe that they had shared a rapport, for fear that she would go home too confident, only to be disappointed later.

As she boarded the bus for home, she told herself that, if nothing else, she had had the opportunity to meet Jackie Cochran and to see Texas. She'd never been south of New York City, and she had found the weather and the wide-open spaces of the terrain interestingly different from the East Coast. Somehow, the people and their accent seemed to reflect the landscape, and she found them fascinating.

The train finally pulled into Kingsburg Station. "Well," she thought as she gathered her things, "no matter how this turns out, I did my best. What's the worst that could happen? I'll still be doing the flying job I love."

Soon, the crisp October days produced a picture-postcard view of the valley's landscape in vibrant oranges and yellows. The war had now permeated the fabric of every town and city in the country. Hostilities had escalated in Europe and the South Pacific and continued to result in more battlefield deaths and injuries. Despite this, the draft produced enough replacements to continue to fight the enemy.

Even with the absence of Angelo, Tina and Tommy's separation, and Federico Capello's incarceration, the families got through the Thanksgiving holiday. Annie spent the day at her family's house, and Tina and the boys had dinner with the Benedetti's. Later that day, Tommy stopped by to pick up his sons and take them back to his mother's house for a visit. Between the family discord. the country at war, and coffee having been added to the ration list, there didn't seem like much to celebrate.

Early December brought snow and freezing weather, and the whistle of the wind made it seem even colder. One night, after both boys had gone down to bed without a fuss, Tina returned to the living room and turned the radio on, hoping to muffle the eerie outdoor noises with music from "Your Hit Parade." Then she sat down to add the finishing touches to a dress she had been making for Eva's Christmas present. An hour later, she heard Junior crying in his crib, and she managed to soothe him back to sleep before he could wake up Peter.

She took advantage of the opportunity to make herself a cup of hot tea. She had just tilted the teapot over her cup when the doorbell startled her. *Who can that be at this hour?*

She hurried to the door, bracing for bad news. But when she opened it, she saw Tommy standing there, shivering.

"Come in. What's wrong? Why didn't you use your key?"

He stepped inside and blew into his hands. "I didn't want to scare you."

"Why are you here at this time of night?"

"I had to tell you in person."

He followed her into the kitchen.

"Tell me what?" she asked, with apprehension.

"They released my old man. I just picked him up and took him home."

"What? That's wonderful!" She threw her arms around his neck, but then remembering herself, she took an awkward step back and motioned for him to sit at the table. "How? Why did they let him go?"

"They couldn't find any real evidence."

"Of course not." She grabbed the teapot. "Do you want some tea?"

He shook his head.

She sat down and continued, "It took them long enough. Thank God that's over."

"Well, not completely. They'll still be watching him, and he can't leave town."

"Even so your mother must be so happy to have him home."

"Yeah, but I still want to know what made them pick him up in the first place."

Tommy rose and Tina touched his arm, then walked him to the door and watched him leave.

Back in the kitchen, she took one more swallow of tea. While rinsing out the cup, Tina reflected on her father-in-law's ordeal, and her joy turned to anger. Who or what had triggered the authorities to investigate him? His incarceration had caused so much damage to the family. What a waste it had been to put them all through the past nine months. *Would they ever be the same again?*

The week before Christmas, as snowflakes fell in Kingsburg, Main Street welcomed shoppers with colorful lights and decorations. Despite rationing, buyers looked for the perfect gift to brighten their families' and friends' holiday, and as usual, the Salvation Army bells rang out to persuade shoppers to drop a generous donation into the kettle. But in spite of the festive appearance, the dangerous battles in the news weighed heavily on the shoppers' minds. This year, almost everyone in town had a relative or friend in the service, and the death toll rose relentlessly every day.

Tina and Tommy's situation made the approaching holiday even more troublesome. They had decided that each would have Christmas dinner at their respective family's houses. Their families ridiculed the plan. They hadn't understood the couple's separation. Tommy's parents blamed Tina for caring more about her career than Tommy's, and Dominic thought Tommy should be glad that somebody was supporting their family. Irene stayed neutral and tried to keep the communication going between all the parties.

Tina's main concern was Tommy and her boys, and she tried to block out everyone else's advice. She had to do what she thought would be best for her own family. Despite being the one to tell Tommy to leave the house, she hurt for what he was going through. But she could see that if they didn't separate for a while, it could be the permanent end of their marriage.

Regardless, she had no intention of depriving Tommy and the boys of a happy Christmas. She invited Tommy to come over on Christmas Eve for dinner. He could put the kids to bed and help her to set out Santa's gifts under the tree afterward.

———◆———

Tina smiled as she watched Tommy arrange the boys' presents with care on the floor. "I think you enjoy playing with those toys as much as the kids will," she said.

"I guess I do. I want them to have the presents I didn't get when I was their age."

She nodded. "During the Depression, we were lucky if we found anything under the tree."

"The worse thing for the kids is, they won't have me here with them in the morning, and it's all my fault."

Tina's heart sank. She had worried this would happen. "You can sleep here on the couch. I'll get you some blankets."

She returned with the bedding. He took it and looked up at her. "I hate this, you know. I've missed you."

She sat down next to him. "It's awful for me, too, but you weren't happy here, and I couldn't watch you so miserable."

"I know. I'm sorry. If it's any consolation, I haven't been any happier being away."

She shrugged. "Maybe just a little consolation," she said with a grin.

He leaned over and gently kissed her lips, and she wrapped her arms around his neck.

"You're still the best thing that's ever happened to me," he said as he pulled her down onto the floor with him.

After spending the night with Tina, Tommy assumed that he was home to stay.

"No, Tom," Tina said after breakfast. "I enjoyed being with you yesterday and last night, but it doesn't make our problems go away. Sometimes loving someone isn't enough. If it were, we wouldn't have separated. Nothing has changed with your business, and I can't live with you taking it out on me and the boys."

Tommy kissed the kids goodbye and walked out of their house that day with a snarl on his lips. He couldn't admit that Tina had been right, even though he understood her reason. On the other hand, he had never expected her to welcome his loving overtures. When she did, he knew that she still loved him. Now with his father out of detention, he had a chance of getting his contract back from the airbase, and when that happened, everything would get back to normal.

He wasted no time driving to the airbase to tell Hank the good news. But as Hank waved Tommy to a chair in his office, he said, "I'm sorry, Tom. They've already appointed a new construction company for the job. They waited as long as they could, but they are on a deadline and couldn't afford to lose any more time."

Tommy headed back to Kingsburg, dreading the sight of Tina's face when he told her the news. He stopped at a bar, hoping to ease his anxiety. After downing two cocktails, he realized that although he needed Tina more than anything right then, he couldn't face her tonight with no job prospects. He'd have to find work, and soon, so that when he told her about losing the airbase job, it wouldn't be such a blow.

A couple of weeks later, on an unusually sunny, snow-covered day, Rosie stopped by Tina's house with her kids in tow.

"Hey, I just had to get out of the house with these rowdy kiddos and thought they could play with your boys for a while."

Tina chuckled and let them inside. "Come on in. Junior and Peter are playing out back." She gestured toward the window to the backyard, then threw her coat on. The mothers sat on the steps while their kids jumped into the snow mounds and threw snow at each other.

They made small talk for a few minutes, then Rosie said. "Tina, you haven't said anything to me lately about Tommy's airbase job."

"Oh, he loves it."

Rosie turned her eyes away from the children and looked at Tina. "Then you don't know?"

"Know what?"

Rosie yelled over to her boy, who had thrown a snowball into his sister's face then turned back to Tina. "Oh, Tina, they dropped his contract for good, almost a month ago!"

Tina got hold of Tommy that night at his parents' house and told him to come right over. When he arrived, she tried to appear calm as she directed him into the kitchen where they could talk without waking the children.

Following him with her heart pounding and nostrils flaring, she spoke with barely contained rage. "Why didn't you tell me that you got fired from the airbase job?"

He turned to her. "How did you find out?"

"Rosie just told me. She thought I knew!"

"I, uh—" He lowered his gaze. "I didn't have the heart to tell you."

"And how did you think I would feel if I found out?"

He crossed his arms and grasped both elbows, looking miserable. "I guess I, uh, thought I'd find a job before that."

"Oh, Tommy. Things are just getting worse with us."

———

After a week of not speaking to Tommy, Tina had finally calmed down enough to be civil to him. With no steady work prospects on the horizon, he finally sucked up his pride, and on the days that he didn't have a job, he babysat the boys while Tina worked. He figured it was the least he could do.

A few weeks after the blowup, still with no steady work on the horizon, Tommy ran into an old friend at a bar. After they exchanged pleasantries, his friend mentioned that he had found work as a welder at the shipyards in New York City.

"That's great, Bill," Tommy said with interest.

"Yeah, I've been down there the past three months. They always need more men to build the fleet of battleships."

"I read about that, but it's so far away."

"Yeah, but it's worth it. You go down there for a few months and make a bundle. They've got three shifts working round the clock. The money's great, and you can make your own hours."

"I heard that, too, but where do you live while you're there?"

"I found a guy who was renting a cheap room. There's always somebody looking for another roommate to share the expenses."

"You kidding?"

"Hell, no." He jotted a number down on the inside of a matchbook. "Here, call this guy. He'll fix you up. It's the best deal to make some quick dough."

Tommy hated the idea of being so far away from Tina and the boys. But after giving the idea a lot of thought, he became convinced that the job would be the best way to get back with them once and for all. Too, maybe getting out of town for a while would squelch some of the whispers still going on in Kingsburg about his father's internment. He had to try something.

He wouldn't mention the shipbuilding job to Tina until he had arranged all the details.

Tina rushed around the house, getting the boys fed and bathed. She wanted to have plenty of time to primp before Tommy arrived to take her to dinner. He had told her that he had some good news about a job and wanted to celebrate. He'd even arranged to have his parents babysit while he took Tina out to a fancy restaurant. She had been praying that he'd get a contract for a job big enough to pay what he was worth. *Please God, make it be the right job.*

Tommy picked her up with a bouquet of white roses in his hands. They kissed the kids goodbye and headed for the restaurant. She tried to get him to give her more details about the job, but he waited until after they'd finished eating a big piece of chocolate cake before broaching the topic.

"Tina, you know how hard I've tried to find steady work,"

"I know, Tom, it wasn't—"

"Well, I found something."

With a wide grin and eyes sparkling, she grabbed his forearm on the table.

He pulled back. "Wait. It's not exactly what we wanted."

Tina tilted her head, and her eyes narrowed.

"I got a job at the shipyards in New York City."

"New York? I don't understand. Why would—?"

"They need welders really bad, and they're paying a lot for them. I'm gonna take advantage of it."

"But where will you live?"

"I'll be rooming with another out-of-town welder. Lots of guys are doing it now."

It had never occurred to Tina that Tommy would consider going that far away for work, and that he would stay at least three months to make it worthwhile. When Tommy dropped Tina off at their front door after hitting her with the news, she could say nothing more than goodnight. Her emotions swung wildly from resenting him to hating herself for feeling that way.

Later than night, Tina called Rosie. "He knows we don't need the money so badly that he has to leave us for that long," she grumbled.

"Yeah, but it's from your work, not his. Isn't that why you two separated in the first place?"

"Yes. I couldn't stand him resenting me for it."

"Well, kiddo, why are you so surprised that he would do anything to match your income?"

Later that night, the more she thought about it, the more Rosie's voice of reason made sense. Obviously, Tommy couldn't see it her way. He had too much pride. As a matter of fact, isn't that what had attracted her to him in the first place? As the day of his departure drew near, she broke down and insisted that he stay with her and the boys until he had to leave. In bed on the night before he left, they clung to each other.

"Tommy," Tina said, "I can't believe I'm saying this, but if your going is the only way we can stay together, than maybe it's for the best."

———◆———

Despite Tina trying to convince herself that Tommy had to take the job, it didn't make the lonely nights any better. He wrote twice a week saying how hard he was working and how much he missed her and the boys. She passed the nights answering his letters.

During the days, she had little time to sulk over their situation because the kids and her work kept her occupied from sunrise to late at night. Irene and her father took the children often, and Tina found a woman in her neighborhood to fill in when they weren't available.

WE CAN DO IT!

On a cold and damp February night in 1943, Tina had just put the boys to bed and started straightening up when she heard a knock at the door. She opened it to see Rosie standing on the porch.

"Hey, Ro, come on in. What brings you here this time of day?"

"Got a minute?" Rosie asked, taking off her jacket as she walked in.

"Sure. I just put the kids down." Tina led her into the kitchen. "Let's go in here so we don't wake them."

Rosie slid onto a chair at the table.

"Want some coffee? I have a little bit left in the pot."

"No, that's OK," Rosie said while looking down at the floor. "I'll take a cup of Postum. At least it's hot."

Tina took a cup from the shelf and got out her jar of Postum, the government's wheat bran and molasses substitute for coffee.

"Is something wrong? You're acting kind of funny."

"Well, it's not good news." Rosie swallowed hard. "Frankie just heard from his mother that Eddie is out of jail."

Tina dropped into a chair. "What? When? I thought he had another year."

Rosie shrugged. "She said something about good behavior."

Tina sighed and banged her fist on the table, "Things aren't bad enough? Now I've got to worry about running into him."

———◆———

Tina didn't have time to happen upon Eddie because he showed up at her door a week later.

"Hello, Tina," he said with a grin. "How are you?"

She held the door open only a few inches. "Eddie, you've got a lot of nerve showing up here."

"I know. I'm sorry, but I thought it would be better than meeting you accidently in public." He cleared his throat. "May I come in a minute?"

Before she could answer, Peter appeared at the door and pulled on her dress. "Mommy, Junior took my truck away and won't let me have it back."

Tina picked him up and Eddie continued. "I heard you had a couple of kids."

"Yes. Two boys."

He scanned her from head to toe. "It doesn't show. If anything, you look even more beautiful."

Tina put Peter down and folded her arms across her chest. "What do you want, Eddie? I'm busy."

"I can see that, so I'll make it short. I heard that Tom's business failed because of his father's enemy alien status. That must be rough on all of you."

"New travels fast."

"Small town." He cleared his throat. "Anyway, I had a lot of time to think about what I did to Tom, and I want to apologize for sabotaging his school building job. I just didn't want to lose you to him, but I should've known that you would run to his defense."

She didn't want to discuss it with him, so she replied firmly, "I appreciate your apology, but if you're looking for absolution, you'll have to take that up with a priest. It's probably good that you stopped by to break the ice, but I really have things to do. Goodbye," she said and shut the door in his face.

———

By mid-February, as usual, the fresh snow of early December had turned gray, but freezing temperatures persisted and preserved the towering snowbanks. The family thanked goodness that February had fewer days than all the other months.

Angelo had gotten leave and would be home on February 28th. He would have three weeks with them before going overseas. He'd been assigned as a radioman on an aircraft carrier and didn't know when he'd be home again. His and Annie's baby was due around late February or early March, and everyone hoped that he would be there for the birth.

Once home, Angelo enjoyed seeing the family, but he held back from slipping back into his role as the wise-cracking kid they had known and loved. Not only had his demeanor changed during his many months in the military, but he knew that he had to maintain a certain mindset in order to leave there and arrive ready to fight the enemy he had been trained to hate. So, after a week of being with his family and visiting the familiar places around town, he went to see his boyhood friend, Vinny, injured in battle.

"Hey, Vin," he said, as he entered the room where Vinnie sat alone in a wheelchair.

Vinnie swung his chair around. "Angie, how are you, buddy?"

Angelo peered down at Vinnie's smiling face and tried to hide his glance at his friend's missing right leg as he shook his hand.

"I'm glad to be home, for a while anyway," Angelo said.

"I bet that wife of yours is happy, too. You're lucky to have some-body home waiting for you."

"Yeah, I'm hoping I'll be here when the baby comes, too."

Vinnie gave a silent nod.

Angelo had to ask, but hesitated a moment, "Want to tell me how it happened, Vin?"

Vinnie shrugged. "Nothing heroic. Just didn't get out from under that grenade fast enough."

"You joined up before you got called. That was pretty heroic to me. So, what are they going to do for you?"

"They gave me new leg." He pointed to the prosthesis in the corner. "Even taught me how to walk. But it hurts and I hate it."

"What about work?"

"Well, I can't go back to truck driving."

"Won't the government retrain you for something you can do?"

"I guess so, but I've got a pension coming to me for the rest of my life, so I'm not in a big hurry."

Angelo left feeling sorry for his friend, but at least the war was over for Vinny. It was just about to begin for him, and he shivered at the thought that he might return home injured—or maybe not at all.

Eva had been away on a job when Angelo arrived, so when she got back into town, she was eager to join the family for dinner. With the meal finished, Eva and Angelo found themselves alone at the kitchen table.

"It's good to be home," he told Eva. "But it's not the same with all my friends either injured or scattered around the world fighting this damn war."

"I know. The local bars and hangouts are not much fun for us girls now, with most of the men away."

"Irene told me that you might be leaving to fly army planes soon."

"Yup—if I get chosen and make it through four months of training."

"Well, I know how much you want to do it, but I don't blame Pa for worrying about you. I guess it never occurred to him that you'd join the service. Of course, none of the rest of us thought so, either."

"I can understand that, but it's the closest thing to fighting the enemy that I can do. I can't let this chance pass me by. Besides, you're the one he really has to worry about," Eva continued. "Aren't you scared about going into combat?"

"Sis, I've always worried that I might get hurt or die, but never as much as I do now that I have responsibilities. I'm afraid for Annie and the baby if something happens to me."

Eva blinked away a tear, as she realized that her kid brother had grown up, and she hated that he had to face such weighty issues. "I'll make a deal with you," she said as she gave him a smacking kiss on the cheek. "Let's both agree to put ourselves in God's hands and have confidence in ourselves and each other. And when it's all over we'll throw a big party to celebrate."

◆

Later at her apartment, Eva couldn't take her mind off Angie as she flipped through the mail she'd brought in earlier in the day. It took a minute for the return address on one of the envelopes to register with her. When it did, she tore open the envelope and read the letter of acceptance to the WFTD, signed by Jacqueline Cochran. She dropped onto a kitchen chair and read the details inviting her to report on April 6th to Avenger Field, the new training facility in Sweetwater, Texas.

◆

Angelo needn't have worried about missing the birth of his baby, because Annie went into labor that night. Tina wished she could be at the hospital, but she didn't have a babysitter. She would just have to wait by the phone all night.

The call from Angelo finally came at 6:30 the next morning. "It's a girl, Tina! She's six pounds and ten ounces, and we named her Jennifer Anne."

"Oh, Angie, that's wonderful. And Annie and baby are doing well?"

"Yes. Can you believe that I'm a father?"

"It's going to take some getting used to, but"—her voice cracked—"I know you're going to be a wonderful daddy. Give my love to Annie and give your daughter a kiss for me. I'll be by to see them this afternoon."

Tina called her father and Irene first. She got through to them, but when she tried calling Eva next, her line rang busy. "Oh, of all times for the lines to be jammed. Damn this war!"

Before she could get through to Eva, her phone rang. She answered to hear an excited Eva, who reported her news about the WFTD.

"Oh my God. I'm so happy for you!"

"You are? Really?"

"Of course. Why wouldn't I be?"

"I got the feeling you didn't think I should apply."

Tina hesitated before responding. "Well, it sounded even more dangerous than cargo flying. And army planes? Somehow, I couldn't picture you in the army."

"Still think of me as your flighty little sister, huh?"

"No, I—"

"Come on. You know you do.

"Eva, that's not—"

"Well, don't worry. I'm not going to let that ruin my excitement over getting chosen."

Tina giggled. "I knew you wouldn't, and you shouldn't. It's just that I'll miss ya."

Tina hung up the phone with a sigh and wished she could tell Tommy everything that had happened that week. But he would be at work on the docks, so she would have to wait. She hated him being so far away. It was hard enough day to day, but she missed sharing special family news and events in person.

She quickly reminded herself, she'd practically forced him into taking the shipyard job. She had refused to let him move back into the house until he could reconcile living off her income alone. In her weaker moments, she wished she could take back what she had said. But she also realized that the strain of being apart made her forget the seriousness of their problems. She had to stay strong and ride out this self-imposed separation.

A few days later, after supper with her father and Irene, Eva told her father and Irene about her acceptance to the WFTD training. Irene hugged and congratulated her. Dominic remained silent, walked into the living room, and sat down with the newspaper.

Eva rolled her eyes and followed him. "Can't you be happy for me, Pa? You know how much I've hoped for this."

He sighed and dropped the paper into his lap. "I hated that you learned to fly, but I had to get used to you up there by yourself. Now you're going to fly those big machines that were made for fighting men. Not little girls like you. You ask too much of me. Isn't it bad enough I got to watch Angelo go to war?"

Eva couldn't blame him for wanting to protect her, so she leaned over and kissed his forehead. "I'm sorry, Pa, but I've got to try this."

The last two weeks of Angelo's leave sped by as he and Annie spent them bonding with their new baby. Having that special time with his little family turned into both a godsend and a heartbreak when he had to go.

Eva was at her father's house to say goodbye to Angelo the day he left. She pulled him to her for a goodbye hug. "Now, sailor, keep your head down and get one of those Japs for me, will ya?" she said, hoping her smile masked her sadness.

Angelo's sober look showed her she'd failed. "You betcha, sis. And you remember to keep those silver birds flying straight and level." She could see him trying to hold back his own tears.

Then a somber Dominic and Carmen drove him to the train sta-tion. Angelo tried to keep the conversation light.

"So long, Pa," he said as he turned to board the train,

But Dominic pulled him in for a rib-crushing goodbye hug. "I'm proud of you, my boy. Come back to your family soon."

———

In March, Tommy told Tina that he had signed up to work in New York City a month longer than he'd planned, because his boss offered him double-time to stay. They needed all the good welders they could get, and Tommy was the best. She didn't like the idea, but she knew he couldn't turn it down. As he had promised, he wired her money every two weeks, and since she didn't need much of it, she banked the rest for when he came home. Just in case he couldn't find work, they would have a nest egg to help if they needed it.

Not long afterward, both boys came down with sore throats, snif-fles, and fevers, so Tina called Dr. Chandler.

He made a house call to check them out.

"The boys will be fine," he reported after seeing them. "It's just the virus going around. Keep them well-hydrated and give them three tablespoons of this a day."

He handed her a bottle, then frowned. "I'm more concerned about you. You're peaked. Have you been getting enough rest?"

"As much as I can these days."

"What about eating? You look like you've lost some weight."

"I don't have much of an appetite."

"Hmm. When will Tommy be back?"

"In a couple more weeks. He's trying to take advantage of the war job as long as he can."

"Well, I'd like you to come to my office when the boys are better. I want to run some tests."

When the doctor gave his diagnosis a few days later, Tina had to admit that it didn't come as a complete surprise. She had already considered that she might be pregnant. After all, it had been over two months since she and Tommy had made love, and she'd missed her period. But she had told herself that because her first three pregnancies only came as the result of her diligently taking her temperature, a baby was not likely.

Walking back home, she sighed. *Of all the times to have a baby.* She remembered the baby they'd lost under perfect circumstances. Now, with the constant upheaval of the world at war, and her and Tommy's relationship already under such a strain, it might only result in another miscarriage. She shook her head, looked up to the heavens, and said aloud, "Oh God, I hope you know what you're doing."

Tina decided not to announce her pregnancy to anyone except Rosie. She invited her over the next day, and while the children played together, she blurted it out.

"Oh, Tina, that's wonderful! When are you due?

"September."

"And you weren't even trying! What did Tommy say?"

"I haven't told him. I'm waiting to tell him when he gets home in a few weeks."

"Why?"

"I want to tell him in person."

"I understand, but I don't think I could hold it in that long."

"I'm kind of scared to tell him, so it's also a delaying tactic to wait."

"Scared? Why are you scared?"

"I don't know. We've got so much going on right now."

"That's silly. Personally, I think it's the perfect time to bring you two back together for good. This could be the best thing for you right now."

The war continued to effect life on the Homefront even more. In the kitchen, items like meat, fats, canned milk, and cheese had made it to the ration list. As a result, preparing tasteful meals became a bigger challenge. To offset the problem, more and more recipes appeared in newspapers and magazines.

Tina went to work designing women's slacks and dresses that would meet the government's strict L-85 order, stipulating those designs had to limit the use of nylon, wool, and silk, to conserve them for war use. L-85 also mandated that women's slacks would have narrow legs and only one pocket. Fabric belts could be no wider than two inches, and skirts had to be at least seventeen inches from the floor, considerably shorter than had been the style of the 1930s. Tina and Irene had to hire two new seamstresses and acquire more sewing machines to keep up with the orders.

Some working women found it difficult to prevent their clothes from becoming tattered, so Tina also designed smocks to protect and conserve their street clothes. Orders increased as more women joined the workforce in factories. Women who could not afford brand-new pants, or wanted to conserve material, brought in old pants to be re-designed. The shop began to make more money than Tina and Irene could've ever imagined during the Depression years.

Irene and Tina even arranged for Mary, Irene's assistant, to teach classes for working women on Saturday afternoons at the high school. The women learned how to sew their own clothes and crochet snoods to protect their hair from getting caught in factory machinery. In addition, Irene and Mary advised homemakers on how to make new clothes out of old ones and mend their own clothes as per the government's call to "Sew for Victory."

In Europe, US General George Patton's men taking Palermo led to the removal of Benito Mussolini. However, soon after, Hitler ordered his troops to occupy Italy, and a fierce battle ensued. Dominic worried about his older brothers back in the old country where fighting had been reported. But the war had made communication difficult, and all he could do was listen to the war news each night on the radio.

At the end of March, Eva finished her last cargo job and prepared for her departure to Texas. Her roommate had told her that she would have to take in another boarder in Eva's absence, because she needed the money. So, if Eva washed out of training, she would have to find lodging elsewhere. Eva anxiously prayed that she would graduate and join the WFTD.

Eva boarded the train for Sweetwater, Texas, carrying one bag holding her essentials, as the acceptance letter stipulated. She knew she would receive a paycheck but wouldn't have much to spend it on. She took her seat on the train and gulped. *Well, this is it. No going back now.* As she looked out the window, she watched the landscape change from the lush green countryside of the east and mid-west to the flat, wide-open spaces of Oklahoma and Texas. They seemed to be endless.

As she got closer to her destination, her doubts doubled. *Four months is an awfully long time to be away from home. How will it be to sleep in a roomful of strangers. And the classes. Will I be able to keep up with the other women, much less pass?* Then she thought of the military discipline of the army. *Maybe Tina was right. Will I be able to take army life?"* Angelo's stories made it sound awfully rigorous. The thought of him getting ready to join the fight across the world, under much worse conditions, told her she owed it to him and all the other boys like him, to do her part.

On April 6, 1943, Eva took a seat amid a roomful of other recruits in a large room with a small podium. Beneath their subdued murmuring, she sensed an underlying, quiet apprehension.

The program began with a welcome and thank you for the women's interest in the WFTD and their willingness to put their lives on hold for the service of the country. The Speakers stressed that the opportunity to fly military planes was a privilege, and that the training would be conducted according to military protocol. Furthermore, they the program would accept no less than those standards from successful recruits. Any variation from that behavior would be a reason for expulsion from the program.

Eva and the others were assigned six to a room, each with an army cot and a locker. After a long couple of days of travel and trepidation, the women welcomed retreating to their beds. But like many of them, Eva spent a restless night in her new surroundings. Though she had often had to sleep away from home while on cargo jobs, her mind and body could not relax in this new environment with a room full of strangers.

The next morning began with the sound of a bugle reveille before dawn, and training got underway. First, Eva and her roommates learned to pass inspection by properly making a military bed and storing their assigned gear in their lockers.

Next came the issue of men's coveralls or "zoot suit" flight wear. Which amounted to a one-piece coverall of sorts with long sleeves and trousers. The smallest size available still swallowed the women's frames. Far from the latest women's fashion, the garments often had to be modified to fit the women. Otherwise, they would trip on the pantlegs and lose their hands in the sleeves. As Eva gradually adjusted to the training routine, she even learned to appreciate the hearty and nutritious food served in the mess hall, one exception being the American version of spaghetti and meatballs. *They must've used ketchup for the sauce.*

Eva discovered that being thrown into close quarters with women from all walks of life could be a challenge. One bathroom for twelve women created chaos on mornings after reveille. Eva tried her best to jump up and get in and out of the latrine as fast as she could. She'd been sharing a bathroom with her whole family all of her life, so she was used to it.

One morning she stood in line with her other roommates outside the bathroom door. "Hurry up in there, will you?" she yelled, pounding on the door.

"I'll be out when I'm finished," a snooty girl from a well-to-do family replied from inside.

Eva turned to the women in line. "Who does she think she is? The queen of England?"

When the girl came out of the bathroom, Eva said, "Finally. Her Royal Highness emerges."

"Hey, I can take as long as I want. This organization is lucky that I'm willing to share my living quarters with an "Italian," and others like you. For all I know you could be one of those spies."

The comment stung, but Eva masked her feelings as she went into the bathroom.

Later, one of the other girls, a southern belle named Rosalind, took Eva aside. "Don't pay any attention to her, honey," she said. "She doesn't speak for the rest of us. We're all in the same boat here, and that's to help fight for the freedom of Americans from all walks of life."

***

In May, Annie told the family that Angelo had been assigned as a radio operator on an aircraft carrier. When Dominic got a letter from him describing his new home, he shared it with her.

Annie took the letter and eagerly began to read. "This place is unbelievable," he wrote. "It's like about a couple of city blocks long with a kitchen, a laundry, a drugstore, a hospital, a barber, a shoe repair shop, and even a movie theater. So don't worry. They're taking good care of me. The guys are all pretty swell, too."

"Of course, I miss everyone an awful lot. Annie sent me a good picture of you holding baby Jennifer. She's getting so big, but you know that because Annie says they go to your house for Sunday dinner twice a month.

"Well, it's bedtime for me, so I'll say goodnight until next time. Love to you and Irene, Angelo."

Annie smiled. "Thanks for showing me the letter, Pa. I'll tell him when I write to him tonight."

A few weeks later, a letter from Angelo told them that transfer was imminent. What he couldn't tell them was his location. The letters were all postmarked with an FPO address for them to use so that their letters would be forwarded to him wherever he was, and the government censored Angelo's responses containing any indications of his location. They suspected that with all the battles being reported in the South Pacific he had to be involved in the fighting.

The family experienced a sense of relief whenever they received a letter from Angelo, but in the weeks between letters, the only thing his loved ones could do was pray and light candles at home and in church.

———

Tina hadn't spoken to Eddie after the day he appeared at her door. However, much to her chagrin, his name continued to come up in conversations with friends and customers.

"So, Tina, have you seen Eddie since he's been back?" asked one nosy customer at the shop.

"Only once. And that was enough."

After the woman left, Irene shook her head. "Those old blabbermouths love to get fuel for their gossip."

"It will pass eventually when they have something new to talk about. I'm just glad I'm not here every day."

"The main thing is that he doesn't bother you at home anymore."

"That shouldn't be a problem now. Rosie told me that he's got a girlfriend. Somebody out of town. Besides, I don't have time to worry about him, what with taking care of the kids and all the work I have to do."

"Did you ever tell Tommy about Eddie's visit to you?"

"No, and I don't plan to."

Tommy hated being so far away from Tina and the kids but knew the money would make the difference between him living with his family and being alone. He couldn't go back to having Tina support him again, so when the boss enticed him with a fifth month's work, Tommy grabbed the opportunity.

"Tina," he said when he called her on phone, "I got offered another month down here, and I took it."

He waited for Tina's reply, but she didn't offer one. "Tina, did you hear me say I'm going to stay here one more month?"

"I heard you," she croaked.

"What's the matter? I thought you'd be happy that I'm going to make more dough."

"Oh, I like the money all right. It's just that the boys miss you, and I could use your help here with them."

"I miss them, too. What about you? Do you miss me?"

"Yes. I told you I do."

"No. You said you needed me to help with the kids."

"Of course, I miss you," she said in a matter-of-fact tone.

"OK, I'll take your word for it. I just figured I should work as much as I can. I can't count on finding work near Kingsburg."

"Your father is home now, and things are different around here now. The war has changed things a lot."

"That's good to know, and I miss you too, but I've already committed to staying on here for one more month. But all the dough in the world couldn't keep me here any longer than that. I promise."

With Tommy gone for another month, Tina realized that this would be the best time to finish up some work projects in progress. If she timed it just right, she could get all her obligations satisfied before the baby's arrival. God, she hated taking the birth for granted. She had done that last time, and it almost did her in when she miscarried. But she couldn't wait until the last minute to get ready, so she made up her mind to think positive.

One afternoon, just as Tina was putting the boys down for their afternoon naps, she heard a knock at the door. She opened it to a Western Union boy.

"Telegram for Mrs. Capello," he said.

Tina took the envelope and shut the door. Thinking it to be from a manufacturer with whom she'd been working, she set it on the table by the door and took the boys into their bedroom. After she got them settled in for their naps, she picked up the telegram, poured herself a cup of tea, and sat down to read it.

"Oh my God! Tommy!" she cried out, as she read the message:

"EXPLOSION AT SHIPYARD STOP TOMMASO CAPELLO SUFFERED BROKEN LEG AND CONCUSSION STOP RECEIVING TREATMENT AT LOCAL HOSPITAL STOP FOR FURTHER DETAILS—."

Tina saw the phone number and called Tommy's family. They rushed to her house to be there when she made the call, but it didn't go through until a half an hour after they arrived. Tommy's father paced, and his mother wept. Tina heard the doctor say that Tommy was badly hurt. She gave the phone to Tommy's brother, Carl to get more details while Tina rushed around packing a suitcase to take with her. She planned to leave on the next available train to New York City.

When Carl hung up, he filled the family in about Tommy's condition.

"Well, he's conscious, but under sedation for the pain and unable to talk much. They still aren't sure how much damage was done, or if he'll have any long-term side effects."

Tina hated the sound of that. *This can't be happening. Oh God, please make him be all right. His sons need him, and he doesn't even know that the new baby will need him soon. And, oh God, I need him!*"

After the Capello's left for home, Tina called Rosie. She didn't even wait to hear her friend's hello. "Uh, Ro," she stammered, her throat tight. "Tommy's been hurt! I have to go to him at the hospital in New York, and the boys—" The sobs she had been holding back broke through.

"I'll be right over to pick them up," Rosie said. "You just concentrate on getting packed."

"Oh, Ro, thank you. I need to catch the train as soon as possible, but I'll make more permanent arrangements for the boys before I leave."

———

Tommy's parents gladly agreed to care for Peter, and Junior would stay with Dominic and Irene.

The train ride seemed longer than any other trip she'd taken to New York City. She tried to read the newspaper, then thumbed through a couple of magazines. But nothing she read registered in her brain. All her thoughts kept drifting back to Tommy. *Was the money really so important that it had to keep us apart the past year?*

She closed her eyes and pictured him smiling at the boys. The only thing that mattered was that Tommy was well and able to come back to her and their family.

———

When Tina arrived at the hospital, she spoke with a nurse who showed her to Tommy's room. At her first sight of him, her heart sank. He lay there with a bandaged head and his leg in a sling suspended above the bed. A bottle of liquid hung from a pole beside him. She would later learn that it fed him penicillin, a rare new drug used to fight infection. The drug had been developed as a panacea for war injuries on the battlefield. Few civilian hospitals kept supplies of it, and it would not have been available in Kingsburg.

But then, if Tommy had remained in Kingsburg, he would not have suffered these life-threatening injuries, and wouldn't need the drugs in the first place.

"Oh, Tommy," she said as she leaned over and kissed his bruised face. She had a sense of déjà vu remembering many years before when he was brutally beaten by the police after they trashed his illegal gambling speakeasy.

He stirred and slurred, "Tina? Is that you?"

"Yes, sweetheart."

"How did I get home?"

"You didn't. I came to you in New York. How do you feel?"

"My head hurts. Where are the boys?"

"I left Peter with your parents, and Junior with mine. They're fine."

"I still don't know how I got here. What happened?"

Tina knew that he'd been told about the accident but that he was suffering from memory loss, so she reminded him. "There was an explosion at your work. You got pretty banged up."

"I missed you. I'm glad you're here, but what about your work?"

"My work can wait. I need—I want to be with you right now." She chuckled. "I need to make you follow doctor's orders. I know how you are about doctors. You think you know better than them. Do you need anything from the nurse right now?"

He didn't answer. He had fallen back to sleep, so Tina wiped her eyes and sat down in the chair next to his bed to wait for the doctor.

While sitting there, she recalled that from the beginning, money had been the only thing that had kept them from being together. She had opposed being with him from the start. He was a gambler, and she hated his business and his reputation of being a small-time hood. He stood for all the things she had worked so hard to dispel in the eyes of the people living on the north side of town.

Tina stirred as the doctor walked into the room.

"Oh, Doctor. I'm Tommy's wife."

The doctor told Tina that Tom's considerable strength would help him. "He'll be back walking in a couple of months. It's just a matter of time."

"What about his head?"

"Unfortunately, I can't be as sure about the head injury. It's still too early to know if he'll suffer long-term-pain and/or memory loss."

"When will we be able to know for sure?"

"A few months, at least. It will take that long for his injury to heal. We should get some idea about the memory by then."

Tina hadn't heard what she had hoped to from the doctor. *Oh, I can nurse his leg and his superficial injuries easily. The memory loss is another story. What if he never fully recovers from that? What will our life be like?* She couldn't help thinking of Eddie with his business thriving as if nothing had happened. It didn't seem fair, after he'd sabotaged Tommy's school project and ruined his business.

———◆———

WASP training continued for Eva. The twelve-hour days proved to be grueling, with half of the day devoted to flying and the remainder to classes on subjects like hydraulics, meteorology, Morse code, aerodynamics, physics, and plane maintenance.

"Ugh," she complained one night, as she and her roommates wearily returned to the barracks. "I could use a night off. Whaddaya say we sneak out, go to town, and hoist a few."

"You know we have to wait for the weekend," Hope, one of her more serious friends, told her.

"Oh, you're no fun!"

Eva had no problem with the training, but the constraints on her free time played havoc with her freethinking personality. Though Eva worked hard, she found the military discipline and army regulations confining and began to have second thoughts about her ability to adapt to its restrictions long term.

The rules and tight control imposed on her began to wear thin. When that happened, she thought of Angelo and his circumstances in combat and answered his latest letter.

For the rest, she liked the class work and loved learning to fly the military way. She got along with her flight instructors and soaked up everything she could from their flying knowledge

In June, Tommy's doctor discharged him from the hospital, and his brother, Carl, traveled by train to pick him up. At home, Tina spent the day cleaning house and preparing for his arrival. She vacillated between being ecstatic and apprehensive. He sounded pretty good the times she had spoken to him on the phone, and he seemed alert and anxious to come home.

This is the day she had longed for, but now panic had taken over. She told herself that he would be the same old Tommy. But how could he be, after going through what he had experienced?

Tina stood at the door and watched him walk up the steps of their house with the use of a crutch. Her eyes quickly darted to his bearded face and then to his thin profile. A sudden chill swept over her and made her gasp. Then he smiled at her, and she saw the man she had fallen for many years ago. She ran to him and threw her arms around him.

He dropped the crutch and encircled her with his arms. "I'm home," he said with a smile. "Sorry I'm late."

"Well, it's about time," she said with a giggle.

Tommy spent the following couple of weeks getting acclimated to home again. The doctor had been right. His leg, though out of the cast, had lost muscle mass, but with regular exercise and home cooking, he continued to improve.

Despite recurring headaches, Tommy helped with the boys until they got too rambunctious, and the noise caused a ringing in his ears. At least he didn't have to worry about money for his care, because he had received a settlement from the company. Though he couldn't work, he knew that money was coming in.

Tina continued to work as much as she could, despite getting progressively drained by the pregnancy. She still had not revealed it to Tommy because she feared that him worrying about her and the baby's health would put more of a strain on him and slow his recovery. She had been able to hide her fuller figure for now, but she knew that when he got stronger, he would turn to her for intimacy and discover her secret.

She didn't have to wait that long.

"Hey, I go away for a couple of months, and you get a little flabby," he joked as he watched her make the bed one morning.

She looked down and clutched her stomach. "I guess I have gained a couple of pounds. I hoped you wouldn't notice."

"Just more of you to love," he said with a wink.

"Tommy," she said as she sat down on the bed. "I wasn't going to tell you yet, but since you noticed—I'm almost five months pregnant."

Tommy's jaw dropped. "Sweetheart, that's wonderful. How long have you known?"

"Since before your accident. I was going to tell you when you came home after the first three months. But when you stayed in the city, I didn't want you to worry about me from down there."

He wrapped his arms around her. "And how are you?"

"I'm fine, and so is the baby." She smiled. The doctor thinks this one is going make it, because he hears a strong heartbeat."

"I wish I'd known you've been going through all of this."

"I'm just glad you're here now. I was so afraid when I thought I'd lost you."

He smiled. "I'm not going anywhere. I'm staying right here with you. No more separations."

———

July 1943, Jackie Cochran announced to her fliers that the WFTD would have a name change. They were to be called WASP, or Women Airforce Service Pilots. Eva and the class of 43-5 accepted their new moniker with little fanfare and continued their training.

By August so many male pilots had been sent overseas that the Army Air Forces turned to the WASP to take their places in a variety of stateside flying jobs. No longer just ferrying new planes from factory to army bases, they branched out to towing targets, tracking and searchlight operations, simulated strafing, radio control flying, and administrative and utility flying.

In September, after being so focused on flying and her studies, Eva hadn't given much thought to the WASP graduation ceremony. Because of that, when she called Dominic and Irene to say she had passed her exams and would be home after *graduation,* she surprised herself. As it turned out, she had never been so proud of herself as on the day Jackie Cochran pinned her wings on her white uniform shirt in view of the army brass and guests.

Although graduation day represented all the hard work and sweat, she and her fellow graduates had endured together, saying goodbye and going their separate ways was bittersweet. That is, until she and two of her favorite classmates, Hope and Rosalind, received orders to report to Camp Davis in North Carolina at the end of their leaves.

When Eva arrived in Kingsburg, her former roommate picked her up at the train station and dropped her off at the Benedetti home. She walked into what seemed like an empty house and yelled, "Anybody home?"

Carmen came running down the stairs. "Just me and the chickens. Is that you, Eva?"

"In the flesh," she said. "How are ya, kid?"

"I'm good." He eyed her khaki-colored skirt and the wings on her white shirt. "Pretty sharp. Who'd a thought I'd have a sister in the service?"

"And it looks like you grew a few more inches," she said looking up at him. "Where's Pa and Irene?"

"Pa's working in the garden, and Irene had some work to do at her shop."

Eva walked out and found Dominic hoeing in the garden with his back to her,.

"Hi, Pa. I'm home."

He turned and wiped his face with his handkerchief. "Eva." He dropped the hoe and wrapped his arms around her.

"How are you, Pa?"

He shrugged and stood back. "You look different, but good," he said.

"It's the uniform. It makes everyone look better."

He eyed the wings on her chest. "I guess this means you're really an army pilot now."

She nodded. "Are you OK with that?"

"They must think you're a good flier, or they wouldn't have given you those. So," he said with a smile, "I guess I'm just gonna have to be proud of you."

Eva wanted to see everyone, so after spending time with the family, she called her friends the next day and arranged to meet them at their local hangout that night. The place looked the same, but somehow smaller and older. She spotted a few of the regular barflies, and her girlfriends, but other than that, the place looked deserted.

She found her friends glad to see her and anxious to hear what she had been doing. But before long their eyes began to glaze over as she described her training and the airplanes she had been flying. She said goodbye to them long before closing time and went home missing the WASP friends with whom she had spent months living, training, commiserating, and encouraging.

She spent some time at Tina's house with Tina, now six months pregnant.

"The boys have really sprouted up! I bet they must really wear you down. How do you keep up with them?" she said to Tina.

"I have to admit, it was hard before, but it's a real challenge now with this extra load." Tina patted her stomach.

"You're happy though, right?"

Tina nodded and grinned. "I wouldn't have it any other way."

The following day Eva went out to the airport to find out if any fliers or staff had heard from Glenn lately, as he hadn't answered her last few letters.

"Didn't you hear?" said a waitress at the coffee shop. "His plane was shot down over England a couple of months ago."

Eva spent the rest of the day walking around town by herself, crying silent tears. Glenn had been so much more than a boyfriend. He had changed her life by introducing her to flying. She couldn't imagine what her life would be like if that hadn't happened. When she had cried all the tears that she could for him, she went home to her family even more committed to being the best WASP she could be in tribute to him.

The highlight of her leave turned out to be the graduation party that Irene gave in her honor. Annie brought baby Jennifer, and the family shared stories about Angelo that brought him close in spirit. After the party, Eva spent the rest of her time at home, anxious to begin her new adventure.

YOU'RE IN THE ARMY NOW!

Later in September, Eva reported to Camp Davis, North Carolina, situated near a swamp along the Atlantic Ocean. It was a large facility with hundreds of men carrying out a variety of training exercises. Gunnery squads set up with an arsenal of artillery blasted at targets being towed by airplanes.

"More lead! More lead!" the officers yelled at their charges.

Meanwhile, a steady number of planes came and went on the tarmac.

A week after Eva's arrival, a Piper Cub raced down the runway in preparation for takeoff. Inside the cockpit, Eva's gloved hand pushed the throttle forward, lifting the plane off the ground and into the sky.

Just as she sniffed smoke and saw flames on the floor, the traffic controller came over the radio.

"Holy shit!" he said. "653 you're on fire. I repeat, 653, you're on fire! You're cleared for landing. Bring her back!"

The plane jerked, coughed, and shuddered as it touched down. Eva threw open the hatch and jumped down from the plane, pulling her helmet off. She marched up to Sgt. Gunderson, working on a plane in the hanger, with fire in her eyes and venom on her lips.

"All right, Gundy, who's the jackass that signed off the Form One?"

The mechanic pulled his head out of the plane's engine. "What?"

Eva held up the form in question. "The red line was signed off. You're supposed to repair the problem before you sign it off."

"Look, lady, if it's signed, it's fixed."

"Oh yeah?" Eva lifted her greasy gloved hand and smeared dirty oil on his face. "Well, nice job!"

She left the hanger and ran directly to Major Draper's office. Still covered in fresh oil, she stood fuming in front of the adjutant's desk. "I want to see the major right now."

The adjutant took one look at her face and didn't hesitate. "I'll tell him," he said and walked into the major's office, leaving the door open. She could hear them from where she stood.

"Major, it's one of those woman pilots. She wants to talk to you."

"I don't have time to talk to another goddamn female."

"Uh, she seems pretty hot under the collar, sir. I don't think she's going to take no for an answer."

As directed by the major, the adjutant showed Eva in.

"Hello, Major. I'm Eva Benedetti."

Draper didn't look up. "What's the problem, miss?"

"I just had a very close call in one of the planes, sir, and it was due to the negligence of one of your mechanics."

He finally put his pen down and looked at her. "That's a pretty strong accusation, Miss— what is it?"

"Benedetti."

"Miss Benedetti, are you prepared to file a formal complaint and testify to your statement?"

"Well, uh, I hope that won't be necessary. I just want to call your attention to the problem so that you can correct it."

"Very well," he said and went back to his paperwork.

Eva just stood there until he looked up again. "Is there something else, Miss Benedetti?"

"So, can I tell the others that the mechanics will be more conscientious from now on?"

"I'm sure they are doing the best job they can, given their limited resources."

"But these planes are barely operational."

"They're all the army has right now, and parts are almost impossible to get. After all, there is a war on, Miss Benedetti."

"I'm very well aware of that, Major."

"Would you rather we send these planes to our men overseas?"

"No, sir, I—"

"I told Miss Cochran that sending you girls here was a bad idea. You don't have what it takes to do the job, but she used her feminine wiles to persuade the general. Now that you're here, the only thing I can suggest is, if you can't take it, resign. Personally, I think the whole lot of you should quit. The experiment failed. The army can just write off the expense of your training as part of the war cost."

"Yes, sir," Eva said.

"Now, is there something else, Miss Benedetti?"

"No, sir."

He waved her off. "Then good afternoon."

With clenched teeth and hands, Eva turned to walk out, but the sound of his voice stopped her.

"Oh," Draper added, pointing to her smeared face and uniform, "and I don't believe a 'real' lady would let herself be seen looking like that."

Miles away at the Pentagon in Washington, DC, Jackie Cochran spoke with General H. H. "Hap" Arnold. The two had just previewed a film clip from a newsreel being shown in theaters across the country. The film touted the WASP as a brave group of "beauties" relieving men of transporting planes, thus making them available to fly combat missions overseas. But the film then added that the men would actually prefer to date them.

Cochran flipped off the projector and sighed in disgust.

Arnold shrugged. "You wanted publicity."

"The country's not going to agree to commission them into the Army Air Forces if they think they're just frosting on a cake. From now on, I don't want any reporters within a hundred miles of my girls."

The following day, Eva and her fellow WASP, Hope, Veronica, and Rosalind, walked to the mess hall past a group of enlisted men who hurled catcalls at them. As they entered, they found the space buzzing with army pilots, nurses, various officers, and WASP from all over the country.

They got into line behind a group of pilots who turned to look them over. Rosalind, thinking that the guys were admiring them, winked at one of them.

"Good morning, Lieutenant," she said in her southern drawl. "Fine day for flying, isn't it?"

The pilot scowled and turned to look at his buddy.

Rosalind frowned. "Well, that's not very neighborly."

"Forget about it," Veronica said. When they left the line with their trays, Eva scanned the room and spotted some empty chairs. "There's some seats at that table."

The group headed toward the table, but three guys who crowded in front of them grabbed the seats. Looking around the room, they noticed a guy waving them over to his table. As they approached, the young officer cleared the table of the male pilots who were sitting with him.

"Thank you so much," Rosalind said. "That was nice of you. I'm Rosalind. "This is Hope, Veronica, and Eva."

"Don't mention it, honey. Name's Kiley. I've only been here a few days, and I can't figure why some of these guys give you ladies such a hard time."

"We don't know either. We're just trying to do what we can for the war effort," Rosalind said.

"Well, having you gals to look at around here sure makes my war experience more enjoyable."

"I don't think that was the army's reason for putting us through that expensive flight training," Eva said with smirk.

"What I don't get is why some beautiful girls like you want to risk your little necks in an airplane."

Eva sighed with irritation. "That's it," she said as she plucked his food from the table and deposited it on his tray.

"Hey," he blurted out. "What are you doing?"

"Saying goodbye," Eva said. "You're leaving. Thanks for the seats."

Kiley looked at the others. "What's wrong with her?"

Rosalind shrugged. "You'd better go."

Kiley got up. "Shit, those guys were right about you broads."

The women looked at each other and smiled.

"Well, it was nice of him to get us a table," Hope said.

Rosalind shook out her napkin and placed it in her lap. "Yeah, even a bit of misguided warmth is a nice break in this iceberg."

"Oh, he was just flirting with us," Veronica said.

Eva picked up her fork. "Well," she said, "he needs a new line. That one's got whiskers."

Rosalind shook her head. "Forget it, Eva. We're here to do a job, just like them."

"Yeah?" Eva said in irritation, "so why isn't Draper letting us do it? We're supposed to be towing targets, but he won't even check us out on the A-24s."

"I know," said Veronica. "I feel like a beginner again in those little Piper Cubs."

"I sure miss those AT-6's we flew in training." Hope sighed. "They spoil you for anything else."

"Yeah," Rosalind said, picturing the plane in her mind. "That sleek, lanky body, with muscle in all the right places—what a ride."

Veronica laughed. "Hey, aren't you confusing the plane with that guy you dated in Texas?"

———

Late one afternoon, Eva walked toward the flight line. She'd been ordered to deliver some documents for her supervisor to another air base. Two planes stood ready, so she approached Gundy.

"Which one should I take?" she asked

He pointed to one of them. As she began a visual check of the outside of the plane, he turned to walk away.

Not taking any chances, she called out to him, "Any problems with this one?"

He answered with a scowl.

"Hey, that's a fair question, considering what happened to me the other day."

"Check the Form One."

"I'm asking you."

Gundy shot back at her, "Look, the plane is ready to go. Fly it or don't. It's up to you."

At that moment, a ground crew member, Pfc. Cash, approached them in haste.

"Hey, Gundy, LT sent me out to tell you to grab a pilot and go rescue a flier who went down over the swamp."

Eva spoke up. "My errand can wait. Let's go."

Gundy hesitated. "Uh, I usually go with Stevens."

"So where is he?" she asked.

"He took off towing about an hour ago, Sarge," Cash said.

Eva looked over at Cash. "Better tell the lieutenant that downed pilot will have to wait about four hours."

"That ain't gonna fly, Sarge," Cash said to Gundy.

Gundy looked up at Cash then over at Eva. "Oh, all right. What the hell."

Eva turned to climb into the plane, but Gundy grabbed her arm. "Wait! Not this one." He pointed to the other plane. "That one."

"Why? What's the diff— Oh," she said.

Gundy jumped onto the wing of the second plane and got in. "Get my toolbox, Cash."

Eva tried to hide her disgust with Gundy as she watched him settle into the plane, knowing that he had tried to sabotage her. As she taxied the plane down the runway for takeoff, he turned rather pale and tapped his foot wildly.

"Don't do much flying?" she asked.

"Not with girls."

"So, I'm your first?"

He nodded.

"I promise I'll be gentle," she said and opened the throttle, pressing them back into their seats as she executed a silky-smooth takeoff. Leveling off, she said, "That wasn't so bad, was it?"

He shrugged in an obvious effort to look nonchalant.

"Well, then—" She began a series of maneuvers to show her skills—first a dive, then a chandelle, and then a snap roll. But watching Gundy turn green in the middle of a spin was the best revenge she could've hoped for.

"Had enough?" she asked.

Gundy gulped and nodded. A few minutes later, she made a smooth landing in a very tight area of the swamp. Darkness was falling as she taxied to a stop.

She looked over at him and smiled. "Well, it was terrific for me. How was it for you?'

"You're a good pilot."

"Thank you."

"You're welcome."

They sat for a moment in awkward silence. Then, Eva reached over to a pocket next to her and picked up a plastic packet with a tube attached to it.

"Uh, I noticed these in a lot of the planes here. What is it?"

"Oh, uh, nothing you have to worry about."

"Look," she said, "if I'm going to fly these things, I need to know."

Gundy gulped and said, "Uh, when a pilot's in the air for several hours, sometimes, you know, uh, nature calls."

Eva laughed. "A portable potty? You're kidding."

He corrected her. "Relief tube."

Eva inspected it more closely and could see it was made to accommodate the male anatomy. "Great idea, but I don't think they had me in mind when they designed it."

Laughing, they exited the plane.

"Say." Eva stopped. "Just one more thing, and then I won't mention it again."

"Yeah?"

"What was wrong with the other plane?"

Gundy hesitated a moment, then said, "Sticky throttle."

There was silence as she absorbed what he had said.

"I'm sorry," he said. "I was just following orders." The magnitude of what he had just revealed left her speechless.

As Gundy clicked on his flashlight to survey the downed plane, animals, birds, and insects raised a racket. When an unfamiliar animal called out in the distance, Eva jumped.

"What was that?" she asked.

"Just an alligator."

"Oh, is that all?"

"Come on," he said.

Eva shuddered as she looked around and made her way through the thick reeds. After a few moments, she saw the plane's pilot approaching through the twilight.

"Hey, Gundy?" Eva said.

"Yeah?"

"Next time you have to come out here, you have my permission to wait for Stevens."

———

As 1943 progressed, Jackie Cochran decided that the country should know more about what the WASP were doing to support the war effort. *Life* magazine had made them the cover story in their July 19th publication. In addition, a movie newsreel featured Cochran leading members of the press and the brass on a tour around the facility at Camp Davis. They observed gunners shooting at planes flown by the WASP as they towed targets and completed other tedious but necessary flying tasks. Cochran stressed to the reporters that the women's job was to supplement, not replace, the male fliers.

In the meantime, General Arnold, upon Cochran's urging, began looking into militarizing the women. The general tried to use an act that had been implemented in 1941 to commission civilian pilots directly into the Army Air Forces. It would be the path of least resistance, but that act had specifically stipulated men. They would have to get someone to take a bill to Congress.

———

Jackie Cochran burst into Arnold's Pentagon office and stormed up to his desk. "This better be good. I left—"

"Jackie, I didn't expect you so soon."

"The colonel made it sound urgent, so I left Fort Worth immediately and flew half the night. Through the worst storm I've ever seen, by the way, to a hotel that gave away my—"

"I'm sorry you—"

"Just tell me I'm here because they've agreed to commission my WASP into the army."

"Sit down, Jackie," he said with authority.

"No thanks. I'm fine."

The general gave her a stern look, so she sat down.

"We're considering having your girls become part of the WACs."

Her nostrils flared and her eyes narrowed. "Over my dead body."

"Colonel Hobby is quite willing to take them."

"I'll bet she is."

"It makes sense."

"To whom?" she snapped.

"Now Jack—"

"I've always assumed that when we went military, they would be under my command."

"Well. That was how—"

"That was the only reason I agreed to allow them to start flying as civilians. It was a shortcut through the army's door while we able to sell them as part of the Air Forces. I won't be a small cog in that bitch's wheel."

Arnold cleared his throat. "That 'bitch' is a colonel in the United States Army, and you're going to have to deal with her and this proposal. I've made arrangements for her to meet with you today."

That evening, after Cochran's meeting with Colonel Hobby, she joined Arnold at the Officer's Club for cocktails.

She took a swig of her drink and began, "That woman doesn't know her ass from a propeller, and I won't subject my girls to her. She doesn't know the first thing about what they need, or how pilots think. How would it be if your fliers had to report to a man who would rather take a train than travel by air? Why, I have to go down to

Camp Davis tomorrow to set that son of a bitch Draper straight about what the WASP are capable of flying. He's refused to let them tow targets. I'd like to see Colonel Hobby fight for my pilots. She doesn't even know what an A-24 is, let alone what it does. I'll be damned if I'm going to sit and watch her screw up what I've built, and I—" She noticed him smiling. "What's so funny?"

Arnold continued to smile. "Nothing."

Cochran realized she had won and smiled back. "You know I'm right, don't you?"

His look confirmed her question. "This could mean a delay for militarization."

"I'd rather stay civilian than kowtow to *MRS*. Hobby."

"You sure?"

Cochran lifted her nose into the air. "I've got every confidence, General, that you'll find another way to take care of this."

After mass on a Sunday morning at the end of June, Rosie walked up to Tina carrying her baby and holding her toddler's hand.

"How about we go see the new movie playing this week? It's got Claudette Colbert in it!"

"Well," Tina thought a minute, sighed, then nodded. "I'd love to. I need a night out." "OK, how about Wednesday night?"

"It's a date." Tina grinned and thought how good it would be able to just sit and relax for a couple of hours.

She and Rosie had always enjoyed seeing movies together before they married. Movies expanded their world, taking them beyond the confines of their lives to previous time periods and exotic locales with unfamiliar cultures and customs.

Now, as the war overseas continued, the film industry attempted to document the rigors of battle with a plethora of war movies. Though dramatic feature films brought people to the theater, newsreels kept them abreast of the latest news at home and abroad. These films gave them their only opportunities to get a glimpse of war battles, world leaders, sports figures, and candid shots of their favorite movie stars, who often urged the audience to buy war bonds to support the troops.

When Wednesday night arrived, Tina and Rosie got set to enjoy their favorite kind of movie, a love story with the war as a backdrop. *So Proudly We Hail,* starring three top stars, Claudette Colbert, Paulette Goddard, and Veronica Lake, was based on the real work of army nurses. The film presented the women's bravery as they struggled to keep wounded soldiers alive in Mobile Army Surgical Hospitals in the South Pacific.

They watched in awe as these women endured horrible living conditions and were expected to carry out their duties while fighting off malaria with very little food, even less sleep, and overhead bombing raids.

Rosie left the theater shaking her head. "Jeez, after seeing what those women had to go through, I'll never complain about taking care of my family again."

President Roosevelt used his radio fireside chats, started during the Depression, to encourage the country to come together for the common cause to beat the enemy. Many did just that. By September of 1943, over one hundred Kingsburg homes had replaced the blue star in their front windows, representing an active soldier, with a gold star recognizing a service member who would never return from the war. By then the town, and the entire country, had changed some part of their way of life to accommodate the needs of the conflict overseas. It touched everyone's life in some way, and most people's lives in many ways.

Rationing of food broadened to include everything from meat to coffee. The book of coupons issued monthly to each family rarely lasted the month. With nearly every staple from grains to produce on the list, feeding a family a nutritious yet palatable meal became a challenge requiring imagination and creative thinking.

When families ran out of ideas, they turned to newspapers and magazines that provided no shortage of recipes to try. Most of them offered substitutes for scarce ingredients, especially meats. For instance, fat drippings took the place of butter in many dishes and desserts.

With produce scarce, families in both the city and the country tried planting Victory Gardens to ensure they would have enough vegetables. Luckily, the Benedetti's and Capello's always had reserves of vegetables grown in their summer gardens and stored in their cellars to get them through the long winters. That, along with the chickens they raised for eggs and slaughter, and milk from their cows, became a godsend for them during the war.

———◆———

Things had become routine at Tina and Tommy's house since he had come home from New York City in June. Tina left the boys home with him sometimes while she met customers at the shop. His cast had been removed in August, and though it took a few weeks for him to build the strength in his leg again, he now could walk comfortably without a crutch.

He still suffered from headaches and recurring nightmares, but they had lessened considerably. He wished they would go away for good, but he had learned to live with them. However, he couldn't accept the other post-accident side effect: his inability to make love to Tina. He'd never before experienced a loss of his virility, and he struggled to keep from slipping into depression.

"It's OK, Tommy. Just lie here and hold me," she would say while rubbing her tummy. "I'm not exactly a bathing beauty with this baby getting bigger every day."

He wouldn't buy her attempts to make him feel better. They had enjoyed having sex during her two previous pregnancies, right up until a month before she gave birth. With all that had happened to him the past year, he feared he would never recover from this consequence of the explosion. All the settlement money he received couldn't make up for that.

—◆—

Carmen began his senior year of high school in September of 1943. Though he had registered for the draft on his eighteenth birthday in May, he still hadn't received a draft notice. He, like his friends who hadn't heard from the draft board, woke up each day wondering if their number would come up in the daily lottery. The family sat on pins and needles with him, praying that he would be able to finish school on schedule.

But only a few days into the school year, he received his notice to report to the induction center in Long Island, New York. When Carmen showed the notice to his father and Irene, they did their best to console him, but with moisture building in his eyes he fled. He soon found himself sitting on a swing in the deserted playground. It didn't seem that long ago that he had played with his friends on that spot. How could he be expected to take up a gun and kill another person?

Tina, Tommy, and their family gathered at Dominic and Irene's house the night before he was to leave, to say goodbye. The following morning, a tearful Dominic saw him off at the train station. He said as he hugged him, "May God, and your saintly mother watch over you and keep you safe from harm."

—◆—

Despite Eva's issues with Major Draper, she still loved being at Camp Davis to fly army planes. She nevertheless missed her family and treasured their letters from home. She always read them right away and answered them as soon as she could. She reread the letter she received from Carmen, telling her that he had received his draft notice to report. Though she had figured it would be inevitable, it hit her hard.

She still thought of Carmen as an awkward adolescent and couldn't picture him leaving home all alone. *He'll get eaten alive by the army.* In her travels she ran into youngsters in the army who reminded her of him. She had hoped and prayed that the war would be over before his number came up. This war had no mercy for young lives. They had become expendable for the world's battles.

On an October day soon after Carmen left, Tina chatted with her customer in the shop while measuring the woman's hem. She held the attention of every woman in the room as she described the movie she had seen with Rosie. That is, until she stood up and experienced a sharp labor pain. When she gasped and grabbed at her belly, Irene rushed over to help her.

"We better get you to the hospital," she said.

"No, no. It's just the first one. I'll be all right."

"Come on. I'm taking you home then."

Irene got her into the station wagon and headed to Tina's house. Two blocks before they arrived, Tina's pains came closer together, and her water burst.

"Looks like this one is ready now!" Irene said as she turned the car toward the hospital.

That evening, as Tommy paced with nervous energy in the waiting room, Tina gave birth to a seven-pound baby girl. Tommy had been with Tina during her first two deliveries at home, but the doctor now preferred using the newly renovated delivery room in the hospital, with all the latest equipment. A special "father's waiting room" had also been added, and the staff insisted that all new fathers remain in the room during the birth of their babies.

Tommy and Tina rejoiced in their healthy new baby and named her Theresa. Tina had finally gotten her girl, and Tommy had to admit that he had secretly longed for a daughter to protect and show off to his family and friends. Despite his appreciation and joy, he looked to the sky and prayed that God would restore his body and allow them to conceive another child.

The morning after Eva received Carmen's letter telling her he'd been drafted, she joined Hope in the Operations Office to get their plane assignments for the day, grab their flight gear, and review their maps. They had come to trust Gundy and Cash's choice of ship for them and anticipated a good day ahead. That is, until Veronica walked in with some personal news.

"I was right. I started. Wouldn't you know it, the first chance we get to tow targets, and I get my period. I'd better report to the flight surgeon."

Eva looked up from her maps. "I wouldn't."

"But I can't fly while I'm on my period. You know the rules."

"Forget the rules. The plane won't care that you're wearing feminine protection. What Draper doesn't know can't hurt you."

Hope added. "She's right. You don't think he's personally going to check to see, do you?"

After receiving her tow target assignment, Eva walked to the hangar, but stopped before entering when she overheard Gundy talking to a couple of the sergeants who had been assigned as cable operators to fly with the female pilots. She peeked around the doorjamb.

"This is bullshit. I'm not going up with that broad," said a sergeant named Camden.

"Why don't you give it a try, Camden? You might find out she's not so bad," Gundy said.

"Like hell."

"I'm with you, Camden," Sgt. Savoy said.

Gundy shook his head. "Well, she's waiting outside. What are you going to do?"

Camden looked over at Savoy, "Come on. We're going to Draper's office."

The two men breezed past Eva on their way out without looking at her. And Eva walked into the hangar.

"Hey, wasn't one of those guys my cable operator?"

Gundy shrugged. "Not if they have anything to say about it."

"And do they?"

"Not from what I've heard about Cochran."

———

Eva climbed into the A-24 Dauntless plane with an air of command presence. She'd had a good amount of experience flying this type of plane. What she'd never done was simulate an enemy plane. After settling in she turned to look at her cable operator in the backseat.

"You ready, Savoy?"

Savoy grabbed the cable attached to a muslin sleeve target at the back of the plane.

"Ready as I'll ever be."

Eva lifted the plane off the ground and flew above the beach below. When she'd leveled off at an altitude within firing range, she turned her throat microphone on and spoke to the artillery officer on the ground. "Ready to proceed?"

"Roger. Give us some lazy eights."

As she performed the lazy eights, Benjamin let out the cable. Having never experienced this before, Eva peered down below at the gun sites and saw officers walking up and down the rows of shooting trainees.

Just as she relaxed and began to enjoy the ride, the explosions underneath the plane lifted her off her seat and caused her to grip the controls harder to prevent the pelting from jarring the aircraft.

"Hey, lady, keep it straight and level, will ya?" Savoy yelled.

"What the hell is that?" she said.

"What do you think?"

"Why aren't they aiming at the sleeve?"

Savoy struggled to stay upright. "They are!"

"Jeez, we're sitting ducks up here." Eva grabbed the stick and leveled off the plane, then she pushed the throttle forward and the plane climbed out of the firing range. Taking a deep breath, she sent the nose into a dive and the plane headed for the ground.

Savoy held on for dear life as Eva flew closer and closer to the artillery line.

"You crazy female. You're going to kill all of us!"

Eva buzzed the plane over the gunners, who dove to the ground for cover. After pulling out of the dive within a few feet of the soldiers' heads, she landed safely and looked over at a pale-faced Savoy, and grinned.

"That was actually fun."

THE SET-UP

Eva sat on her cot reading Tina's letter announcing the birth of Eva's new niece, Theresa. She smiled, glad that Tina had finally gotten the girl she wanted. Before she could finish the letter, the order to report to Major Draper arrived. It didn't surprise her. She figured that her incident with towing targets would make it to him sooner or later.

"You wanted to see me, sir?" she said when she entered his office.

"You'll stand at attention when you address me, Miss Benedetti."

Eva clicked her heels together. "Yes, sir."

"Sgt. Savoy reported that you almost killed him and everyone on the firing line the other day."

"No, sir, I didn't. I was trying to simulate a dive bomber attack, so I—"

"Those were not your orders. We have procedures for these things, and it's your job to follow them, not show us your barnstorming skills. Towing targets is a large part of a WASP's duty while you are here. You don't know the first thing about it, and you never will, if I have anything to say about it. You're dismissed."

Eva nodded and turned to walk out the door. Draper followed behind her and waited to speak until she got to the middle of the reception office, where five men of various ranks were working.

"Oh, also, Miss Benedetti," he called out to her, "the flight surgeon tells me that you haven't reported for your monthly physical since you've been here. Consider yourself grounded until we have an accurate schedule of your menstrual cycle."

The men in the room chuckled, and Eva turned, red-faced, and hurried out of the office.

———

The next day, Eva finally sat down on her bunk to answer Tina's letter. After her months at Camp Davis, she missed her and the rest of the family. Hope interrupted with a knock and an excited question. She had been looking forward to spending her twenty-four-hour leave with her husband and wanted Eva's opinion of the new dress she had ordered through the mail.

"Well, what do you think?" She spun around. "Is this dress a little too obvious?"

Eva gave her the once-over. "Isn't that the point?"

"Yes, but Frank's used to a little more subtlety."

Eva chuckled. "Hope, you've only got twenty-four hours. You don't have time to play hard to get."

Hope had only been gone a few minutes when Rosalind and Veronica knocked and walked into Eva's room wearing party dresses.

"Why aren't you dressed?" Rosalind asked Eva. "The guys will be here soon."

Eva looked up. "I told you I'm not going."

"You have to," Veronica said. "There's going to be six pilots. Roz and I can't handle all of them."

"Speak for yourself," Roz corrected her.

Veronica rolled her eyes and pleaded, "Come on. Let's show Scarlett O'Hara here what a couple of Yankee gals can do."

———

The long line at the entrance to the nightclub had become rowdy and getting in looked bleak for the three WASP and six male pilots. A huge crowd had stormed the door and tried to push past the scowling face of a doorman.

"Come on. Let's try to push through."

"It won't help," Lt. Chapman said. "I've seen this guy before. He's a mean son of a bitch. You'd think Roosevelt himself was in that joint."

Rosalind eyed the bouncer. "Oh, he looks like a big ole teddy bear to me."

As Roz went off to talk to him, Eva's eyes turned to see another pilot with an enviable war record on his chest walk up to their group of guys. Chapman introduced him as Lt. Paul Henderson, a friend from basic training.

"Henderson here got sent overseas. Lucky son of a bitch. And I landed here."

As they caught up on their experiences, Eva learned that Paul had been sent back to the States with a leg injury he sustained in combat when he bailed out of his disabled plane.

"Lucky bastard. Nothing left to do for the duration but impress broads with his Purple Heart."

Rosalind ran up to Eva and yanked her arm. "Come on. I got us all in." She then led the way inside, winking at the doorman as they filed in amid boos from the crowd in line.

A few hours and many drinks later, Eva and Paul sat engrossed in sharing their adventures in the sky, as Rosalind and Chapman continued to tear up the dance floor and coax the couple to join them.

"Y'all fixin' to sit there all night?" Rosalind asked.

Eva and Paul looked at each and shrugged. He took her in his arms, and they got pushed onto the crowded dance floor. Meanwhile, Veronica had had a few too many, and her new-found cohort, a navy lieutenant, tried to persuade her to leave with him.

Rosalind broke it up after the "teddy bear" bouncer was ready to collect from her for letting them inside. Avoiding him she ran to Eva and Paul, she rushed them out, and the group found themselves out on the street. Chapman then wasted no time coming up with an alternative.

"Hey, what do ya say we head to the Victory Hotel and rent a couple of rooms, so's we can keep this party going?"

Chapman and the guys from the base all agreed that it was a great idea, but the women balked. Huddling together with her friends, Eva said, "I don't want to go to a hotel with the guys."

"What's the big deal?" Veronica slurred.

"I'm with Eva." Rosalind said, as she and Eva each took one of Veronica's arms.

"I've had enough of them for one night. And you, my dear," she said to Veronica, "have had enough of everything for one night."

———

Two taxis pulled up at the camp entry gate, and the group tumbled out. Chapman invited Paul to bunk with him and the other guys, but Paul told him he wanted to have a word with Eva before going to the men's barracks. He then walked with the women and asked Eva to wait before she went inside with the others.

Pointing to the steps, he said, "Let's sit here a minute, OK?"

Eva shivered and sat down. Paul took his jacket off and put it around her shoulders.

"I wanted you to know that I had a really nice time tonight," he said.

"Me, too."

"You socialize with Chapman and those guys much?"

"Rosalind has gone to a couple of movies with him, but this is the first time we've all gone out together."

"The WASP haven't made a very big hit around here, have they?"

Eva smiled and said with sarcasm, "Gee, I don't know. We seemed to be pretty popular tonight."

He smirked.

Eva continued, "You've only been around for a few hours. How can you tell?"

"Those guys were trying to set you up."

"What? How do you know that?"

"Chapman can't hold his tongue any better than his liquor. He was spouting off to me in the latrine about how the major has a plan to get you girls transferred out of here."

"A plan?"

"Not that the guys wouldn't have relished their duty, but their real reason for getting you to that motel was to put you in a compromising situation."

* * *

A few weeks had passed since that night, and Eva had received five letters from Paul. He wrote of his work, the war, and how glad he was to have met her. He never mentioned Draper's scheme to get the WASP transferred off the base, but she couldn't help but associate Paul with his revelation, and the memory made her cringe. Still, she had saved all his letters, and Hope watched her add the latest letter to a pile wrapped with a hair ribbon.

"You like him, don't you?" Hope said.

Eva shrugged.

"Oh, answer those letters. What could it hurt?"

"I know enough about flyboys not to look for trouble."

"Oh, go ahead," Hope coaxed. "It could be worth it. Go out with him."

"I don't have the time."

"Look, I manage to do this job while my husband is in the service."

"That's different. You had Frank before the war."

"Yes, but I didn't marry him until the war started. Even though we have to be apart."

"I know, but—"

"Eva, we shouldn't have to give up everything for this war. If we do, then the enemy has already won, haven't they?"

Over time, Eva and Gundy's relationship had evolved into a friendship. The two had come to respect each other's talents, and Eva always felt safe in a plane that Gundy had checked out. He'd also started including her in his weekly poker games with his friends Laslow and Peters.

One night, they gathered at a worktable in the hangar as usual.

"Come on, Benedetti." Gundy said, after taking a swig of bourbon. "We haven't got all night."

"All right. I'll see you—" Eva tossed in two chips. "And—" She threw in more chips. "And raise you three."

Gundy smirked. "I'll raise you—"

The sounds of sirens and trucks caught their attention, and the group jumped up to look outside. They watched a fire blazing in the distance, and Eva spotted some of her sister WASP running toward it.

"What is it?" Eva screamed at them as they rushed past.

"Those are gas flames. It's a plane!"

"Oh my God!" Eva said. "Rosalind is flying tonight."

Eva tried to run toward the crash, but Gundy grabbed her and held her back. Eva wouldn't have it and pulled out of his grasp.

"Wait here," Gundy insisted. "I'll get a jeep."

The two then made their way as close to the burning plane as they could get and jumped out amid the chaos on the ground. Women pilots cried out the names of their friends as fire hoses drenched the flames and fireman shouted to the crowd to get back.

Eva yelled to a familiar face, "Who is it?"

"I think it's Millie Withers."

Eva squeezed her eyes closed in anguish, but then looked up into the smoky sky, and breathed a heavy sigh of relief.

———◆———

Jackie Cochran arrived the next day to investigate the crash. Before meeting with Major Draper and speaking to the mechanics, she met with the all the WASP. The women gathered in the conference room, still reeling from Millie's death. It was their first opportunity to tell Cochran about the condition of the planes they were given to fly.

"There's no point in using the Form One," Eva said, "because the mechanics don't make the repairs."

"Yeah, we never know what to expect from any of the planes when we go up," Veronica said.

Rosalind chimed in. "All we do know is that we might not make it down in one piece."

"What about the men fliers?" Cochran asked.

"What can they say?" Hope shrugged. "They're only here because they've washed out of training or fouled up somewhere else."

Cochran peered over the group. "Do you all feel this way?"

The women all agreed with the accusations. Cochran nodded, thanked them for their input, and walked out.

After the meeting, Eva approached Cochran on her way back to the barracks.

"Miss Cochran? I'm Eva Benedetti. May I have a minute with you?"

Cochran sighed. "Just one, Miss Benedetti. I've had a really long day."

"Of course. I just wanted to let you know that I am much more suited for the ferry command, and I'd like to request a transfer."

Cochran nodded. "You and a half dozen others I just spoke to."

Eva looked down and cleared her throat. "Oh."

"I'm afraid a transfer is not that simple."

"I don't understand. Why—"

"Because I need you here."

"I'm sure—"

Cochran raised her hand to stop her. "Let me save us both some precious sleep time. Your request is denied, Miss Benedetti. End of discussion. Good night."

The next day, Cochran called the squadron of WASP back in to meet with her about the issue. While waiting for her, the women passed a hat to collect donations for Millie's family. As civilians, despite dying in the line of duty, the WASP received no funeral benefits. The sound of Cochran's voice turned their attention to her.

"I realize that Millie's death has had a profound effect on you. Mixed with grief for your friend is your concern for your own safety. That's only natural. Because of this, I've conducted an investigation based on the complaints made last evening. Which included actually taking some of the planes up myself.

I have found some of what you have said to be true. These planes are not the newest available. Those go into combat, and rightly so. However, although the flying times on many of the ones I flew are actually quite low, repairs are still needed. Unfortunately, a fact of war is that spare parts are often hard or impossible to get, and mechanics are overworked. Another fact of war is death. And although you are not being asked to engage in combat, the work you do is dangerous, and the possibility of accidents is always a consideration.

However, I cannot stress to you enough the importance of your job here. And I ask that you use this opportunity to strengthen the commitment you made when you joined the WASP, to serve your country in this time of need, and by doing so, further the cause for militarization of women pilots in the United States Army Air Forces."

Eva breathed deeply as she walked out to the flight line with Rosalind, Veronica, and Hope.

"I think she's serious about making us military," Veronica said with surprise.

"She always has been." Rosalind said.

"That's not the way I understood it."

"So, what's the problem? It's what we all wanted."

"Not me. I don't want to be in the army after the war."

Rosalind squinted. "I thought you hated Muncie."

"Yeah, well. From what I've seen, I hate the army more."

Eva and Hope veered off together toward their respective planes.

"Are you OK, Eva?"

Eva hesitated, then said, "Cochran's right, you know? We all knew that we might be signing our death warrants when we agreed to do this job."

"We just have to wipe that out of our minds, Eva. If we don't, we'll stop trusting our instincts up there, and that will do us in for sure."

The war took a backseat in Tina and Tommy's household after their new baby's birth. Junior, now five years old, obviously wasn't sure what he thought of this tiny bundle of pink blankets and noise. Although he had gotten used to Peter competing for attention, he didn't understand why his parents had to bring home this crying little stranger that had become the center of their world.

Of course, the younger Peter reacted to their lack of attentiveness by getting into things he shouldn't and crying for no apparent reason. Luckily, Dominic and Irene offered to take Peter home with them for a couple of weeks, and Tommy's parents took Junior.

Tommy did his best to pitch in with baby Theresa whenever he could and tend to the household chores. Tina had gone through so much the past several months with his injury and the boys, so he tried to give her extra care. It helped that he didn't have to work, and he made every effort to make things as easy as possible for her.

She could see how determined he was to help and be there for her, and she let him know whenever possible. She realized that despite all they had been through the past year, they were meant to be together.

"Tommy, we're so lucky to have each other and our beautiful family."

He smiled. "And if anyone had told me years ago that you and the kids would be in my life, I would have told them they were crazy."

———

The first working day after Millie's crash, Eva jumped out of bed in her usual fashion, dressed, and went to the mess for breakfast. Once there, she realized she had no appetite, so she nursed a cup of black coffee. She picked up her orders and donned her flight suit and parachute before heading to the flight line. Just after she exited the building, she broke out in a cold sweat. Walking to the plane, she looked up at it and thought she might vomit. Her body froze, and she couldn't bring herself to board. Eva looked over at Cash, who saw her struggling.

"Benedetti, you look like you need a doctor."

A couple of days later, Eva went into the hanger looking for Gundy. As she walked around the planes, Gundy approached her.

"Where ya been, Benedetti? You haven't gone up in days."

"The flight surgeon says I need a break."

"You sick?"

"Just a little queasy."

He shook his head. "Queasy or uneasy?"

"Both, I guess."

"Tell me, Benedetti, why the hell did you join this outfit in the first place?"

"To help us win the war."

"This isn't going into *Life* magazine," he said with sarcasm. "What's the real reason?"

"I wanted to fly."

"Then grow a set of balls and do it."

"But the planes are wrecks."

"So?

"So, you've got a lot of nerve talking to me like that, after what happened to Millie."

Gundy smirked. "More nerve than you, apparently."

Eva took a swing at him. "Why you bast—"

Gundy blocked her punch. "Relax, Eva. You know any plane you take up has to go through me or Cash first."

She stopped as she took in his words, then answered with voice quivering, "Thanks, Gundy."

———

Reassured by Gundy, Eva went back to work and back to their weekly poker game. After a profitable night for Eva, Peters shook his head as he placed his hand in his empty pocket.

"I had the corner on this game until you got here," he said to Eva. "Why couldn't you just do like my sister and give the boys a whirl at your local USO?"

Eva smiled. "It's more fun beating the pants off you this way."

The guys turned off to go to their barracks, and Eva headed toward hers. Suddenly, a jeep pulled up next to her. Major Draper was in the driver's seat.

"Pretty late for you to be out here by yourself, isn't it, Miss Benedetti?"

"I'm, uh"—Eva decided to agree with him—"Yes. I guess so."

"Hop in. I'll take you home."

"That's OK. I'll walk."

"Get in the jeep, Miss Benedetti. That's an order."

Eva climbed into the jeep, and Draper drove them into the darkness.

"I understand you're a little tired of swamp duty."

"I'd like to do the work I was sent here to do."

Draper pulled over, stopped, and placed his hand on her thigh. "I could arrange that, you know."

Eva looked at his hand, put her hand gently on top of his, and peered into his smiling eyes. Then digging her nails deeply into his hand, she lifted it off her leg and threw it aside. "I'd rather take my chances with the alligators," she said, then jumped out of the jeep and ran toward her barracks.

———

A few days later, Eva received a call from Paul. He'd heard about the crash but didn't know who had gone down. When she told him she was fine, he insisted on seeing her.

"Look, Eva, I know you told me in your letter that you didn't think we should see each other, but I'm going to be about a hundred miles from there on Sunday. Can't you grab a plane and fly out to meet me for a few hours?"

Eva balked, but Paul wouldn't take no for an answer. "Please, Eva. We'll just be a couple pilots having some lunch. What do you say?"

"Oh, all right. I'll see what I can do."

———

Eva set her plane down at the field where she was to meet Paul. She jumped down from the wing and dragging her parachute and B-4 flier's bag, she made her way to the Operations Office. She removed her helmet, fluffed her hair, checked in with the sergeant behind the desk, and asked him where she could freshen up. He directed her to the Bachelor Officer Quarters, where she found a comfortable-looking bedroom and a bathroom.

She went into the bathroom, removed her shirt, and wiped her sweaty torso with a wet washcloth. After drying and sprinkling herself with powder, she pulled a clean shirt out of her bag and put it on. She looked at herself in the mirror and attempted again to fluff up her hair, scrunched from her helmet. She saw no improvement, so she took her overseas cap out of her bag and plopped it on her head. Her rosy, wind-blown cheeks required no rouge, but she applied some lipstick. Seeing the result, she shrugged her shoulders and headed outside.

Eva checked her watch as she walked into the sunshine and looked toward the sky. A couple of planes arrived, but she saw no sign of Paul, and took a seat on a bench to wait. After a few minutes, she caught sight of a P-51 pursuit plane landing, and she watched in awe as the gorgeous fighter screeched onto the runway.

Her excitement grew while she walked toward it as it taxied into the flight line. The sight was stunning, and she was taken aback by its beauty and the momentary blindness caused by the sun reflecting off the shiny fuselage. As if that weren't enough, Paul stepped out of the hatch looking handsome and larger than life, and her heart leaped to her throat.

As he jumped to the ground, he said, "I'm sorry. I wanted to be here first to meet you."

"That's all right." Eva gazed at the plane. "I wouldn't have missed that landing for anything."

He glanced over his shoulder. "Pretty impressive, huh?"

"Really something to watch."

"And she handles so well."

Eva peeked into the cockpit. "Can I take a look?"

Sure," Paul said. "Climb in."

She settled into the seat and fingered the controls as he crouched on the wing next to her. "How many horses?"

"Thirteen eighty."

"And the top speed?"

"About four thirty-five, full throttles."

"Incredible." Eva tried to imagine the sensation of flying that fast.

As she marveled for nearly a minute, Paul cleared his throat. "You know, this happens all the time." He grinned. "I never know if a girl is after me, or my plane."

She woke from her daze and got the message that she was ignoring him. "Hey, didn't you say something about lunch?"

Paul jumped down. "You bet," he said, and watched with approval as she climbed out of the cockpit. "This is the first time I've seen you in uniform."

She touched her white blouse and khaki pants. "Not much of one, I'm afraid. We're supposed to be getting a better one soon."

"I was just thinking how terrific you look in this one."

Eva blushed and changed the subject. "The Officers Club is over there."

"Not today. I've made other plans," he said, and drove them to a small bar and grill off base.

They took seats in the back of the place and ordered sandwiches.

"It's pretty much a dive, but I thought it would be more romantic here than on the base."

Eva smiled. "What happened to 'just two pilots having lunch'?"

He shrugged his shoulders. "I lied."

Eva smirked.

"Well, it got you here, didn't it?"

His honesty made her smile. "So, tell me how long you've been flying that beautiful plane?"

"'Bout six months, I guess."

"Is that what you bailed out of?"

"No. That was a P-39."

"I've never met a member of the Caterpillar Club before," she said, referring to pilots who had successfully parachuted out of a disabled aircraft, their feat certified by the parachute manufacturer.

"Well, it's not official. I lost the ripcord after I hit the ground and couldn't prove I'd done it."

"Would you mind telling me what happened?"

"I'd rather hear something about you. Where are you from, and how did you end up here?"

Eva gave him an abbreviated version of her upbringing and skipped to how she became interested in flying. He hung on every word she said and asked to know more, but she abruptly changed the subject. She wanted to know the same things about him.

"I was born in Kansas but grew up in Southern California," he said. "When I was about fifteen, I used to hang around Long Beach Airfield and schmooze the pilots into giving me free rides. Since then, planes have pretty much been my life. I realized that the best way to get to fly regularly was to join the Army AF. And before I knew it, I was overseas. But—"

Paul took a deep breath. "I'm back now, and I don't know about those other guys at your camp, but the thought of a beautiful girl like you flying army planes makes *me* very excited." He winked at her. "If you know what I mean. And if you say you won't see me again, I'm going to be in a hell of a mess."

———

The following day, Eva tried to brush Paul's words out of her mind as she suited up in the ready room. She turned her attention to Hope and grumbled, "I don't know why I even bother to suit up to fly. I spend the whole day waiting, and unless there's a swamp search or an errand, I'm grounded."

Hope shook her head in sympathy and said, "You know, I wouldn't mind a break from towing. I swear I do lazy eights in my sleep."

"Do you mean that?"

Hope nodded. "Take my ride, Eva. No one will know."

Eva paced around the Operations Office until Hope's name was called. The two inched closer together, and Hope handed her the form and whispered, "Go out to the flight line and tell Gundy what we're doing. Then go get into the ship."

Eva wanted to hug her but refrained. "Thanks, Hope. You're a doll."

KEEP CALM AND CARRY ON

Eva pushed the throttle forward with a grin on her face as the A-24 Dauntless sped down the runway. After reaching the proper altitude, she was careful to maintain it, lest she call any attention to herself in Hope's plane. She didn't even mind the stray flak that peppered the plane from time to time. She stayed on task until she spotted smoke billowing in the sky. Her eyes followed it to the ground, where she saw a lot of commotion and emergency vehicles gathered.

"That doesn't look good," she said to her cable operator.

"Looks like a downed plane."

As she set her plane down on the runway and taxied in, Eva prayed that it wasn't another WASP in that plane. She jumped down from the cockpit and ran to the hanger.

She found a lot of commotion in the hanger, and her eyes searched for Gundy. She spotted him talking to two officers. When she caught his attention, he broke away from the officers and joined to her.

"Hope never had a chance, Eva. The plane flipped right over and landed on the canopy."

"Oh my God." She prayed that she'd heard him wrong. "It was Hope?"

"I'm sorry, Eva. I told her I'd send somebody else, but she said she'd better go so Draper wouldn't find out where you were."

"Oh, no, no, no." Eva grabbed for a nearby bench, dropped down on it, and wept.

<hr>

The other women tried to comfort her for almost two days, but she couldn't let go of the feeling that she should've died instead of Hope. Still in deep despair, she would not leave her room until Major Draper ordered her to report to him. She forced herself to get dressed and dragged herself to his office.

Draper commented on the "unfortunate accident" and confirmed with Eva that she had been very good friends with Hope. He rose to his feet behind his desk. "Then I'm sure that you won't mind accompanying her body to her hometown in Missouri."

Eva winced at his reference to Hope's "body" but said she'd be honored to.

"Very well," he said. "Miss Cochran has asked us to arrange for your travel. That's all."

Eva blurted out, "How many times does this have to happen before something is done about these planes?"

"A far as I'm concerned, Miss Benedetti, I've said all I have to say about this issue. You're dismissed!"

<hr>

The day before the funeral, Hope's father and her husband, Frank, met Eva at the Joplin, Missouri, train station. She made every effort to maintain her composure while offering her condolences to them, despite wanting to burst into tears. They told her about the plans for the service and offered to buy her a meal, but she declined, feigning fatigue. The men dropped her off at the Well-Wisher Motel on Route 66.

When she entered the desolate room, a chill ran through her veins, as an overwhelming sense of loneliness enveloped her. She couldn't remember a time when she had felt like this. Even after the death of her mother, she hadn't faced it alone. No matter how much she had complained about her family, they had been there when she needed them.

After the crash, her fellow WASP had refused to let her blame herself for Hope's death and tried to keep her spirits up. Now, as she faced burying her best friend who had died in her place, she experienced a kind of despair she had never thought possible. She could only think of one person who might be able to get her through the wretched task that loomed over her.

The following day, Eva stood in the vestibule of the Catholic church with Frank, Father Madison, and the funeral director. Hope's father walked up to the funeral director and held out a folded American flag. The man looked over to Eva.

She whispered, "Members of the WASP are not really entitled, because we're civilians, not military." But seeing the anguish in Hope's father's and Frank's eyes, she nodded to the director to drape the flag over the casket.

With that, the procession began, and the mass followed. The temperature was moderate that fall day while the mourners gathered around Hope's graveside. Eva sat in between Frank and Hope's father, holding each of their hands. As the ceremony reached its conclusion, the priest sprinkled holy water over the casket and committed Hope's body to the earth with prayers for life everlasting.

When Eva looked up through soggy eyes, she saw Paul emerge from behind the standing mourners. Her heart fluttered in her chest with elation, but she put her arms around a weeping Frank until he got up to press his face to the casket. Paul then made his way over to Eva and enfolded her in his arms.

"Thank you for getting here so fast," she said. "I was ready to cave in until I saw you."

He kissed her on the forehead. "You'd have held it together. Come on, I'll buy you some lunch."

"No," she said, "Hope's family and friends are getting together at their home, and I need to be there."

After she and Paul excused themselves from the gathering, they spent the rest of the afternoon at a nearby park, talking about the conditions at Camp Davis. They had a light dinner at the coffee shop adjacent to the Well-Wisher, then walked to the lobby.

"I'd better get myself a room," he said.

She took his hand, and shifting her eyes down, said, "You're welcome to share mine."

He hesitated. "I'd like nothing better. But maybe this isn't a good time."

She raised her eyes. "It couldn't be a better time."

"Uh, I don't know if—"

She pulled him to her, planted a long kiss on his lips, and led him to her room.

Inside the motel room, Eva changed into her nightgown and robe and sat on the edge of the bed, having second thoughts about asking Paul to stay. She'd done it because she couldn't face another night alone with her feelings of guilt about Hope. She flashed on Hope's casket at the cemetery, and Frank watching his wife disappear into the ground.

It reminded her of her mother's funeral, and all of those pent-up emotions she'd been carrying over the years. Drained by grief, for not only her mother and Hope but for the remorse she carried on her shoulders, she curled up in a fetal position and sobbed.

A few minutes later, Paul came out of the bathroom, wearing only his skivvies. He walked around to the other side of the bed and lay down on his back. After a few minutes, he reached over and took her hand.

Eva had never lacked attention from the opposite sex. If her black hair and deep blue eyes didn't attract them, her buxom figure drew them to possibilities of exhilarating exploration. She thrived on that and had mastered the art of teasing her many suitors over the years without ever giving herself completely to any of them.

But this was not a frivolous flirtation. With emotions heightened after Hope's death and funeral, Eva needed to cling to someone. Paul seemed to sense that and rolled her over on her back and wiped her watery eyes. Without hesitation, she welcomed the intimacy when he swept a kiss over her forehead and lips, opened her robe, and caressed her breasts.

The next morning, they remained in bed, holding each other until the last minute before they had to get ready to part. Paul donned his uniform and stood at the window, peeking out the blinds, while Eva dressed in the bathroom. When he saw the taxi pull up, he tapped on the bathroom door, and Eva walked out. They wrapped their arms around each other and stood in silence. Then he kissed her long and hard, picked up his bag, and walked out the door.

Later that morning, Hope's father took Eva to the train station and saw her off with tears, thanks, and well wishes. It was all so final, with both knowing that they would never see each other again and would have to carry on with mere memories of Hope.

Eva stared out the train window with the realization that, despite her loss, a new and overwhelming emotion had been awakened in her. She had fallen in love for the first time and learned last night how beautiful and thrilling the physical expression of that love could be. She now understood what all the fuss was about and knew that Hope was looking down at her with thumbs up.

When Eva disembarked, she expected to see Major Draper's driver waiting for her. Instead, she spotted Rosalind and smiled.

"How did you get the car? Where's Draper's lackey?"

Rosalind grabbed Eva's bag. "That horny guy really believes he's going to get lucky tonight."

Eva chuckled. "Thanks. I wasn't looking forward to that ride back with him."

Rosalind put the bag in the back seat. "How was it?"

"Brutal. The service was very nice, though. And you should've seen the turnout."

Once inside the car, Eva said sheepishly, "I called Paul. He got there in time to keep me from making a fool out of myself at the grave."

Rosalind smiled and shook her head. "That gorgeous boy's been begging to see you for weeks, and you pick a funeral for the big date. My, you do know how to show a man a good time."

Eva could only grin and turn her head toward the passenger window.

She learned during the ride home that Hope's crash had been listed as "pilot error," but that Cochran would be arriving in a few days. Maybe she would get to the bottom of it. Eva didn't believe there had been any pilot error and knew who she could talk to for the real story.

She went looking for Gundy that night. When she approached him, he insisted that it had been Hope's fault, saying that pilots often got too cocky up there. Eva would not hear of it and kept insisting that there was more to it than that.

Finally, Gundy directed her outside the hangar, out of earshot of the others.

"Forget about this, Eva."

"I'm not going to let this go until I know what happened."

Gundy shushed her. "It won't bring her back."

"No, but it might save someone else."

"How?"

"I need more ammunition against Draper. He's negligent, and he can't get away with it."

Gundy stopped and pulled her into a corner between two buildings. "This crash wasn't caused by negligence."

"What was it then?"

Gundy hesitated, and she had to ask again, "Gundy, what was it?"

"Sugar," he whispered.

Eva thought she'd heard him wrong. "What?"

He told her that they had found evidence of sugar in the gas tank. "The engine died. She never had a chance."

It took Eva a minute to digest what he'd said. Then she asked him how that could've happened.

"We can't be with these planes every minute. There's plenty of opportunity."

"Could the enemy really be on this base?"

"How can you ask that, after everything that's happened to you since you've been here?"

Eva paced around. "Jeez, Gundy. Draper was sure I'd be in that plane."

"This is between you and me, understand?"

Eva nodded. "Who else knows about the sugar?"

"A couple of the mechanics—and Cochran."

"She's here?" Eva said with surprise.

"She was this morning. Took off around noon."

"What did she say?"

"She stormed around here, cursing, then told us to list the cause as a sticky throttle and threatened us with combat duty if we told anyone."

———

Eva couldn't get over what Gundy had told her. She couldn't share it with anyone at the camp, and the silence was building up and distracting her from her duties. Just as she thought she'd reached the point of no return, she got a message from Paul that he would be arriving at Camp Davis that Friday on an errand and asking if she could arrange to see him that evening. The thought of seeing him lifted her spirits and made the two days until then tolerable.

After they each fulfilled their work assignments that Friday, they picked up sandwiches at a coffee shop, and drove to the nearest motel. They spread the food on the small table and began to eat.

"You know, we could've had dinner at a nice restaurant," he said as they ate.

"This is just fine. I don't have much of an appetite."

"Roz called me to tell me you were still upset, uh, about Hope," he said.

While they finished eating, she admitted, "I wanted to call you, but I didn't want to be a pest."

"Eva, the last thing you could be to me is a pest."

Eva smiled and told him what she'd learned about Hope's plane, and what she suspected. "I've always known that sabotage exists," she said. "But I never thought it would actually be directed at me."

"You don't know that for sure. Besides, we all live with it."

"But that plane was meant for me."

"It was a coincidence, Eva," he insisted.

Eva couldn't buy it. "But Gundy said—"

"Gundy should've kept his opinions to himself."

"No. I had to know. And, I have to do something about it."

Paul shook his head. "Like what?"

"I've requested an appointment with Cochran."

"Knowing her, she's already swept this under the carpet. She doesn't want to lose her program."

"But she doesn't know it was directed at me, and how Draper has treated me all this time."

"Do you really think it will make a difference?"

"I don't know," she said through tears. "I just know that it's my fault that Hope is dead, and I've got to make it right."

Paul got up from the table and stretched out on the bed. "Come up here," he waved her over.

She wiped her tears away, grinned, complied, and fell into his arms.

◆

Later, as they lay in spoon fashion under the covers, Paul broke the silence. "Marry me, Eva."

She turned over and looked at him. "What?"

"I want to marry you."

Eva smiled and said, "Oh, I get it. Eat, drink, and marry for tomorrow we fly."

"Sure."

"You don't have to do this, you know. I won't crack under the pressure."

He jumped up in anger. "Look, just forget it, OK?"

Startled, Eva asked him what was wrong.

"I didn't mean for it to be some kind of psychotherapy."

Eva looked at him with surprise. "It's just that I—"

"Has it ever crossed your mind that I might love you?"

"You do?'

"Wasn't it a little bit obvious?"

She looked down and shrugged. "I, uh, hoped you did, but—this"—she pointed to the mussed sheets—"is new to me, and I wasn't sure how you felt about it. But I wouldn't be here with you if I didn't love you."

Paul grinned. "Well, I love you, too. So, you'll marry me?"

"Oh, Paul," she said as she bit her lip, "there's so much going on. Can I have a raincheck?"

He lifted her chin and kissed her softly on the lips. "You just tell me when you're ready to use it."

———

As the days progressed Eva became more and more determined to find out who had sabotaged Hope's plane. She managed to get permission from Cochran to fly to Washington, DC, for a meeting with the famous aviatrix.

In hopes of persuading Cochran to investigate and find the culprit, Eva shared her history with Major Draper.

"This all began when I first arrived at Camp Davis. I had an incident in the air that was the result of negligence. I made the mistake of complaining to Major Draper. Ever since then, he's tried to get rid of me. He almost did, this time, only Hope took the plane intended for me, and now she's gone." Eva took a deep breath to keep from crying. "Will you please talk to Draper?"

"I appreciate your grief and determination, Miss Benedetti. But you must know that I have been fighting for you, and all the WASP, to be militarized. It continues to be an uphill battle, and I can't jeopardize our chances by conducting an investigation that may lead nowhere."

Eva could see that Cochran wasn't going to back down, so she said, "I do believe that if we're going to do this job, we deserve to be militarized."

"Good," Cochran said, "because you and your fellow WASP have proven that women pilots can fly anything the military can build."

———

Eva heard from one of her poker buddies that Chapman had bragged to some navy pilots that he made sure at least one WASP wouldn't be taking somebody's job. But when she tried to get Paul to help her, he wouldn't hear of it.

"Chapman's an arrogant SOB, and he tends to exaggerate his exploits. That's all."

"You believed him," Eva said. "The night I met you when he said they were trying to get us kicked out of here."

"That was different. He went along with that plan because he thought he could get into somebody's panties," Paul said. "He'd never kill anybody."

"What if he was ordered to do it?"

Paul shook his head.

"So, you won't help me dig up some more evidence?"

"Like what?"

Eva thought a moment. "Aren't you friends with the guy he went on furlough with?"

"I've known him a while."

Eva pressed him. "Then ask him if he knows anything about this."

"No, Eva. I'm not setting Chapman up for a court-martial on a bunch of hearsay."

"I can't believe you're going to let him get away with this."

"I don't think he did it."

"Then prove him innocent," she said.

"That's not my job."

"Well, it's my job to avenge Hope's death."

"Are you sure it's not also about relieving your conscious for Hope being in that plane instead of you?"

His remark stung, and she lashed out at him. "That's a rotten thing to say."

"I'm sorry. Look, Eva, I'm just afraid you'll get into trouble if you pursue this. It won't bring her back."

———

Eva tried one more time with Cochran from a phone booth.

"What's the name again?" Cochran asked.

"Chapman. Lt. George Chapman."

"And that's all you have?"

"I know it's not enough," Eva said. "But I thought maybe you could—"

"This is the worst possible time, with militarization hanging in the balance. I'm not about to give the press anymore ammunition against us."

"But—" Eva tried again.

"Even if you had his admission in writing, I wouldn't pursue this," Cochran said. "It's over, Eva."

———

A few weeks later, Eva still hadn't gotten over her disappointment that Cochran had refused to investigate Chapman. On top of that, it still irritated her that Paul had defended him. She hadn't talked to him since then and had begun to miss him. She couldn't help but blame Chapman for their argument. Then, out of the blue, one of the nurses stopped by the room Eva and Rosalind shared to borrow a sweater.

"Are you going to the bash for Chapman tonight?" Nurse Carmichael asked.

"What bash?" Rosalind said.

"The party they're throwing for him. Didn't you hear? They're shipping him overseas next week."

"So, he's finally going to get to see combat." Eva said, knowing that he would get more money and glory over there.

"Yeah, but not from the air. They've transferred him to the *walking* army."

"I didn't know they could do that," Rosalind said.

"Well, they did, and he's livid."

Eva wished she could gloat. Instead, she tried to hide her jubilation when she realized that Cochran had found another way to get justice for Hope's death.

———

The next day, Eva reported to the Operations Office, expecting to get assigned to another swamp rescue. Instead, her orders told her to fly to Fort Benning to get signatures on some paperwork.

"Here. Better take this and draw up your flight plan," Sgt. Brown said, as he handed her the papers. "You need to leave within the hour."

Eva took the form and bumped into Chapman on his way out the door. She figured that would be the last time she had to see him, so she wished him well in his new assignment. He responded with a grin and a tip of his hat.

Later, on the flight line, Eva gave her flight checklist a once-over before climbing onto the wing of her A-24. She maneuvered herself into the cockpit and donned her helmet. With permission to take off, she sailed above the runway, and looked down to watch the land shrink as she ascended above Camp Davis.

At an altitude of about three thousand feet, with excellent visibility, she relaxed and became one with the aircraft. Nothing could take the place of being enfolded within the clouds. This is when she forgot the rigors of training, and the men's belittling.

Her bliss didn't last long. Within a few minutes she heard and saw the bottom of an A-25 dive bomber begin a slow roll directly overhead. "What the hell?"

Fearful of being hit, she dropped her altitude and attempted to pull out of the way. As the A-25 lowered also and leveled off, Eva looked over and saw Lt. Chapman's sneering face in the pilot's seat. His token salute mocked her and made her uncomfortable in her seat. She adjusted the parachute strapped to her back and opened the throttle to increase her speed.

Within a few seconds, the A-25 began to roll above her again, and its landing gear came dangerously close to Eva's wing. Perspiration drenched her upper lip and underarms, and she gripped the controls tighter. When she realized he wasn't going to move, she executed a stall and began to descend into a spin, but Chapman did the same.

Once out of the spin, Eva looked over and saw Chapman with a nasty scowl on his face, while pointing to her and then the ground.

"You, bastard!" she screamed.

Realizing that she had to get away from him or he'd pursue her until she downed, she began a chandelle to allow her to climb and turn in the opposite direction quickly. To accomplish this, she started with a dive to gain speed. Chapman obviously thought that she was trying to put more distance between them again, so he dove to stay on her tail. When she suddenly began to climb in preparation of the chandelle, his plane was beneath hers. She climbed even higher, but he maintained a dangerous distance below her.

"Get out of the way, you idiot!" she screamed, but he didn't budge. *He's got to be either crazy or drunk.*

She had to get away from him, so she increased her altitude to complete the chandelle. Making the 180-degree turn, and assuming he would get out of the way, she felt her landing gear clip his wing. She struggled to remain in her seat when she hit his plane again. Finally, now in control, she looked back to see his plane spinning toward the ground.

She yelled at the top of her lungs, as if he would hear, "Bail, you idiot. Bail!"

Chapman didn't bail, and Eva watched in horror as the plane slammed into the ground.

A few days later, Eva sat alone in the mess hall, staring straight ahead and nursing a cup of coffee. When she heard her name called, she turned and saw Paul standing over her.

"Hello, Paul."

"OK if I sit?"

"If you like."

He sat down and told her he'd heard about Chapman.

"That I killed him?" She wondered if he'd heard that story.

"No. That he attacked you."

"That's not what people are saying."

"They don't know what they're talking about. I know how he was. In fact, I was afraid your suspicions about him would leak out, and he might retaliate. That's the main reason I didn't want to help you nail him."

"I assumed it was because he was your friend."

"Some friend. When I think that it might've been you that—" He hesitated, before saying, "Now I know how you felt about Hope. I would've killed him with my bare hands if he had—"

Eva stopped him. "Funny how that 'eye for an eye' thing doesn't always work. Ever since the crash, I've had the same dream over and over. I'm trying to grab Chapman's hand, but I can't reach it, and he falls to the earth."

Paul smiled. "Most of the pilots I know, that have been overseas, have had some variation of that dream."

"When will it stop?" she said with hope in her voice.

He took a deep sigh. "I'll let you know."

After a moment of silence, Paul placed his hand over hers. "Eva, you don't need this misery in your life. Let's get married now. I'll be getting new orders soon. I don't know where, but if you resign, we can be together there, and—"

She sat up straight. "I don't want to quit the WASP."

"But they've given you nothing but grief since you've been here."

"So what? I get to fly."

"But you're so vulnerable up there."

"And you're not?" she shouted, as others in the room looked over at them.

Paul whispered to her, "Goddamn it, Eva, you're a woman!"

She squinted. "What's that supposed to mean?"

"It means you have no business in those planes."

"So, what happened to, and I quote —'Just thinking about you flying those planes gives me a hard on,'" she said, her voice dripping with sarcasm.

"I fell in love with you. That's what happened!"

Her eyes widened. "That doesn't give you the right to tell me I can't fly!"

Paul looked stunned for a moment, and then shook his head. "You know, it doesn't really matter." He stood up and shoved his chair under the table. "Do what you damn well please. Just don't tell me about!"

A week later, Draper called Eva into his office, and she stood at ease in front of his desk, trying not to fidget.

Draper got straight to the point. "We've completed our investigation into the death of Lt. Chapman. Of course, we only have your side of the story, but we do know that Chapman had not filed a flight plan that day, nor did he have authorization to be in that plane at that location. I don't know why he would've 'stalked' you, as you have said, but since we'll never know, there will be no official action taken against you."

Eva had to ask. "What about *unofficially?*"

He smirked. "Don't press your luck, Miss Benedetti."

Eva's 1943 Christmas present came in the form of a telegram from Jackie Cochran. She screamed when she read it and rushed to find Rosalind to tell her the news.

"You'll never guess what this says," she held up the wire in front of Rosalind with a big grin.

"Well, obviously nobody died," she joked.

"Cochran's sending me to pursuit school!" Flying pursuit planes had been her dream since climbing into Paul's pursuit plane on their first date. "Yeah, and from there I'll go to Long Beach to join the Ferrying Command."

"I'm so happy for you—I just wish I was going with you."

"Don't worry," Eva said. "We'll get you there somehow."

Though there was no snow on the ground, the week before Christmas in Kingsburg the temperature was well-below freezing. Tina pulled her collar up as she approached her father's house to borrow her mother's favorite roasting pan. No one was home, so she used her house key. Carmen was at boot camp, and Dominic was taking it hard. With three of his children off serving their country, the family home had never sounded so hollow.

As she walked through the empty rooms, the silence triggered the sounds in her head of the boys arguing and Eva vying with her for their mother's attention. The scene became so real that Tina smelled the aroma of her mother's cooking mixed with her father's sweat from a long day on the railroad tracks and Angelo's scent of hay after milking the cow in the barn.

Tina essentially put most of her work aside following Theresa's arrival, focusing on recovering from the birth and tending to the three children and Tommy. His leg had become progressively better during that time, and he suffered less from the headaches and nightmares.

It helped that they had both committed to putting their family first and their work second. He hadn't made any decisions about his job possibilities and had thought it best to wait until after the new year to decide.

Tina hadn't signed any contracts with manufacturers, but she had a couple of interesting and profitable prospects. Now that Theresa was approaching three months old, the household had fallen into something of a routine, and she and Tommy had more time to themselves.

As Tina and Tommy had done the previous Christmas Eve, they tucked the kids in for the night, then found themselves putting Santa gifts under the tree that Tommy had chopped down in the woods behind their house. Though few toys were available in the stores because of the war, Tommy had taken some time to refurbish Junior's toys for Peter, and his ten-year-old nephew's small two-wheeler for Junior. Baby Theresa had plenty of rattles and stuffed animals handed down from Peter.

Together they stood back and looked at the trimmed tree with the presents under it and smiled.

"Luckily they're too young to care about what they get," Tommy said.

"Yes. Let's hope next year will be better."

Standing behind Tina, Tommy wrapped his arms around her and kissed the back of her neck. "I think this one is pretty terrific."

"Certainly, better than last year."

He turned her around in his arms and they smiled at each other. "I don't know. I rather enjoyed Christmas Eve last year."

Remembering their lovemaking on the floor under their feet, she said, "It was nice, wasn't it?"

He pulled her in close to him, and gave her a deep kiss, while thrusting his pelvis into hers. She reached down to touch his swollen crotch. "Hmm, nice. How long has this been going on?"

"About a week or so, but I thought I'd save it for this special night."

"This will go down as the best Christmas gift ever," she said, as she led him into their bedroom.

Tina read Eva's Christmas letter telling her about her transfer to California for pursuit training.

She didn't know the difference between a pursuit plane and a bomber, but she got a sense of Eva's excitement, nodded her head and smiled. She flashed on the many times that she had disapproved of Eva's cheekiness and audacity, thinking those traits would lead her astray and be her downfall. *How wrong could I have been? It never occurred to me that those very characteristics would allow her to do such an amazing service for her country.*

Tommy enjoyed being home with Tina and the kids, but now that he had recovered from his accident, he missed working. He had spent so much effort creating his business after his success with Miss Snow's school building, only to watch it taken from him by false rumors of his father's association with Benito Mussolini. It had ruined his livelihood and almost destroyed his marriage. He still wished he knew where the government got the information that had brought his family down but dwelling on that wouldn't help him revive his business.

Now, with the economy thriving from the war industry, he wanted to take advantage of any opportunities he could for the duration. Luckily, he had been able to save some of the money he received from his injury settlement thanks to Tina and her profitable business. If he could find at least one guy to help him out, he knew he could start bidding on projects again.

In the meantime, he started picking up small repair jobs around town, just to keep his skills sharp. He took a job to replace a water heater and a toilet at a house on the north side. While there he noticed a For Sale sign in front of the house next door. Like many around, the dwelling stood like a bastion of affluence from the last century.

On his way out, he took a closer look at the place. He saw chipped paint on the eaves and a roof in need of replacing. The loose clapboards on the sides could use paint, as could the front porch. The windows required updating, and the yard had been neglected.

Despite this, and the possibility that the inside could be worse, he knew he could restore it to its original state. He envisioned wagons, tricycles, and a baby carriage on the porch and the kids playing ball in the front yard. What better way to sharpen his building skills?

On his way home that day, he stopped at the realtor office for the price of the property.

The buyer had listed it below market value because of its condition. Still, it was a pretty good chunk of dough in comparison to a house on the south side.

All he could think about was how his family could finally have a house big enough for them. The new baby required more space, and what if they got lucky and had more kids? He had considered adding on to their house, but it would've left them with no yard for the kids to play in.

"And the house is on the north side," he gloated as he described it to Tina later. "Won't that be a kick in the pants to the neighbors?"

Tina loved the place when she saw it and agreed that the time had come to move out of their cute honeymoon cottage and rent it out.

Tommy managed to get the selling agent to accept his lower offer. The owners had died, and the anxious family had wanted to take the money and run. He wasted no time getting started on the inside, which required quite a bit of work. It included seven bedrooms (one considered a maid's quarters), three large bathrooms, a good-size kitchen, a huge dining room, and much more. He knew he couldn't handle everything that needed to be done, so he asked some contactor friends for help. He'd have to tackle the exterior during the summer.

Kingsburg and nearby towns in Central New York continued to thrive with war-related enterprises. Tommy had thrown his heart and soul into creating a beautiful home for his family, and in February, he had just about finished when his business finally won a contract for major repairs to a local building. He hired two new guys from out of town who needed the work. Having bid on a few other projects and lost to other, more-popular contactors, he appreciated that this latest company agreed to give him a chance to prove himself again.

NEW BEGINNINGS

Eva hated leaving Rosalind and the other friends she had made at Camp Davis but having the chance to fly fighter planes excited her. These planes were made for combat: smaller, faster, and much nimbler than any aircraft she'd flown before.

With her two-week training behind her, she now sat in the single-seater cockpit of a brand-new P-51 on the flight line in Long Beach, California.

When the mechanic jumped on the wing, he shouted to her above the roar of the planes.

"They tell me this is your first assignment in one of these." Eva nodded. "Well, remember, this ship runs hot. So—"

His words brought her back to her first date with Paul, when he'd let her sit in the cockpit of his pursuit. As she taxied out with the force of the momentum pinning her back against the seat, she shouted, "What a ride!"

This began weeks of her picking up new planes at the Long Beach factory and ferrying them to various air bases around the country. In between, she flew war-weary planes from one airfield to another. The work could be rigorous and lonely. After delivering a plane, she would check into a motel, eat alone, wash her undies in the sink, and lay her clothes under the mattress to iron out the wrinkles before she fell onto the bed, exhausted.

The loneliness was the hardest part for Eva, who had always been a social butterfly. The alone time also gave her a chance to wonder how and where Paul was. But she hated that they had parted at odds the last time. She often replayed their last encounter in her mind. *Jeez, the man told me he loved me and asked me to marry him, and I yelled at him.*

Now she realized that he had meant well by suggesting that she quit her job and marry him. After what had happened to Millie and Hope, he knew how dangerous the job was. But, still, she hated that he didn't consider her job as important as his.

She performed a necessary army job that could be dangerous, just as he did. She couldn't help feeling committed to her job, and she didn't understand why her feelings were not important to him. She tried to tell him in a letter but tore it up because she didn't know how to write it. She decided it would be best said in person and could wait until she saw him.

Occasionally she would meet up with some fellow WASP in route to somewhere else. One evening, after meeting up with two friends, they decided that for a change they would go to a restaurant for a decent meal. When they asked the waiter for a table, he answered by taking them aside.

"I'm sorry, but we can't seat you." The women looked at each other in surprise. "We don't allow women wearing slacks to dine with us."

"But we're Air Force pilots, and this is our uniform," Eva said.

"Of course, you are." He looked down his nose at her. "And I'm General MacArthur."

Eva made a move toward the waiter. "Why, you little twit. Where's your boss?"

One of the other pilots grabbed Eva's arm. "Come on. Let's just go."

Before they turned toward the door, the waiter straightened his tie and spoke under his breath. "Pushy females. You give them a job in a factory, and they think they own the world."

But regardless of incidents like that, she wouldn't have traded her job for any other. It gave her the chance to fly some of the most beautiful and state-of-the-art planes in aviation. She couldn't help but compare it to Kingsburg. Growing up there, very few things ever gave her the opportunity to be in control of her destiny and show her that, literally, the sky was the limit.

———

By early 1944, American and Allied forces had reached their stride due to the overwhelming amount of war equipment available to them. All the sacrificing of food, oil, and rubber made on the home front began to pay off in battle. As a result, General Arnold ordered the targeting of Germany's war manufacturers. The relentless Air Force bombing of oil refineries, rubber factories, and military motor vehicle sites lessened the capabilities of the Axis's offensive and defensive power against the Allies.

Meanwhile, the army continued to plod its way through Anzio and the Alban Hills of Italy, on to Rome, the Arno River, and the Apennine Mountains in their effort to push back the Germans. They continued their relentless attacks on the enemy, and despite considerable casualties, managed to hold their positions on the ground. At the same time, the Allied troops in northern Italy had the Germans pinned down.

On the first day of May in 1944, Tommy and Tina moved into their new house on the north side of town. They beamed as they walked into the newly remodeled home.

She sighed. "Well, this is finally it."

Tommy put a box down and pulled her into his arms. "Happy?"

Her hug and kiss confirmed it. "I can't believe we're finally here."

Although they had taken some clothes and household goods to the house over the past couple of months, tonight the whole family would sleep in their new bedrooms. Tina loved the paint colors she had chosen for all the rooms, but new kitchen appliances and bathroom fixtures would have to wait until the war's end. In the meantime, Tina did her best to make do with available fabrics and colors for the curtains and flooring.

They had sent the three children to the grandparents that afternoon so that they could put things in their places without the little ones getting in the way. As they carried their belongings from the truck to the house, Tina saw a couple of the neighbors watching them with interest. She waved to them and smiled, and the ladies shouted out, welcoming them to the neighborhood.

As she expected, the old woman right next door to them peeked behind drawn draperies but would not show her face. The woman's behavior didn't surprise Tina or Tommy, because Irene had told them that she had overheard more than one conversation between some of the neighbors about their move to the north side. Tina hadn't told anyone, but she'd also heard about a couple of people who hadn't gotten over the fact that Tommy's father had been arrested for being a follower of Mussolini. Would the family never live that down?

That night, Rosie and her family stopped by to see the newly furnished house.

"Oh, Tina, this is beautiful," Rosie said as she walked through the rooms. "But it's so big," she joked. "Aren't you afraid you'll lose one of the kids in here?"

Tina laughed. "That's the best part. We won't be on top of each other anymore."

"There's so much more to clean, though."

"That's true, but at least it won't be as cluttered."

Rosie plopped down onto a kitchen chair while the husbands stayed in the living room with the kids.

"Well, kiddo. You finally made it out of the south side."

"Maybe, but my heart will always be there. It's where my family and best friend live."

———◆———

On June 6, 1944, the Americans, with the help of British and Canadian troops, assaulted the beaches of Normandy, France, from the ocean. The surprise attack proved successful, despite thousands of American injuries and fatalities, and paved the way for US forces to liberate Paris months later. At the same time, Americans on the home front demanded retribution from Japan for the attack on Pearl Harbor.

Admiral Chester Nimitz and General Douglas MacArthur were happy to oblige by leading successful operations along the New Guinea coast and sinking a Japanese convoy at the Battle of the Bismarck Sea. But the Japanese forces proved to be a brutal foe. On November 20, 1944, in one of the bloodiest battles of the war, the Japanese fought the Marines on Tarawa in the Gilbert Islands, killing one thousand Marines and injuring two thousand more in the process.

Because families in Kingsburg and the valley had suffered an inordinate number of fatalities at Tarawa, St. Paul's Catholic Church held a joint memorial service with three churches of other religious denominations. Though the Benedetti family had not suffered any personal losses from the battle, they attended alongside their neighbors to share their support and their grief.

———◆———

After supper a few weeks later, Tommy and Tina had just put the kids to bed when the phone rang and Tommy answered it as quickly as possible, so it wouldn't wake the kids. Irene identified herself.

"Tommy, Dominic has had a heart attack. The doctor sent an ambulance to bring us to the hospital. I think Tina better come quick."

Tina threw open the hospital doors and ran right to the information desk. "I'm here about my father," she cried. "Dominic Benedetti."

The receptionist checked a list. "Mr. Benedetti suffered a heart attack, and the doctor is with him upstairs. I'll let the doctor know you're here." She pointed to the waiting room. "Please take a seat."

Tina flashed on the last time she had waited in the same seat for word on Carmen, after he'd been injured in Liberty Lake years ago. She couldn't help but remember Dominic's obstinacy during Carmen's treatment. She had been so angry at him then. Fortunately, Carmen survived, and afterward, her father became more understanding toward all his children. But now this. Just when things were looking up for her and Tommy, and the war had finally turned in America's favor.

"Hello, Tina," Doctor Channing said, startling her. "I'm glad you're here. He's had a severe attack, but he's a tough old guy, and he has that in his favor. We're doing the best we can until the specialist can get here from the city."

"Can I see him?"

"Yes, I think that would help both him and Irene. She's very upset."

Tina flinched when she saw her father lying in bed, his face covered by an oxygen mask, his helpless body dwarfed by the bed amid the equipment in the sterile room. Irene jumped up and opened her arms to Tina.

"Oh, Irene," Tina said, "what happened?"

"He had just lifted a pot of water onto the stove, then he grabbed his chest. I ran in as fast as I could, but he had dropped to his knees. I helped him lie down and then called for help. Oh, Tina, I'm so scared."

Tina squeezed Irene's hand, then bent over and spoke softly into her father's ear. "Pa, it's Tina. I came as soon as I heard."

He opened his hand, and she grabbed it. "I love you, Pa. You're strong. Show us how tough you are, and you'll be better soon."

He nodded and closed his eyes. Tina motioned for Irene to step out of the room with her.

"I'm sure it's going to be a long night until that heart doctor gets here. Are you all right? Do you need anything from home?"

"Oh, I don't know," Irene said weakly. "I can't think right now. Can you stay until the doctor gets here?"

"Of course. I'll call Tommy and tell him what's going on. The kids are asleep, and there are bottles of milk in the icebox in case Theresa wakes up."

After Tina called Tommy, she left the waiting room to send a telegram to Carmen, still in boot camp, saying she would keep him posted and let him know if he should ask for leave. As for Angelo, she certainly couldn't get hold of him, and Eva might be flying planes anywhere in the continental United States.

After watching Dominic have a fitful night , Tina called Father Marino at the church rectory and asked him to come to see her father right away. The priest soon arrived, and his presence and reassuring voice as he prayed at Dominic's bedside calmed her father down and got him through the night. Before leaving, Father Marino assured Irene and Tina that he would continue to pray for Dominic and would add his name to the prayer list at all the masses.

Tina and Irene continued to wait for the specialist to arrive. When he did, he examined Dominic, evaluated the charts, then spoke with Tina and Irene in the hallway.

"His heart has suffered considerable damage, but he made it through the night, and that's a good sign. He seems pretty fit. What kind of work did he do?"

"Foreman on the railroad."

The doctor nodded. "I've prescribed some medication, and he's going to need a lot of rest."

"What are his chances, Doctor?" Tina asked with trepidation.

"I'm afraid it's going to be up to a higher authority than me, so we'll have to wait and see if he makes it through the next few days with no more attacks."

"We're glad you're here. Will you stay until he's better?"

"Unfortunately, that's not possible. I have other patients in the city. I will be here for another day so that I can evaluate his tests and advise Dr. Channing."

After the doctor left, the women sat in silence until Tina suggested that Irene go home for a while.

"No, not yet, but you should go. You have a family to take care of."

Tina knew Irene was right. "OK, I'll be back later. In the meantime, please go down to the coffee shop and get something to eat." Tina hugged her. "You need to stay strong for Pa."

Over the next worrisome days, Dominic continued to improve, and ten days after his attack, he was released from the hospital. At home and recovering, Dominic struggled with depression as his health began to improve. No matter how often the doctor and his family told him that he had passed the critical stage of his illness and would improve with time, he refused to be as optimistic as they were.

"I'll never be as strong as my old self again. What good am I to anyone?" he said one day when Tina and Tommy visited.

Tommy gave Tina and Irene a signal to leave the room. They tiptoed out but listened at the door as he told Dominic that he, too, had felt like that after his accident, and knew what he was going through.

"Remember how you encouraged me to keep going, for Tina and the kids' sake?"

Dominic nodded. "Well, it finally sank into my thick skull that I had to do it for them. Now we need you to be strong for Irene and all your kids." Tommy grinned at his father-in-law. "Including me."

Kingsburg and nearby towns in central New York continued to thrive during WW2 with war-related enterprises. Thousands of miles away from the battlefields, Kingsburg residents, like those in most American towns, had been doing their part for the war effort for nearly three years. Some who had come of age during that period barely remembered their lives before December of 1941. Their adolescence revolved around fear, loss, rationing, working mothers, and war casualty reports. Names of faraway places like Anzio, Midway, Guadalcanal, Bataan, Casablanca, and Normandy had become part of their lives.

Carmen, who had just finished boot camp, came home for three weeks that August before shipping out. Of course, he didn't know for sure where he would be sent. All he did know was that he didn't want to go. He hadn't been crazy about boot camp, but he did his best and made it through. Unlike Angelo, he didn't receive any additional training. He and the other inductees going with him would receive on-the-job training. In other words, to use Eva's term, he'd have to "fly by the seat of his pants."

By then, many of his friends and their brothers had already been sent overseas, and as Eva found out when she was home, many of the "hot spots" in town were dead. Dominic and Irene gave Carmen as much of his favorite home cooking as he could eat. He found the house was too quiet without Eva and Angelo teasing and bickering, so he spent some time at Tina and Tommy's house. He was good with the boys, and they loved having him around. When his leave came to an end, once again a heartbroken Dominic stood by as one of his children departed to join the fight for his adoptive country.

In July, Eva had finally received the letter from Rosalind that she'd been hoping for. Rosalind would be transferred to Long Beach to join her, but she didn't know when she'd arrive.

Later that week, when a bedraggled Eva walked into the Long Beach Operations Office with the weight of her parachute on her back, she heard her name.

"Eva!"

Eva looked over as Rosalind ran to her. "Roz. You made it!" she cried, hugging her friend. Then she took a step back. "You look wonderful."

"You, too."

Eva shook her head. "I look awful. I flew two days to Colorado and spent the last week hitching rides on milk runs to get back."

"Is it always like that?" Rosalind asked.

"Pretty much." She grinned. "And I love it."

"I just checked in. Come on and buy me a cup of coffee."

———◆———

For the first few weeks after Rosalind's arrival, Eva enjoyed taking her around Southern California in between assignments. From the mountains to the sea to the desert, they took in the local color and bathed in the dry, sunny weather. Eva mentioned that she had included some of Paul's old stomping grounds that he had told her about.

"You miss him, don't you?" Rosalind said.

Eva shrugged and grinned. She could hardly admit to herself, let alone to Rosalind, how much she missed him, and how the places made her feel closer to him.

One evening Eva, Rosalind, and Patty, a fellow WASP, headed toward the Officers Club for a night out. Eva stopped short as they entered, hearing a familiar voice bellowing across the room. She looked around and spotted Paul, encircled by a table of giggling nurses who appeared uncomfortable with his drunken behavior.

Patty shrugged her shoulders. "There's always one jerk in the crowd."

Eva watched as Paul grabbed a nurse, pulled her onto the dance floor, and began to dance toward them.

"You know that guy?" Patty asked. Eva nodded. "Well, come on. Let's get a drink."

Eva and Rosalind didn't move, so Patty asked, "Who is he?"

Rosalind nodded toward Eva, whose eyes were glued to Paul. "An old flame."

"It looks like it's still lit."

Paul and his partner worked their way toward the threesome. "Well, if it isn't the mighty WASP. Hey, Eva, Roz."

Eva remained silent.

"Good seeing you, Paul," Rosalind said, then turned and walked away with Patty.

Eva finally spoke. "Hello, Paul."

"Nice uniform, and you look like a million in it," he said, referring to the stylish new Santiago Blue uniform.

"Thanks."

Paul turned to his dancing partner. "Doesn't she look like a million?"

The nurse gave an embarrassed nod, pulled herself out of Paul's arms, and walked away. Paul stood swaying in front of Eva, his whiskey-soaked breath in her face.

"How are you, Paul?"

"How do I look?"

"You look fine."

"Yeah, not bad for a pilot about to be grounded."

"What?"

"Why so surprised? It's your fault. You and your friends."

Eva squinted. "I didn't realize—"

"They don't need injured old combat pilots to fly in the States anymore." He raised his voice. "They've got the WASP!"

His voice drew attention from Tim Hanley, a fellow ferry pilot and friend, who had joined Rosalind and Patty at their table.

Eva tried to steady her voice as she said, "We're just doing what we can—"

Paul finished her sentence. "—for the war effort. What a line of crap. You're doing it for the same reason I am. Because you love it."

"And I have just as much right to do it as you do."

"The difference is that we put our asses on the line over there. Some of us are scarred for life. We deserve privileges!"

"Tell that to Millie's and Hope's families."

Tim had heard enough. "Hey, Benedetti," he called, "want to dance?"

Eva walked over to him and grabbed his hand. "I'd love to, Tim."

"Hey, I'm talking to her," Paul yelled.

"Well, she's done talking to you." Tim led her onto the dance floor.

Paul lurched toward them, then reared back and took a swing at Tim, who deflected the punch, pushed Paul away, and resumed dancing.

"Don't be a sap, guy," Paul yelled out. "She's only after your airplane. 'Course, if all you want is a good time, she's your girl, but then maybe you've learned that already."

Eva had heard enough and stopped dancing. Tim grabbed Paul by the collar and poised himself to throw a punch, but Eva spoke up. "Tim. Don't!"

Tim backed off, and Eva moved in between them.

"Let me," she said and slugged Paul in the face as hard as she could.

———

The next day, Eva, in flight gear, walked to her assigned plane, climbed onto the wing and then into the seat.

"I should've figured you'd throw a pretty mean punch," Paul called out as he walked toward her plane wearing flight gear.

Eva looked down at him. "How's your face?"

He climbed onto the wing, took his sunglasses off, and leaned his swollen cheek next to hers. Eva winced and gulped. He kept his face close to hers while she glanced at her watch.

"It hasn't been eight hours from bottle to throttle. You sure you're OK to fly?"

"Yeah, sure. Listen, I had plans to be very civil when I saw you, but Mr. Whiskey changed that. I'm sorry." He pointed to the oxygen mask in the cockpit. She handed it to him, and he breathed deeply into it.

"Where are they sending you?"

He exhaled. "Bakersfield."

She knew it wasn't where he wanted to be. "I'm sorry."

"Couple of sorry pilots we are, huh?"

When he handed the mask back, she nodded, her heart sinking. But he broke the mood with an abrupt remark. "Well, uh, you, uh, take care up there."

"OK. You, too," she said and watched as he gave the plane an affectionate pat, jumped down, and walked away.

———

As 1944 progressed, the odds of the WASP becoming militarized got slimmer. Although Cochran and Arnold still tried to push for it, the climate in the country had changed. The remarkable response by the nation, growing from one totally unprepared for battle to a superpower in the world's fight against fascism, had changed the military's needs.

With plenty of trained male pilots now available, the demand for the WASP to supplement the Army Air Forces had begun to be questioned by male civilian fliers and their political representatives. Articles appeared in the newspapers, denouncing the continued work of the WASP and calling for their disbandment. They even criticized the long-awaited Santiago Blue dress uniforms, designed with Cochran's help and issued to the WASP.

While the fight for militarizing the WASP heated up in Washington, the rank-and-file civilian male pilots planned to fight back by picketing Congress. Eva got firsthand knowledge of the scheme when she overheard Tim and the other men plotting their protest as she walked into the room. When the other guys left the room, Tim hung back.

"Don't take it personally, Eva."

"But you guys are my friends."

"It's our jobs."

"And it's not mine?"

"That's different. Some of these guys have been doing this work for years. They've got families."

"So, we women are supposed to forget what we learned, forget what we can do, and what? March quietly back to the kitchen?"

———

Later that afternoon in the WASP alert room, Eva told her WASP friends what she'd learned about the protest.

"Those guys are serious." she said. "They're going to Washington, DC, this week to lobby against us."

"When are we going to let people hear our side?" Mary asked.

Maggie jumped in. "She's right. They think we're a bunch of glamour girls in fancy uniforms."

"You know we have strict orders. No publicity from us," Rita reminded them.

The next day, Eva and Rosalind spent part of their day off shopping in downtown Long Beach. Eva loved having so many stores all in one place. Kingsburg's Main Street couldn't hold a candle to this.

As they walked toward the bus stop loaded down with packages, both had to admit that joining the WASP had changed their lives for the better.

"That's why we have to fight against their disbanding us," Eva said, as they boarded the bus. "We can do this. I can co-pilot that bomber tomorrow. How tough can it be? We deliver the ship to Jersey and find a ride to Washington."

Rosalind shrugged. "I still don't know why we're going."

"Look, some of the WASP hate Cochran and don't want to see her made colonel. They're all going to the Capitol to lobby against her. The men are sticking together against the WASP. That leaves us, and if we don't stand up for ourselves, who will?"

The women landed at Camp Springs Army Airfield in Maryland and took a bus to a hotel in Washington, DC. As they got ready for bed they listened as the battle for and against WASP militarization continued over the radio airwaves. Unfortunately, the WASP detractors' voices outnumbered the supporters'.

"As far as I'm concerned," said a member of Congress, "the bill is about as unpalatable as it can be. I am wondering what we are going to say to these boys who have been combat pilots, and have been wounded, and come back, and want to keep flying.? No. They cannot do that because they say, "We have to have somebody in there who is a very attractive lady pilot."

When Eva and Rosalind arrived by taxi in front of the Capitol building the next morning, male picketers met them with signs and chanting. As the women approached, the men yelled out to them.

"Not more WASP! Why don't you give it up and go home?"

"Yeah, and take your high-dollar uniforms with you."

Eva screamed back into their faces, "Like hell we will!"

"Ooh, tough broads, huh?"

Rosalind urged Eva to try to get inside, and when one of the picketers heard her Southern drawl, he mimicked her. "They should've never let you off the plantation, honey chile."

The women tried to ignore them and pushed forward. Then a voice behind them yelled, "Flying prostitutes, that's what you are. Well, we're not buyin' what you're sellin'."

Eva turned around and grabbed his sign. That created a tug of war. Rosalind caught sight of their friend, Tim, from Long Beach. He began to push through the crowd to get to her and Eva, who had just been shoved to the ground by one of the men. When Rosalind saw

Eva down, she jumped onto the back of the guy and began pounding him with her fists.

Tim and his buddies finally made their way through the mob, and Tim punched Eva's attacker in the gut. The brawl grew in intensity until a group of military police broke up the donnybrook. Just then, reporters threw open the hearing room doors, and ran out shouting, "The men won. The WASP bill is dead!"

The crowd grew as people began to flow out of the hearing room. Reporters started grabbing male pilots and WASP for comments. The MPs grabbed Tim, Eva, Rosalind, and as many picketers as possible and tossed them into a paddy wagon. The police sergeant deposited them into holding cells, where they stayed until the next morning.

At zero six hundred, the demoralized bunch marched out and stood in front of the commanding officer. He peered over the sorry group and said, "I've got better things to do than play referee to a group of glamour boys and girls. You pilots all think you're God's gift to the war effort. Well, I've got news for you—"

He stopped and looked at their tired and humble faces and shook his head.

"Oh, to hell with it. I should contact your COs, but I think a night in jail has tarnished your pretty wings enough. And given the unusual situation, I'm not even going to file a report on any of you. Now lift your airborne asses out of my station."

On the street, Eva, Rosalind, and Tim separated themselves from the others and walked off.

"Well, that was truly humiliating," Rosalind said.

"Yeah, but worth it," Eva said.

Rosalind shook her head. "Maybe, but I don't know what we accomplished."

Eva laughed. "The look on that guy's face when you jumped him was almost enough for me. Scarlett O'Hara would've been proud."

Rosalind smiled, and Eva looked over at Tim. "Thanks for your help."

"Picketing is one thing," he said as he hailed a taxi. "Pushing women around is another. Come on. A bunch of us are staying at a hotel down the street. I'm sure you can get a room."

"No, thanks," Eva said. "We've already got one."

"Oh, OK. Well, I'd like to say it was swell, but—"

She smirked. "Never mind. See you at home."

Heading toward their hotel, Eva and Rosalind walked by a corner newsstand, where they saw the paper's bold headline: WASP TRAINING ASSAILED BY THE HOUSE.

They bought a paper and sat down on a curb to read more. The more they read, the more obvious it became that the WASP were flying on borrowed time. The newspaper reports quoted Cochran as saying she would rather "junk" the group than continue without militarization. The press had taken the men's side and encouraged the public to write the WASP off.

"Well," Eva said as she folded the paper, "Cochran finally met her match. We're in trouble now."

"Maybe not. They still have to vote on it"

Eva shrugged. "Well, we'll see."

"So, what are we going to do?"

"There are still plenty of planes to deliver." She sighed. "Let's go home."

FINAL APPROACH

Irene and Tina's shop continued to do a good business with working women through 1944. Not only did they need work clothes, but the extra money earned at their factory jobs allowed them to have their old dresses altered to reflect the latest style. Tina tried to help Irene, but she still had a contract to fulfill for a local manufacturer, and the three children kept her busy.

One spring evening, Tina had just turned out the light in the nursery after rocking Theresa to sleep and putting her in her crib, when Tommy's yell from the living room startled her and woke the baby.

"What's wrong, Tommy?" she shouted over the baby's screams.

"I got it! I got it!"

Tina lifted the baby out of the crib and headed for the living the room. "This better be good. I just got her to sleep."

Tommy waved a telegram at her. "I got the contract in Schenectady!"

"That's wonderful," she said, leaning in to kiss him, then dropping into the rocking chair with Theresa. She said a silent prayer of thanks that he had gotten the job. Not because of the money, but because he needed to know that his customers valued his reputation.

Located about sixty-five miles southeast of Kingsburg, the job would be to restore a government office complex. He contacted a couple of the guys he'd worked with at the shipyard, and they agreed to begin work in March of 1945. Now, knowing he'd been accepted back into his business, he could relax and enjoy the rest of the year, and their new home on the north side, with his family.

The family barely had time to celebrate Tommy's success, because the first week in April, an anxious Dominic showed Tina a telegram he had received from the War Department. It informed him that Carmen had been slightly injured in battle and hospitalized for shrapnel and infections.

"Poor Carmen! He must be so scared," Tina cried. "I wish I could be there to take care of him. Oh, why do we have to have wars? Because some boys grow up to be men that want to rule the world at all costs to human life. Did they not have loving mothers?"

A few weeks went by with no updates on Carmen's condition, and the nervous family waited on pins and needles. They finally got a letter from Carmen with his Purple Heart medal enclosed and a note saying, "I'm much better, and this is for you, Pa." The family breathed a collective sigh of relief, but they knew there would be no liberation from worry until both Carmen and Angelo came home for good.

Tommy and Tina had tried to give Junior and Peter each a room of their own in the new house, but they didn't like sleeping alone and kept running back and forth during the night.

One evening after Tommy put them down for the night, he joined Tina in the living room, where she sat listening to the war news on the radio. Despite the good news of battles won across the continent, the casualty numbers continued to rise.

A knock at the door startled them, and Tommy jumped up to answer it before the kids would wake up. Rosie and her husband Frankie stood on the porch.

"Uh, hi, Tom," Frankie said.

"Hey, this is a surprise. Come on in." Tommy stepped back to let them inside.

"Sorry to bother you," Rosie said.

"No bother. It's good to see you. Tina," he called, "we've got company."

Tina walked into the foyer. "Hi, you two. Come on in. I'll put some coffee on."

"Thanks, but we're fine," Rosie said, lowering her gaze as she and Frankie entered the living room. "We just finished dinner."

"Well, take your coats off and sit down."

Rosie and Frankie walked over and sat on the edge of the couch.

Tina and Tommy shared a confused glance. Normally Rosie would be talking a mile a minute.

Tommy cleared his throat. "So, how's work going, Frank?"

"It's keeping me busy."

"Rosie, how's Frankie Junior's cold?" Tina asked.

"Oh, he's back to his old self and getting into trouble again."

"That's good. Sometimes I think it's worse on us parents to see our kids sick than it is on them."

Everyone nodded.

Tina couldn't take the tension anymore. "OK, what's going on? You both look like somebody died."

Frankie started. "Well, first of all, you know, I hated that Eddie sabotaged your school project. It was a criminal and lousy thing for him to do to you. I wouldn't talk to him the whole time he was jail. He is my cousin, though, and after he got out, I figured he had paid his dues."

Tommy shrugged. "Hey, Frank, I never blamed you for what Eddie did, I—"

"I know, and I appreciate that."

"So, what's the problem?"

"Well, after Eddie got out of prison, he talked me into going in on a big deal he was trying to put together for some property outside of town, to build a motor lodge and restaurant along the highway. It sounded like a good idea because with all the factories around here, the place is full of out-of-towners needing a place to stay. Rosie and I talked about it, and we both thought it sounded like a sure thing. So, we gave Eddie our savings to get the deal going."

Tina listened in silence, wondering how Rosie, of all people, could keep such a big secret for so long. She looked over at Tommy and tried to read his face but couldn't.

That's when Tommy spoke up. "Frank, what you do with your family is your business. Just because I hate the guy doesn't mean you have to. I never held what he did to me against you."

"I know, and I appreciate that." Frankie cleared his throat. "But that's not why I'm telling you this."

Tommy and Tina exchanged puzzled glances as Frankie went on.

"That weekend, after making the deal, Eddie and I went out to celebrate our new project by hitting all the bars in the neighborhood. We ended up at Pete's Bar and Grill, and by then we were both pretty well tanked. There were a few servicemen there on an overnight pass, and we got to talking with them. And, well, you know Eddie. Before long he was running off at the mouth and started braggin' about what a great businessman he is, and our new project."

Tina sat back and folded her arms. "Sounds like Eddie."

"Well, he went on to tell these guys that he spent time in prison, and because he's such a good salesman, he was able to talk his way into special privileges with the guards. It started with getting simple things, like more food, and less work time. The way he tells it, he had one of the guards under his thumb, by convincing him that he got railroaded into jail."

Tommy shook his head. "That guard must've been a real patsy."

"Yeah, well, he wasn't the only sucker who believed Eddie." Frankie took a deep breath. "Eddie blurted out that he made a deal with the prison warden for an early release in exchange for information that Tom's father had ties to Benito Mussolini!"

The truth hung in the air as Tommy and Tina stared at Frankie in shock.

"Oh my God!" Tina cried and covered her mouth.

Tommy pounded the arm of the chair and jumped up. "So, it was him! That bastard! I'll kill him!"

"I'm so sorry," Rosie said. "I couldn't believe it when Frankie told me."

"It surprised the hell out of me when he said it," Frankie said. "For a minute I thought he was bullshitting the guys to impress them, but when he saw the look on my face, he realized that he'd screwed up."

Tommy paced around the room in silence while Frankie continued to apologize for being related to the guy, and Rosie tried to comfort Tina. After the couple left to go home, Tina couldn't get over the shock that Eddie, the guy she had almost married, had done such a rotten thing. Though she had often questioned her love for Eddie while they were engaged, it never occurred to her that he was capable of doing the things he'd done to Tommy out of vengeance.

Tina and Tommy sat up later than usual that night trying to absorb what they had learned, then tossed and turned until daybreak. The next morning, they told Dominic and Irene. Bad heart or not, when Dominic heard about Eddie's dirty deed, he threatened to "beat the shit out of the whole Pecora family." Tina didn't know whether to be worried that her father's heart would give out on him again or be happy to see him act like his old self.

They arranged for a babysitter to stay with the children that night while they went to Tommy's parents' house to tell them and his brothers' families that Eddie had been responsible for turning their lives into a nightmare.

They heard a lot of cursing and threats of retribution from the family. After letting the family vent their anger, Tommy told them not to worry. He had a plan.

The next day, Tommy went to Eddie's restaurant and slid into a booth where the waitress put a menu in front of him.

Tommy pushed it away. "You can take that back and tell your boss he's got a visitor."

"I'll see if he's here."

Tommy tilted his head toward the door. "I saw his car outside. Now tell him it's important."

A few minutes later, Eddie sat down across from him. "What d'ya want, Capello?" he said. "I'm busy."

"Quit the act. Frankie told me the bullshit lies you gave the penal authorities about my father, just so you could get out of jail sooner. Well, I'm not going to let you get away with almost destroying my family."

Eddie started to get up. "I got nothin' to say to you, Capello."

"If I were you, I'd stick around and listen. I've got a proposition for you."

Eddie took a deep breath and sat back down. "I'm listening."

"I've got a couple of options to make you pay for ruining my livelihood, almost wrecking my marriage, and disgracing my whole family. I could go to the authorities, and that would bring your entire family to their knees, or— you can sign your restaurant property over to me and leave town for good."

"You must be crazy. What do you know about running a restaurant?"

"Nothin', but what do you care? It's the only way you're going to save your ass from landing in jail again for good."

Uncharacteristically, Eddie kept his word. He signed the restaurant over to Tommy and left town, telling everyone he had a lucrative business deal out of state. Tina doubted that anyone believed him. She didn't care. All she knew was that her family's life was back on track after a long siege of turmoil and sickness. Now, if only the war would end, and her brothers would come back to them, safely.

In October, Jackie Cochran released a letter to her fliers that read, "To all WASP, General Arnold has directed that the WASP program be deactivated on 20 December 1944."

The letter included a statement from General Arnold to the women, commending them for their fine work when the country needed them, but concluding, "The situation is that if you continue in service, you will be replacing instead of releasing our young men. I know that the WASP wouldn't want that."

Eva, Rosalind, and a group of their friends gathered to commiserate over the letter.

"It's not as if it's a complete surprise," Rosalind said. "It just never occurred to me that they would pull the planes right out from under us."

"Not this quick anyway," Eva added.

"What are we going to do now?" Rosalind said.

Eva shrugged. "Look for another job."

"Here it is!" Eva said, weeks later, as she opened an envelope from American Airlines replying to her inquiry about a pilot's job.

Rosalind's head shot up from her own mail. "So, do they want you?"

"Oh, yes. They've got a uniform and a set of wings for me."

"Really?"

"Yeah. They say I'd make a wonderful stewardess."

Now November, with time running out for the WASP, Eva and another WASP were waiting for their assignments when Eva overheard the sergeant talking to a male flier.

"Couldn't find anything else for an ace like you to do but ferry?"

"I'm happy to get any flying time these days," the lieutenant said.

The sergeant pointed to Eva and the other woman. "Lucky for you those girls are turning in their wings in a few weeks."

"Ladies," he called, "meet one of your replacements."

Even though Eva couldn't help but resent the pilot and others like him, she tried to be civil. "Just get back from overseas?"

"Nah," he said, "I've been grounded up in Bakersfield the past few months."

Eva's heart raced. "You know a flier by the name of Henderson? Paul Henderson?"

"Sure. He a friend of yours?"

She tried to act nonchalant. "Yeah. How is he?"

"Crazy, if you ask me. The son of a bitch volunteered for combat again."

Eva tried to hide her fear. "When? Why?"

The lieutenant shrugged. "Beats the hell out of me, but he should be leaving any day now."

———◆———

"Eva, you fool," Rosalind called through the bathroom door. "Are you just going to let him go?"

There was no answer.

Rosalind pounded twice on the door and shouted, "He shouldn't have to go over there again."

When Eva still didn't respond, Rosalind placed her hands on her hips. "Damn it, Eva. He could get killed this time!"

Eva replied by turning the shower on.

Rosalind narrowed her eyes. "How can you be this way, Eva?" she yelled as she jerked the bathroom door open and charged through it. "How can you be this way? I've never met anyone so stub—" She stopped in her tracks. Eva sat on the toilet, sobbing into her towel.

"Oh, honey," Rosalind said, putting her arms around her."

"I love him. What am I going to do, Roz?"

Rosalind pulled back, looked into her eyes, and said, "Go get him, Eva."

The next day, Eva arranged for the day off and managed to talk the sergeant at the Operations desk into giving her a plane to take her to Bakersfield. She asked for a pursuit but ended up with a primary trainer. Parked on the far end of the field, it obviously hadn't been touched recently. She took one look at the open-cockpit plane that had taken a beating from dozens of student fliers and cringed. She had to wipe off the seat and windshield just to taxi up to the hanger for a quick inspection and a tank of gas.

While she waited, she donned her leather flight suit, helmet, and goggles, all necessary in the open cockpit. It took her a few minutes after takeoff to get accustomed to the feel of the plane and its top speed of one hundred thirty-five miles per hour. Once she did, she found herself appreciating the scenic ride. She especially got pleasure in dipping the nose to buzz some golfers on a golf course below. The weather was delightful, as usual in Southern California, so she relaxed and enjoyed the ride that would take her to see Paul again.

As she neared Bakersfield, the weather changed. Thunder cracked in her ears and flashes of lightning darted around her as rain began bombarding the cockpit. Wind tossed the little plane around, and Eva struggled to keep it level. When changing altitude failed to remedy the turbulence, she flicked on her throat microphone.

"Field tower, this is PT-19 792. Approximately fifty miles out. Request landing instructions."

The response in her headset kept breaking up, so she tried to connect one more time while trying to get her bearings. Without warning, she experienced a thud and drop in altitude. She turned to follow the sound, just in time to watch the right wing break away from the fuselage.

Without thinking, she recited "Hail Mary full of grace, the Lord is with thee. Blessed are thou among women, and blessed is the fruit of thy womb, Jesus. Holy Mary, Mother of God, pray for us sinners, now and at the hour of our death."

After one more attempt to receive landing instructions failed, she searched below for a place to land, but couldn't see anything. With the plane rapidly losing altitude, she knew she had run out of options. Though she doubted anyone could hear her, she followed protocol, and called in.

"Field tower, this is WASP Benedetti. PT-19 972 #40–3852, prepared to bail!"

She took off her seat belt, flicked off the switches, and patted the plane. Then, making the sign of the cross over herself, she climbed out of the cockpit and jumped.

As she free-fell out of the plane, she tried to remember her training, searching frantically for the ripcord. Now clutching it, she couldn't thoroughly enjoy the sensation of floating   until she pulled the handle and the chute opened. As she floated down, she grimaced while watching her plane dive into the ground and burst into flames.

Though she tried to control her landing, she found herself on a farm, face to face with a pig in a pen, surrounded by slop and manure. She apologized to the farmer, and he seemed glad to drive her to the Bakersfield base. On the way, she sniffed a bad order and realized it came from her clothes. She looked down and saw her hand still clutching the ripcord handle. She smiled, put it into her pocket, and gave it a pat.

When the farmer left her at the gate to the base, she was a bedraggled mess as she carried her unraveled parachute up to the sentry.

"Excuse me. I'm looking for a Lieutenant Paul Henderson."

The guard grimaced, hesitated, and called for help to deal with her. After a few minutes, a jeep pulled up and drove her to Paul's barracks. When the jeep dropped her off, she approached a couple of soldiers, and asked them if they knew where Paul was.

"Company D, huh? Oh yeah, they're leaving in a couple of days."

Eva nodded. "That's it."

"They took off on a 48-hour leave. Guess they went into the city."

"Thanks," she said, but could overhear one of them say, "Henderson left just in time. Nobody deserves to spend their last twenty-four hours with the likes of that."

Defeated, Eva wandered through the camp until she spotted the Officer's Club. *Maybe someone in there knows where Paul is.*

Walking into the dim, nearly empty club, she stopped cold when she saw Paul sitting by himself at the bar, nursing a drink. Her heart leaped, and she could hardly contain herself. She took a deep breath, walked up to the bar, and sat down next to him.

The bartender asked her what he could get for her.

Before she could answer, Paul threw her a brief, side-eyed glance and said, "I didn't know there were any of you WASP still up here."

She tried not to smile. "I'm, uh, on a special assignment."

He turned slowly toward her and squinted. "Eva?"

She jumped off the stool, and they stared at each other for an awkward moment.

"What are you doing here?"

"Paul, you can't go over there again."

"Why not?"

"I'm in love with you. That's why."

"That doesn't give you the right to tell me I can't go!"

She tried to keep a straight face. "Like hell it doesn't!"

They both laughed, and she fell into his open arms. When they separated, he stepped back and looked her up and down.

Eva looked down at her dirty and rumpled clothes. "Oh my God!" she exclaimed. "I must look awful." She reached up, pulled her helmet off, and fluffed her hair.

He smirked. "Who are you kidding? You know I can't resist you in this getup."

Paul was able to get his orders changed so he could stay in the US while Eva returned to Long Beach to resume ferrying until the WASP program ended on December 20.

The last day arrived much too quickly. Gloom shrouded the barracks as the women dressed in their uniforms. Then they taxied their military planes in for the last time.

Eva, Rosalind, and some of the other women promised to stay in touch as they said goodbye with tears and hugs. They all agreed that they had been given a rare and special opportunity that they would always be proud of and never forget.

"I'll send you my address after Paul and I get settled," Eva said, as Rosalind gave her her home address.

"I'm not sure of my plans," Roz replied, "but my mother will forward any mail to me." She hugged Eva, giving her an extra squeeze.

The family expected Eva to return to Kingsburg after her WASP job ended. Instead, Eva called home with some news.

"Hi, Pa. How are you and Irene?"

"We're doing OK."

"Good. I called to tell you that I'm not coming home right now. The army has sent Paul to Riverside. Not too far from where I am in Long Beach, and he wants me to join him there so we can get married on the base."

He balked. "You mean you're going to get married without your family there, and in a strange church?"

"I'm sorry, Pa, but Paul can't get away for another three months, and we don't want to wait that long."

He didn't respond. "Uh, Pa?" she said. "Are you there?"

"Eva? It's Irene. Your father gave the phone to me. You're getting married? What's going on?"

"I told him I'm not coming home to get married. I'm sorry. I wish I could, but Paul has to stay here to finish his tour of duty. But we'll be home in about four months."

"Oh, I'm sorry to hear that, too."

"Uh, Irene, I have to hang up now. This call is costing me a fortune. I'll write to you tonight to give you more details. I love you both. Bye now."

That night she wrote a letter to her family telling them that Paul had arranged a transfer to March Airforce Base in Riverside, California, where he had scheduled a wedding ceremony with an army chaplain. She would be joining him in Riverside, where they would spend the weekend at The Mission Inn, a historical landmark in the city, and then move into military housing on the base.

On December 16, 1944, the Germans launched a surprise attack on the Allied western front in the Ardennes region of Belgium. The battle took place during frigid weather conditions, with some thirty German divisions attacking battle-fatigued American troops across eighty-five miles of the densely wooded forest. Paul and Eva checked the radio periodically for updates on the battle. The US suffered grievous casualties, but finally on January 25, 1945, they, along with all Americans, rejoiced in celebration when the Allies proclaimed victory and headed for Berlin.

But the battle in the Pacific still raged on. On February 19, 1945, Allied troops invaded Iwo Jima, an island off the coast of Japan, in a battle that lasted until March. Though the battle proved to be one of the bloodiest of the war, Americans finally claimed the island.

Finally, on May 8, 1945, in Germany, American services joined Soviet and British forces to encircle Berlin. Together they attacked the German headquarters and brought the German army to its knees. German generals signed an unconditional surrender that ended the war in Europe.

The papers plastered the victory in Europe news all over their front pages. Radio news broadcasters heaped accolades on the US and her Allies for defeating Hitler's Nazis.

Later that month, Dominic shared a letter from Carmen with Tina and Tommy. In it he reported that he would not be one of the lucky ones to be sent home first. He had not been able to accrue the required eighty-five points given for special circumstances, and as an infantryman, he would have to remain in the army. He feared that his new assignment would be in the Pacific, as the war there had escalated.

"No, no,'" Tina cried out. "Hasn't he done enough for his country in Europe? He's just a kid, and he's exhausted."

Tommy put his arm around her. "Honey, he's a man now."

"You don't understand. He'll always be a six-year-old boy to me."

Many in Kingsburg used the end of the war in Europe to hoist a few at local bars. But under the surface, everyone knew that the real celebration would take place when Japan laid down their arms for good.

In hopes of prompting that, the US Army and Marines took to the land and sea to launch an attack on Japanese positions on the island of Okinawa. A war-weary US awaited news as casualties mounted on both sides.

One of those American casualties was Rosie's older brother, a sailor. His death hit Rosie hard. "Oh, Tina, he always tried to protect me, but who was protecting him?"

Tina comforted Rosie as best she could and helped by babysitting her kids when Rosie needed to be with her parents. Since her brother had been lost at sea, there was a mass said in his honor at St. Paul's Catholic Church.

It was one of too many services that the people of Kingsburg had attended since the beginning of the four-year-old war. No one that Tina knew had ever guessed that the war would last this long.

"People aren't supposed to live like this year after year and die so young," she said to God as she begged for her brothers to return home safely.

On Monday morning, August 6, Tina had just put bowls of cereal on the kitchen table in front of the boys and on Theresa's highchair when she heard Tommy yell to her from the living room.

"Tina, come here, quick. Listen to this!"

"What? Just a minute. Peter," she said as she handed him a spoon, "here, sweetie."

"What's going on?" she said, as she walked into the living room.

"We bombed Japan! Listen—"

Tina hurried to take a seat next to him on the couch. "Sixteen hours ago," the reporter read, "an American airplane dropped a single bomb on Hiroshima, an important Japanese army base. That bomb had more power than twenty thousand tons of TNT. It had more than two thousand times the blast power of the British 'Grand Slam' which is the largest bomb ever yet used in the history of warfare."

Tina and Tommy listened in amazement as the President's statement revealed that, unbeknownst to everyone except a select group of scientists, the US had been working covertly for years on a formula for an atomic bomb that could kill thousands of people at one time.

It took a second, even more powerful bomb, dropped three days later by US forces on the Japanese city of Nagasaki, to force Japan's Emperor Hirohito to announce Japan's unconditional surrender via radio address on August 15.

This time, the town of Kingsburg pulled out all the stops for their celebration. Adults and children took to the streets, screaming and congratulating each other while throwing streamers and releasing balloons. School band members marched down the streets blaring their instruments with a cacophony of noise that was music to everyone's ears. The townspeople could almost be heard breathing a collective sigh of relief, as if a ton of bricks had been lifted from their chests.

SOFT LANDING

Not long after, Eva and Paul took their vacation in Kingsburg to introduce her family to her new husband. Dominic and Irene greeted them with open arms, as did Tina and Tommy.

"I'm so happy for you, Eva," Tina said." It's hard to believe that my little sister is married. And Paul seems like a great guy. I'm just sorry that you'll be living so far away."

"You should be used to me being away by now."

"I know, but that seemed so temporary. It sounds like California will be your permanent home."

"Yes, and I'm so excited. You know how badly I always wanted to move away from Kingsburg. But you'll come to visit us, right?"

Tina pulled her sister to her and squeezed as hard as she could. "Of course, we will. I promise."

The following days, as the dust settled, families waited impatiently for their sons to return home. Up and down the streets, people experienced joy and apprehension at the thought of seeing the boys who had left years ago and would now return as men.

The Benedetti's were no different. Three weeks later, Dominic and Irene took Annie and little Jennifer, wearing a pink dress and white pinafore, to the train station. They found a spot on the crowded platform where, Annie paced up and down with Jennifer in her arms. Irene and Dominic craned their necks looking through every window as the passenger cars passed by them.

"There he is!" Annie cried when she spotted her husband making his way to them with his duffel bag over his shoulder.

"Angelo!" Dominic yelled out while Irene and Annie waved to get his attention.

Annie thrust Jennifer into Irene's arms and took off running. Angelo dropped his bag.

"Oh, Angie!" Annie cried as she threw herself into his arms. "I was afraid I'd never see you again."

Angelo met her lips with his and continued to give her fevered kisses until Jennifer's piercing cry reached them. "Mommy!" she wailed.

Dominic and Irene beamed as they approached them. Angelo reached out to Jennifer, but she stretched her arms out to her mother, and he gave her an awkward kiss instead. "You're such a big girl." he said, rubbing her back.

Dominic held out his hand. "It's so good to see you, son. Are you all right?"

Angelo took his hand, but then pulled him into a quick hug. "Yes, Pa. Are you?" He pointed to Dominic's heart.

"Oh, I'm OK. Even better now that you're home."

"Irene," Angelo said as he wrapped his arms around her, "the ole man been taking good care of you?"

Dominic laughed and said, "Come on. Let's get out of this place. Tina's got a big dinner waiting for us at her house."

Irene had used most of their rationing stamps so the family could gather around the table to enjoy Angelo's favorite meal of cheese ravioli, meatballs, baked eggplant parmesan, and chocolate cake with chocolate frosting. As they reminisced about past family dinners, they couldn't help sensing the absence of Carmen and Eva at the table. But, as usual with young kids, Tina's sons and daughter and Angelo's two-year-old girl pretty much monopolized everyone's attention.

Angelo had tried to get Jennifer to warm up to him during dinner, with no success. After their meal, he grabbed Junior and pulled him to the floor.

"Hey, If I remember, you were pretty ticklish before I went away," he said as he tickled his nephew until he screamed for mercy.

While they roughhoused, Peter jumped on Angelo's back, screaming and punching his uncle. Before long, the noise attracted Jennifer, and she wandered over to tug on her father's arm. Angelo tickled her until she giggled, then drew her to him for a hug and smothered her with kisses. An outsider peeking in would have heard chaos, but it was music to the family's ears.

———◆———

That night, Angelo and his family went to Annie's parents' house. They would live there until they could find their own place. He and Annie started looking the next day, but most of the available housing had been taken up during the war by out-of-towners who needed a place to live while working at the factories. Many of the companies had started laying off, but it would be a while before housing would become available, if at all. All Angelo and Annie could do was put their name on the waiting list at a few places and wait.

In the meantime, Angelo had been thinking about looking for a job where he could use the radio operator skills that he'd learned in the navy. He figured he could make more money and not have to trim produce anymore.

But he hadn't dropped in at Sarducci's since he'd been back, and he was anxious to see his old boss. So, he stopped at the store one afternoon a month after he returned home.

"Oh, it's so good to see you, my boy," Mr. Sarducci said, grabbing Angelo's shoulders and looking into his eyes. "You looka fine."

"I am, and glad to be back and see you again. You're looking good, too."

"Maybe, but four years older and starting to feel my age. Annie kept me posted about you while you were gone. And that daughter of yours is beautiful. Say, come into my office. It's noisy out here." He pointed Angelo up the stairs.

"Oh, I heard about Mrs. Sarducci," Angelo replied. "I'm so sorry."

"It was her time, I guess. She was suffering so. But I really miss her." He sighed, then nodded toward a chair. "Sit down, my boy."

Angelo sat down wondering if he should tell Mr. Sarducci that he wasn't planning to come back to his old job. "So, how's business?"

"Like lots of other stores, we've been busier during the war. More outsiders working in the factories, you know. We've had to keep growing with them. Had to hire a few more cashiers and another manager. I've heard tell, that some of those workers are planning to stick around here after the war."

"No kiddin'," Angelo said, still wondering if he should tell Mr. Sarducci about his radio work.

"I been lookin' forward to you coming back to work. That is, after you've had some time off with your family."

"Well, as a matter—"

"Yes, I've made my mind up to retire. Been doing this a long time, and I'm ready."

"So, you're going to sell the store?"

"Not if you come back and manage it for me. You're the closet thing I have to a son, and you know the business. What d'ya say?"

Angelo hadn't been ready for this. This place had been his second home for many years, and he knew he could run it. But he had a family to take care of now. They came first. "I don't know, I—"

"If you're worried about money, don't be. I will make you my partner. I already talked to the lawyer about it. We'll split the profits until I die. Then the place is yours."

Angelo couldn't speak for a moment because he could hardly catch his breath. Then he jumped up and embraced Mr. Sarducci. "Sir," he said, "I'd be honored."

Angelo ran home to tell Annie and the family his news.

"I'm so glad," Annie said. "Sarducci's is a good business. I know, because I handled the receipts when I worked there, and it's grown so much during the war. It also has lots of possibilities. But are you sure it's what you want to do?"

"Yeah, I'm sure. I know the work and feel at home there, and I've got some ideas for new things I'd like to try. Besides"—he smiled and gave her a hug—"it's where I met you!"

Now with Angelo's job secured, they concentrated on finding a place to live. They finally found a one-bedroom apartment over a bar. It had a small kitchen, a living room, a tiny bedroom and a toilet. Since they had no furniture, they borrowed a couch, chair, and kitchen table from family members. Annie's parents let them take the bed from their spare bedroom. Despite the cramped quarters and the smell of beer wafting up to them from the bar downstairs, they loved having their privacy.

In January of 1946, Carmen came home, and Dominic and Irene hosted a welcome home party for him at their house. Practically the whole neighborhood showed up, and Dominic cooked them all the traditional Italian foods. No one except Irene and Tina knew that Dom had bought some beef and pork from a guy he knew that dealt with black market goods.

"What the hell," he had said. "The war's over!"

Tina could see that Carmen was uncomfortable with all the adulation being showered on him. "You don't seem to be enjoying your party," she said to him quietly when no one else could hear.

"Oh, it's good to see everyone again. Everyone is so nice."

"But?"

"It's just that it's an awful lot of praise for killing so many people."

At that moment, Tina realized that Carmen was no longer the child of six she remembered. He was a man who had been forced to grow up fast on the battlefield and would never be the boy she knew before he had been sent into that hellish war.

Carmen's first week at home seemed like liberty to him. He bounded out of bed in the mornings with the anticipation of a kid on his first day of Christmas vacation. He spent days getting reacquainted with the family and town again, and nights at the local hangout, drinking with old friends and new.

As time passed, he slept later in the morning and grew restless. He questioned why he had survived the war when men had lain dead or dying all around him on the battlefield. It occurred to him that he had traded the horrors and devastation of the war in sunny Italy for remorse and frigid weather in Kingsburg.

After mass on a snowy Sunday morning in early February, he drove his father's car in the opposite direction of home and fell deep into thought. Mesmerized by the movement and sound of the windshield wipers, he soon found himself on a rural road heading out toward the country.

Rounding a curve, he spotted a car that had skidded off the road into a snowbank. He pulled his car to a stop and rushed to the disabled vehicle. He rapped on the ice-covered driver's side window. To his relief, the window rolled down a few inches, and a woman peered out.

"Need some help, ma'am?" he asked.

She let out a sigh and closed her eyes. "Oh, thank God you're here. We've been stuck out here for a couple of hours, and we're freezing."

Carmen took a closer look inside the car, where a young boy sat shivering next to her, and two little girls huddled together in the backseat.

They all piled into his car, and he turned the heater up full blast before following the mother's directions to their home.

"I can't thank you enough for this," she said. "There weren't many cars out on the road today. What brought you all the way out here?"

Carmen didn't know how to tell her that he'd wanted to be alone and not have to talk to anyone. "Uh, I just got back from overseas and wanted to see the countryside."

"Well, whatever the reason, I thank the Lord for sending you to us. You must be so glad to be home with your family again, and they must be so relieved that you are all right."

"Uh, sure," he said and cleared his throat. "Uh, your husband will be glad to see you. He must be worried."

"He isn't home. He's, uh, out of town."

"How will you get your car?"

"Oh, I'll call my neighbor for a tow in the morning."

They continued down the main road, passing a mixture of silvery fields and farmhouses, until she directed him to turn onto a dirt road covered in snow.

"Up on your right," she said as she pointed to a white clapboard house with a huge porch. Behind the house sat a barn and what looked to be farmland.

"You've got some nice property here," he said. "What do you plant?"

"Mostly lettuce, but carrots and turnips too."

"So, your husband's a farmer."

"Yup. Uh, you can pull up right over here."

When he turned off the car, the kids jumped out and ran toward the house.

She offered him her hand. "I can't thank you enough for the ride. You really saved our lives. By the way, my name is Susan Dickson."

He shook her hand and smiled. "I'm Carmen Benedetti."

"Won't you come in, Carmen, for a hot cup of cocoa? That's the least I can do."

"Uh, I don't know, I—"

"Is someone expecting you?"

"No. Not really," he admitted.

Inside the cozy kitchen, she put the milk on the stove as he took a seat at the table.

"So how long have you lived out here?" he asked.

"About five years. We came from the big city. It was my husband's idea. He had always wanted to have lots of land and dreamed of being a farmer."

"And what did you think of the idea?"

"I didn't want to leave city life and all of my friends there. It was all I'd ever known."

"But you did."

"I figured marriage was a two-way street and I had to let him try."

"And now you like it."

She shrugged and poured the cocoa. "I don't hate it as much as I thought I would. And it's great for the kids."

He nodded and sipped his cocoa.

"But that's enough about me. How long have you been home? You must be so glad to be back and in one piece."

"Been back about three weeks. I'm still getting used to it. Part of me is still there."

"I've heard that from other vets I've talked to. I guess it takes time."

"Hey, Mom," her son yelled from the other room. "When we gonna eat?"

"In a few minutes," she yelled back.

Carmen gulped some cocoa and said, "I'd better get going. Your kids are hungry."

"You're welcome to stay. I'm just warming up some beef stew, but I've got plenty."

"Oh, I don't—"

Carmen stayed for dinner. He enjoyed being there with the kids and helped clean up.

"Dinner was great," he said as he dried a cup. "Thank you."

She laughed. "Not sure how much of a compliment that is, coming from someone who's been living on army rations."

"Believe me. I wouldn't kid ya."

She smiled. "OK, I'll take your word for it."

"I really do have to go now. The family's going think I got lost."

Carmen left wishing them well and saying he enjoyed the day. Susan thanked him again for coming to their rescue and told him to stop by the next time he was out that way. He thought about them all the way home.

Jeez, they might've died in that car if I hadn't taken that drive to sort out my own problems. Was it just good luck he went out that way? Or had he been directed from above?

Could it even be the reason God had sent him home alive and well?

The thought lifted a weight off him. *Maybe I can stop feeling so guilty about all the guys I left behind.*

The next few days, he found he couldn't get his mind off the family he'd met on the road. He tried keeping busy with chores at the house. With his father not the same after his heart attack, Carmen tackled some of the jobs for him and Irene. Still, he thought about Susan and her family and wondered if they could use his help, too. She hadn't mentioned how long her husband had been gone, or when he would return.

Finally, one morning a week later, he decided to take a ride out there.

He pulled up in front of the farmhouse and parked beside her car in the driveway. He knocked at the door, but no one appeared. He followed a path of trodden snow to the barn and looked inside.

"Susan?" he called out.

"Who is it?"

"It's, uh, Carmen from last week."

She appeared with a pitchfork full of hay. "Oh, our guardian angel. What brings you back out this way?"

"Just been wondering if you got your car out of that snowbank and if it was damaged."

"The fender's a little bent, but it drives fine."

"That's good. "

"How about a cup of coffee? It's freezing out here."

"I'd like that."

He followed her into the warm kitchen. "How are the kids? Are they around?"

"No," she said with a smile. "It's Thursday. They're at school."

"Oh yeah. I should've known."

She pulled a chair out from the table and gestured for him to sit.

"What did your husband say when he heard about the car?"

"He, uh, doesn't know."

"Didn't want to worry him, huh?"

She put the coffee in front of him and sat down. "The fact is, I haven't heard from him in six months."

Carmen cleared his throat and dropped his gaze. "Oh, sorry. It's not really any of my business."

"It's not a secret. I just didn't want to burden you with any more of our problems."

They chatted for a while, avoiding the obvious topic of her husband's whereabouts, and Carmen volunteered to do some heavy lifting and farm chores before heading home.

As he finished milking the cow, she approached him.

"Hey, you're a pretty good farmhand."

"I've been taking care of cows and chickens all my life. We live in town, but Pa has always raised them for food. He also rented a plot of farmland from a friend, and we kids always had to help with planting and picking."

"Well, thank you so much. You've helped us out again."

Carmen left, promising to be back on the weekend. He sighed and shook his head as he headed down the driveway. He couldn't understand what would make a man abandon his pretty wife and cute kids. The guy must be crazy. Carmen had only known them a few days, but he'd grown attached to them and wanted to take care of them.

He did go back that Sunday, but not before stopping at the corner store to pick up a bag of penny candy, along with a yoyo for Billy and little dolls for the girls. It was one of many weekend visits to the family in the following weeks. He found it to be the only place he could relax and get the images of the war out of his mind.

In the weeks that followed, the temperature rose, and the snow began to melt. The first days of spring had snuck up on them as his visits to the house in the country continued.

One Sunday, he made plans with her to pick up supplies at the hardware store the following Tuesday and help her with some damaged fencing on her property.

The repair went quickly, and as he and Susan walked back to the house he glanced at his surroundings "This place needs a lot more work."

"Carmen, you're doing so much for us. Why?"

He paused as he considered how to answer her. Finally, he said, "Susan, it's the only place I feel at home. The only place I can get the war out of my mind." To avoid reaching for her hand, he hastened his walk.

As he washed up at the kitchen sink, he asked, "Why do you stay here? You have to admit, it's too much for you to handle alone. He's the one that wanted this." He wiped his hands and draped the towel over the edge of the sink." You don't still expect him to come back, do you?"

She shrugged and leaned away from him.

"And you don't have any idea where he is?"

She looked down and shook her head.

"What about his family? Don't they know either?"

"I've tried everybody I can think of. No one knows."

"Maybe something happened to him. He—"

"I've tried everything short of hiring someone to look for him. It's pretty obvious to me that he's not coming back." She picked up a clean dish and put it into the cupboard. "I'm not even sure I want him to," she murmured.

Carmen turned, his pulse racing. This time he took her hand in his. "You must know how I feel about you."

With one swoop, she brushed his lips with hers, and quickly turned her back to him.

"At first, I believed that he would come back, and I had no right letting you get close to us. You should be with a younger woman with no baggage. I told myself you were just a guy back from the war who needed something to do while getting used to civilian life again. But now I—"

Carmen spun her around, and wrapping his arms around her, pressed his hungry lips to hers.

When at last he pulled back, he said, "I've wanted to do that since that first day when you rolled the car window down."

She kissed him on the cheek, and grinned. Then, taking his hand, she led him to her bedroom, and he knew then that he would never leave her.

From that day forward she and her children became his family. He knew he would always take care of them, protect them from any harm. The one thing he couldn't do was marry her. She was still married and not legally free.

But he could never tell his family, especially Dominic, about their arrangement. He thought sometimes that his brother and sisters suspected, but they never brought it up. As a result, Tina, Eva, and Angelo's children often seemed confused about why their uncle Carmen never married or had a family of his own.

After a few months in their tiny apartment above the bar, Angelo and Annie knew they had to find another place to live. Tina and Tommy had leased their old house, and the contract wouldn't expire for another year. Finally, two months later, Angelo's name came up on the list for a bigger place.

This time it was in a duplex a few blocks away with the owners living below them. They packed their sparse belongings and moved into the bigger place. They got by, but since Angelo was making more money, he and Annie started talking about buying their own house.

While having dinner with Tommy and Tina one Saturday, Angelo mentioned it to them.

"You know, I've been talking to some ex-servicemen, and they reminded me that I'm entitled to a VA home loan. That means no down payment and a better interest rate."

"That's terrific," Tina said.

Tommy said, "Yeah, the problem with that is there aren't many nice houses available right now in Kingsburg. I know because I hear it from other contactors."

Annie grinned and spoke up. "You did a beautiful job building your first house. How about building one for us?"

"Hmm, that's not a bad idea," Tina said, and looked at Tommy with hope in her voice.

As Tina and Tommy got into bed later, Tina said, "Why can't you build them a house, honey?"

"Jeez, I don't know. I'm pretty busy with my job right now."

"Well, they'd have to find the property to build on first, and that would take some time." She leaned over and gave him a kiss before pulling the blankets up over herself.

"We'll see," he said sleepily, and turned off the lamp.

The next morning Tommy couldn't stop thinking about Angelo and Annie's problem. They needed a house, and he could build it. He remembered a section of land just outside of town that might be available. Maybe it would work for Angie and Annie.

He got hold of the owner the next afternoon. But the guy wouldn't budge, saying, "There's room for six home lots or a commercial building. I want all the money upfront. I won't break it up into pieces."

Tommy didn't say anything about it to Tina that night, but he had an idea.

That week he talked to a couple of his contractor buddies to see what they thought. He found out that Angelo wasn't the only returning vet looking to use his GI benefits for housing. The other builders told him that they had considered the idea but didn't know where to start.

They agreed to pool their money and buy the section of land and divey it up into six lots. They would then each pick two lots and build homes on them. Because it was cheaper to buy materials in bulk, the houses would be similar, but floorplans would vary according to the buyers' wishes.

Tina liked the idea of building Angelo a home, but she wasn't sold on involving Tommy's friends.

"You have to be careful about going into business with friends. It could be a disaster."

"I know. That's why we've decided to make it a separate company. That means we'll get a business license for a new company. Any ideas for a name?"

"Whoa, don't you think we should talk more about this? All I wanted is for Angie and Annie to have a house."

He sat down at the kitchen table, pulled a chair out, and waited for her to sit.

"OK, let's talk."

She sighed and dropped into the chair. "Well, what about your other building contracts still in progress? And what about the financing?"

"My jobs are coming along good, and I still have some money left over from my settlement. And we've been able to save some since I started working again."

"Hmm. That's true," she said.

"Besides, Angelo will be getting a homeowner's loan from the GI Bill. That will pay for the cost of the lot for his house, and the build-out. That leaves me with only paying for the other lot."

Tina smiled and got up and kissed him on the cheek. "I knew I married the right guy. I can't wait to tell Angie and Annie."

———

A few days later, Tina answered a knock at her door and opened it to find her father standing there.

"Oh, hi, Pa." She let him inside. "What brings you here today?"

"Just thought I'd stop in and see the babies."

"Tommy took Junior with him to the store, and the other two are asleep."

"Oh, well, I'll see them later."

She led him into the kitchen. "Can I get you a cup of coffee?"

"No."

"Sit down. What's wrong? You look funny. Are you all right?"

"It's Irene."

Tina sighed. "I've noticed she's been coughing a lot lately."

"Yes. This winter has been hard on her. I'm afraid her lungs are not good."

"What does Dr. Channing say? Has the TB come back?"

"No, but it made her lungs too weak." Her father swallowed hard. "He doesn't know how long they will hold up."

Tina winced. "Isn't there something he can do?"

"Nothing. She just needs to take it easy. He doesn't want her to work anymore."

"How did she take that?" Tina asked, knowing how stubborn Irene could be.

"She said no at first. But the doctor and me made her understand that she had to." He shrugged. "She wants to talk to you about making Mary the manager and hiring another seamstress."

"It's fine with me. Mary has certainly paid her dues. I'll talk to Irene tomorrow."

Tina hugged her father. She couldn't believe he might soon have to face losing another wife. "I'm so sorry, Pa."

———

A month later the family got together to celebrate on New Year's Day, 1947. With the war behind them they could look forward to their future.

Tommy and Angelo used the opportunity to announce to the family their plans for the new house.

"And that's not all," Tommy said, and then explained how he and the other contactors had formed a corporation. "We're planning to eventually buy more of the adjacent land and create a whole new residential development, and we're calling it Kingsburg Heights, because it's on a hill."

"How wonderful. Isn't it wonderful, Dom?" Irene said.

Dominic shook his head. "I don't know. It sounds like a gamble to me. I hope you don't lose your shirts."

"Oh, Pa, be positive," Tina scolded him. "Tommy knows his business."

"Yeah, Pa," Angelo said. "Annie and I are going to have a great house."

Annie took Angelo's hand. "And a new baby! I'm due next summer."

———

"Irene," Mrs. Greene said. "I have this material I found in New York City when I visited my sister last week. Isn't it gorgeous? I haven't seen anything like this around here in a long time."

Irene fingered the fabric. "Yes, it is lovely. Did you have something special in mind for it?"

"Well, I was hoping that Tina could design a formal for me to wear to my son's wedding."

"She'll be in on Thursday. Why don't I make an appointment for you, so you can tell her what you'd like?"

"OK."

Irene scanned Tina's schedule. "How about one o'clock?"

"Perfect. See you then."

Tina hurried to leave for her appointment with Mrs. Greene. She gave last minute instructions to Nanny Alicia, kissed the kids, and made a quick exit. She'd found that it gave them less time to make her feel guilty for leaving. In reality, they loved Alicia and the attention she lavished on them. Her only duty was to make them happy, and they relished it.

Based on Irene's description of Mrs. Greene's material, Tina had already started sketching some ideas for the design. Tina had known the woman for years. She had been one of the first north side ladies who didn't care about Tina's background and encouraged her friends to give Tina a try.

After seeing some of Tina's sketches, Mrs. Green selected one of her ideas. Tina was about to excuse herself when Mrs. Greene pulled out a New York City newspaper clipping and told her to read it. "I'm assuming you haven't seen this."

Tina expected to see an article from the *New York Times* fashion section. Instead, she saw the headline, "FEDERAL SHIPYARD EXPLOSION CULPRITS REVEALED!"

The article read:

"The cause of the explosion that rocked the docks in early 1943, killing two and injuring nine dock workers, has been revealed. Sources say that Eduardo Pecora, Jr. used his father's underworld connections to blow up an area of the shipyard where fellow Kingsburg, NY resident Tommaso Capello was scheduled to work that day. Mr. Capello suffered debilitating injuries to his head and leg. The other victims were not intended targets but became collateral damage. Father Eduardo and son Eduardo Pecora, Jr., both from Kingsburg, NY, will stand trial in New York's federal court, set for Monday, September 10, 1947, in New York City."

A sudden chill came over Tina, and the clipping fell from her hands. The dizziness told her she should reach for the chair next to her, so she dropped into it.

She muttered, "They were so hellbent on bringing Tommy down that they killed two strangers and injured eight other innocent people." Tina took a sip of coffee in the cup next to her. "I can't believe this," she croaked. "The man and his whole family are evil. How did I not see that?"

"Some people are good at putting on a front and never letting their guard down." Mrs. Greene said. "They are actors who do what they need to do to get what they want."

Tina knew that now, but how could she have fallen for it? She had seen through Tommy's tough-guy veneer, knowing that deep down he was sweet and vulnerable. But she had accepted Eddie and his family at face value, and they had taken advantage of that.

Mrs. Greene said, "Just be grateful that you didn't marry into that family and have his children."

Tina had been thinking the same thing.

"Oh, and I'm taking this article to our newspaper. Everyone in town should know what their neighbor has been up to."

Everyone did hear about it, because the Kingsburg newspaper ran with the story on the first page of the following day's edition, revealing that a Pecora family member had provided firsthand information about Eddie Pecora's role in the arrest of Tommy's father.

The damning article read:

"PECORA ADMITS LIES ABOUT CAPELLO LINK TO MUSSOLINI!"

"The truth surfaced during a drunken discussion at a local bar involving Eduardo Pecora and other customers. Pecora bragged that he had used the false allegation to buy his way to an early release from prison. This story has been corroborated by Frank Donato (Pecora's cousin), the bartender, and various customers.

Federico Capello spent several months incarcerated in federal facilities while being investigated for aiding and abetting the enemy. During that time, he and his family denied all ties to Mussolini and his regime but suffered many threats to their life and property from angry citizens.

The most devastating damage done has been the ostracizing of the family members and the loss of their livelihoods. Both the family and many of their supporters are asking for a public apology from the Pecora family."

PRESENT DAY

"Oh my God!" Carly screamed as she finished reading the articles Grandma had included in her scrapbook.

Brooke said, "My mom has alluded to something like that going on in those days. It just never occurred to me that our family knew the people behind it."

Grandma nodded. "It's certainly nothing to be proud of. We've tried to put it behind us all these years by not talking about it. The important thing for you both to know and remember is that the Pecora's did not represent our family or our friends on the south side."

Carly looked at Brooke for confirmation, and they both nodded. "We know."

Grandma wrapped up the story. "Tommy's building venture in Kingsburg Heights was completed a few years later with thirty-five houses. It's still up there if you'd be interested to see it.

He gained even more prominence in the area by being instrumental in an urban renewal project that transformed downtown Kingsburg. Since Eddie's restaurant was located there, Tommy and Tina donated the land to the city. Of course, the prosperity only lasted until the late 1960s, when outsourcing manufacturing overseas became the way the country conducted business.

Tina hired nannies for the kids and continued to sell her designs to local manufacturers until she later went to work for a major department store in the state, designing a line of clothes for summer and winter each year.

Angelo and Annie had a baby boy that summer, but he died in infancy from a weak heart. They went on to have a girl and another boy. Angelo inherited Sarducci's grocery store when the old man died, just as Mr. Sarducci intended. Angelo added on to it, opened another store in a neighboring town, and built it up into the number one supermarket in the area. In the 1950's, he moved the family to Southern California and opened more stores there.

And Tina and Tommy had another girl"—she smiled—"your great-aunt Maria."

"What about Eva?" Brooke asked.

"Oh, after the war, she and Paul settled in Long Beach, where Paul got a job with a major airline. Commercial airlines started to become very popular in the late forties and fifties, and he flew some of the newest passenger planes. Eva resumed her work as a cargo pilot and worked full-time until she started having children. She kept her hand in, though, giving flying lessons, and continuing to fly throughout her life."

"And," Grandma added proudly, "in the fall of 1977 Congress voted to grant the WASP military status, finally giving them the benefits they so deserved."

"That's awful," Carly said, while shaking her head. "They had to wait over thirty years to get them."

She had hung on every word Grandma spoke as she recounted her family's lives during World War Two. She had glanced over at Brooke during the parts about Eva and the WASP and noticed the sparkle in her eyes. Their great-aunt Eva had been incredible. But Carly's idol would remain Tina because she could relate to her best. Tina's commitment to her work had never wavered.

Brooke chimed in. "I love that Aunt Eva paved the way for my generation of women pilots. Now I see why everyone says I take after her"—she winked—"because she was amazing."

"Yeah, right," Carly smirked.

"Grandma, thank you for sharing all this with us," Brooke said. "I guess I never understood how hard the war was on everyone at home. So many restrictions, and how seriously it affected everyone in the country in so many ways."

"But what about Irene and Dominic?" Carly asked. "Did they live much longer?"

"Surprisingly Irene outlived Dominic. His heart gave out on him in 1962. Irene lived until 1971."

—————

Carly only had three days left in Kingsburg, so she and her grandmother spent some alone time in Aunt Maria's attic, where Tina's trunks of clothing and patterns were stored. The fact that she could touch the same items that Tina had touched seemed magical to Carly. She loved to finger and examine Tina's pieces, gleaning all she could from Tina's technique. She held several items up to herself and tried each of them on.

"Grandma," she said as she returned the last item to the trunk, "remember the final project this coming year that will count for most of my grade?"

"Yes, I remember."

"Well, I would love to use Tina's designs as a springboard for that project."

Grandma smiled. "Really? What would you do?"

"I want to highlight the nineteen thirties and forties fashions. You know, what they call *vintage*. It's pretty popular now."

"I didn't realize that, but it's a good idea. How would you do it?"

"I plan to create a blog."

"Oh, yes, the women's church group I belong to has a blog. I always enjoy reading it."

"What do you think?"

"I think that would be wonderful. It would be a way to keep her work alive."

"I'm glad you feel that way, because I'd like to take some pieces home to model them and create a video."

Grandma frowned. "Oh, I don't think that would be a good idea. I wouldn't want anything to happen to them. I'm trying to hold on to them for the whole family to appreciate. The best way to do that is to keep them safe here."

Carly hung her head. Grandma had always seemed to want to please her.

Grandma touched Carly's cheek. "I'm sorry. Say, maybe you can take pictures of you wearing them right here."

That Friday night, while the family sat around the dinner table at Aunt Sandra's, Grandma brought up the subject of taking pictures of Tina's designs for Carly. Long after they had finished their meal, the family sat around the table and brainstormed a plan for sending Carly home with pictures and video for her blog. Brooke's dad volunteered to use his amateur skills to shoot pictures with his digital video camera of Carly and Brooke in front of some historical buildings in Kingsburg.

That weekend turned out to be one of the best of Carly's life. Dylan joined the whole family for videoing her blog project. From sunup to sundown, they scouted out buildings and chose the best examples of the bygone era.

They captured Carly and Brooke wearing some of Tina's original designs on the steps of the old library, the courthouse, and the jail. Carly had never felt as close to anybody, except her mother, as she did to her father's family that day. The pictures turned out beautifully, but Carly knew that the thing she would remember above everything else was the love and belonging she experienced that day.

Carly and Dylan flew back to LAX together. It had been a great vacation, just as she'd expected. The change of scenery had been almost as wonderful as being with the family. Of course, it helped that Dylan had shared so much of it with her. Though she hated to see her visit end, knowing that she held the weekend videos in her bag made her anxious to get home and get started on her project.

Carly had left her car at the airport, so she dropped Dylan at his dorm, since he had to go to work the next day near his campus. Her classes didn't start for another week, so she drove home to Encinitas. She couldn't wait to tell her mother about her blog project and get her advice for promoting it.

Amanda seemed pleased to hear that Carly had spent some of her vacation time working on her school project. Carly often sensed that her mom didn't appreciate Carly's affection for her father's family. And of course, her relationship with Dylan had been a source of contention from the start. But much to Carly's relief, Amanda showed her enthusiasm for Carly's project by jumping in to help Carly with her blog. Since advertising was her mom's field, Carly had her own personal ad expert.

Once the blog was up and running, Carly tried to concentrate on her studies while still spending time with Dylan. But seeing each other as much as they wanted was difficult with the heavy traffic on the road between their dorms. One day when one goodbye turned into a couple of hours, Dylan sat up in bed and said, "I came out here to LA for school so we could be together, but it's not working."

Carly jumped up. "I know. Let's get a place together somewhere in between the two campuses."

As Carly expected, her mom didn't like the idea of them living together, but she and Dylan found a cute one-bedroom apartment and took up housekeeping with furniture found at swap meets and garage sales. They loved it.

Amanda's first instinct had been to fight their decision, but after talking to friends about it, she finally realized that she could lose Carly in the process if she didn't loosen the reins on her. She finally gave in and bought them some basic kitchen and bath items. When she took them to the apartment, Carly smiled in pleased surprise and threw her arms around her mother.

———

A month after the blog's launch, Carly still had only about fifty followers. If the blog's popularity didn't increase, she worried her project wouldn't give her the grade she wanted from the project.

"Give it some time, honey," Amanda said. "I think the blog is really well done. But it might also be a good idea to ask your followers for feedback about some of your ideas. People love to give their opinions, and you might create a rapport with them. You have to engage them."

Carly did just that, and in no time, her followers grew, generating more interest from advertisers. She found herself spending most of her time on the blog, and her grades dropped in a couple of her other classes. She even got called out by one of her favorite teachers for her carelessness.

She also began to realize that living with Dylan gave her less time for anything else. She would never admit it to her mother, but Dylan was a slob. At first, Carly just accepted it. After all, she had never lived with a guy before. Not even a father.

But eventually she couldn't keep her irritation to herself. "Dylan, can't you just once not leave your dirty towels on the floor? And how about cleaning your hair out of the sink? I don't have time to pick up after you."

"Sorry, babe," he said, giving her a peck on the cheek. "But I get in a hurry and forget."

———

By their last semester Dylan's housekeeping skills hadn't gotten any better, but she had less time to notice because her blog traffic continued to pick up. The upshot of that was that her income had increased considerably. However, at the same time Dylan had begun to spend more and more time away from their apartment, and less with her. When she asked him about it, he always had a good excuse.

"The profs are bearing down this semester. You know, how it is. Besides, you're always busy with class work and that blog. I kind of figured you didn't mind."

"I know. I'm sorry. How about we go out this weekend for dinner and hit some clubs? My treat."

"You're on," he said as he kissed her goodbye.

They had a wonderful time clubbing that Saturday night and spent most of Sunday in bed together. In between caresses, they promised to try harder to spend more *quality* time together the rest of the school year.

"Does that mean that you'll spend less time on your blog?"

"I promise," she said with a smile.

———◆———

To prove that she was serious, Carly arranged to have a student friend handle some of the clerical duties of the blog for her and paid her a small salary. She also put herself on a strict blogging time schedule so as not to interfere with her time with Dylan. But two days after she made the changes, she still hadn't had a chance to tell Dylan how she was keeping her promise.

If he wasn't off meeting with a study group into the wee hours, he was crashed on the sofa to avoid waking her up when he got home. Then each morning he ran past her, plucked a piece of fruit from the bowl on the counter, gave her a flying kiss, and ran out the door.

The afternoon of the second day, as she hurried to wrap up her scheduled blog time, she received an email from someone named

Mateo Guzman, an independent film producer who had seen her blog and learned of her expertise in vintage clothing. He explained that he was searching for talent to help with his proposed movie, set in the 1930s, and he wanted to meet her for lunch to talk about the job of costume designer for his project.

"Oh my God!" she screamed. *How fun would that be? But I can't take on such a big project now. What would Dylan say?*

Nevertheless, with curiosity and stars in her eyes, Carly spent a couple of hours researching Mateo Guzman online. She found that he was a film school graduate with some short films on his résumé and had worked on the fringes of the film industry for a few years, Now, he had finally decided to jump into producing a full-length film.

With a few misgivings about telling Dylan, she agreed to meet with the producer. *After all,* she told herself, *what will it hurt to learn more?*

Dylan returned earlier than usual that evening, but before she had a chance to tell him about the changes she'd made in her schedule for him and the email exchange with the producer, she learned that he had exciting news of his own. He had been selected for a two-month internship with a local news station in New York City.

"New York City?" she exclaimed. "How did that happen? You asked to be considered by the journalism internship program in the Los Angeles area."

"I don't know. I didn't ask for New York."

"Well, you can't take it. I've spent the last couple of days trying to clear more of my schedule for you and you're leaving me to run to New York!"

"Carly, I know it wasn't my first choice, but how can I turn it down?" He took a moment to catch his breath. "I got selected from a long list of applicants."

Taking her in his arms, he said, "I'm sorry this is such bad timing, but I can't pass it up. Besides, two months isn't that long, and you've got lots of work to do, too, with your blog and final projects before graduation."

Carly pulled herself out of his embrace with an exasperated sigh. "Well, I had some news, too, but after hearing yours I'm not so excited anymore." At his look of interest, she told him about the potential film project.

"Oh, Carly," he exclaimed, "that *is* exciting. Mateo would be a fool not to bring you on." He brushed her cheek with the back of his finger. "See? The time will pass before you know it."

She knew he was right, but she didn't want to admit it. "I guess so. When do you leave?"

"Next week." He pulled her down onto the couch. "So, let's make the most of the time till then."

Though she hated seeing Dylan off at the airport, Carly's outlook brightened when she thought of her appointment to meet the movie producer for lunch. The next morning, she stepped into a coffee shop near her campus. From a table near the window, a nice-looking guy waved her over. As she settled into a chair across from Mateo Guzman, he admitted having gotten her name from one of her instructors.

"I hope you don't mind how I found you. I figured that the college would be the best place to find the talent I need for this film."

"No, I'm flattered that they recommended me."

"Well, I was most impressed by your blog. You seem to have a lot of insight about the era, and a talent for design."

"Thank you. I have a personal attachment to the time period." Carly went on to explain how she had learned about Tina and had an immediate connection with her and her work.

The two finished their lunch while sharing more about themselves, and he showed her a synopsis of the story, with the main characters and setting. He mentioned that he was still finding more sources of funding, and that he would be in touch.

He held out his hand. "Well, thank you for seeing me today. It was a pleasure to meet you."

Carly left the restaurant intrigued by the project, but with no sense of whether she'd ever see him again.

———

With Dylan in New York, Carly had plenty of time to work on her school assignments and blog. Her grades improved, and she looked forward to the end-of-the-year projects for her classes. She received abundant praise from her instructors and shared their comments with her mother.

"I'm enjoying this last semester and will probably graduate with honors," she told her mother on the phone one evening. "I do miss Dylan so much, though."

"How's his internship working out for him?"

"He's had nothing but good things to say about it. He misses me, though, as much as I miss him."

"I know that you don't like when I mention this, but this separation has been good for you. Your grades have certainly shown that." Carly wouldn't admit it to her mother, but she did have more time for school projects with Dylan so far away.

It seemed that Dylan would always be a source of contention between Carly and her mom. But just because her mother didn't have room in her life for a steady man, Carly didn't have to feel the same way. She had tried but could never understand her mom's point of view.

A few weeks later, Mateo offered her the job of costume designer for his movie. He had gotten the go-ahead from his backers to move forward with the project, and he told her to stand by for updates. She immediately called Dylan with the news.

"That's great!" he responded. "I knew you would get it."

"How's it going there?" she asked.

"Just as busy as ever. Never a dull moment. But I can't wait to get back there with you and my classes. I miss ya, babe. Are you being good?"

"I'll never tell. And what about you and those city women?"

"They don't hold a candle to you."

Soon after her phone call with Dylan, she met Mateo at the local Starbucks to talk about the concept of his film. They then followed up a couple days later. When they got down to the actual costume styles and fabrics, she invited him to her apartment. She liked hanging out with him, and they had developed a rapport. Though softspoken, he had a vision, and he expressed it with self-confidence. It was obvious that he had put his heart and soul into this story.

Though he would want her to choose the clothes for the different characters, he explained that many aspects of each scene would influence the decision. "It's important to consider the set decoration and the lighting when selecting the right costume for every person in the scene," he said.

"It didn't occur to me that there was so much to think about."

He smiled. "With your knowledge of thirties styles and fabrics, and my filmmaking know-how, we should make an excellent team."

Carly spent the last part of the semester preparing her final presentation, which would include designs from her blog and an analysis of the blog's success. The presentation went even better than she'd hoped. All her hard work had paid off.

Dylan couldn't get home to California in time to attend her graduation ceremony. He hadn't seen his parents in months, and they insisted that he owed them a visit to Upstate New York. Carly balked, but she understood family obligations. After all. His parents were paying his college tuition. That didn't make her miss him any less.

With her diploma in her hand, the popularity of her blog, some designing prospects acquired through school, and the movie costumer job, she could now call herself a fashion designer. She often thought of Tina, now knowing how she had felt when she acquired success after so many years of trying.

Dylan made it back to California just in time for his graduation ceremony. Carly took the day off to attend and then celebrate with him that night. In the days after graduation, she and Dylan talked about their future, with both living and working together in the LA area. Dylan accepted a roving reporter job for a local TV station but continued looking for something he said had more depth to it.

Carly had visions of them living in a luxury high-rise building in West Los Angeles, so she began searching for the perfect apartment. Unfortunately, there were none available, so she was forced to put their names on a waiting list.

In addition to her blog and the movie, one of Carly's school prospects came through. She couldn't wait to tell Dylan that a local manufacturer had hired her to design a sportswear collection.

"I'm glad one of us is broadening our working horizons," Dylan said bitterly when he heard her news.

His tone took her by surprise. She hadn't realized he resented her success. "I'm sorry none of those investigative reporter posts came through for you."

"Not your fault." He hugged her. "I'm happy for you. Really, I am."

They made love that night, but she sensed a remoteness between them.

———◆———

A month later, Carly realized that her schedule was once again cutting into some of their time together. Dylan seemed to take it in his stride, and they continued on an even keel. Carly tried to make up for her absences by suggesting his favorite places when they did go out.

One night, he came home from work to an empty house and a note telling him he could find his dinner in the fridge. Carly would be late but promised to make up for it in bed when she got home. He smiled and shook his head as he popped the food into the microwave.

When she got home about nine o'clock, she found him watching TV in bed. She brushed his lips with hers without a word and went in to take a shower. She came out fifteen minutes later in his favorite silky teddy. With a seductive smile, she pulled back the covers and climbed on top of him.

She moved her body up, down, and around his until she felt him stiffen, and then worked herself downward to take him into her mouth. After a few minutes, he pulled her up and turned her over and reciprocated. When her moans told him it was time, he mounted her and brought them both to a climax.

They lay there, still joined together, recovering, and caressing each other.

"That was definitely worth waiting for," he said with a smile.

"I'm glad. I've been thinking about doing that all day."

As they cooled down and cuddled back into each other's arms, they talked nothing about each other's day and fell asleep.

The next morning, as they sat eating breakfast, Carly found out why Dylan had stopped complaining about his job and the number of times she had been too busy for him.

"Carly, we were a little preoccupied last night, and I didn't get a chance to tell you my news."

Carly hoped he would tell her that he'd been promoted to an investigative reporter job at his Los Angeles station. "What's up?'

"I, uh, applied a month ago for an investigative reporter job for a network news company—and I got it!"

"Oh, Dylan. I'm so glad. I know it's what you wanted. When do you start?"

"I, uh, have to be in London in two weeks."

"London?"

"For how long?"

"At least six months."

"Six months!"

"Yeah. Look, babe, I tried getting something local, but this is the opening they had."

"That doesn't mean you have to take it!"

"Of course I do. It's the kind of break I've been hoping for. I don't want a career doing nothing but interviewing people on the street and covering grocery store openings. That's not why I went to journalism school. I thought you knew that!"

"But—"

"Your career is going in the direction you hoped for, and that's great, but I had plans, too, and this is the break I need right now."

Nothing Dylan said after that registered with Carly. All she knew was he was going to be six thousand miles away. All the plans that she had made for them came crashing down.

Christmas came and went, and they had little to say to each other. They avoided arguing, but that only left a silent void in their relationship. As his departure date approached, Carly weakened a bit. She remembered Grandma's story about Tina reconciling herself to Tommy's going to New York City to work so they wouldn't part on a bad note.

She tried doing the same, but she was not a good enough actress to hide her feelings. As a result, sarcasm took over whenever they talked about the logistics of his trip and her plans while he was gone. The day finally came, and he told her he would take an Uber to the airport to make it easier on both of them.

He wrapped his arms around her and gave her long and lingering kiss at the door.

"Take care of yourself," he said. "I love you."

The realty of his leaving hit her, and she panicked. Hugging him tighter, she said, "I love you, too. Take care of yourself over there."

Carly walked back through the empty apartment. Dylan had only been gone a few minutes and she missed him already. Six months seemed like an eternity to be apart. She remembered waiting months for him to arrive from New York when he came out to go to school. She had survived that because of the promise of them being together until they graduated.

That time had flown by, and now they faced a long separation again. Only now, the difference was that she had come to rely on him for her physical and emotional needs. She had almost forgotten how to function without him but would soon be forced to remember.

—◆—

With Dylan so far away, Carly called her school friend Alexis and arranged to meet her for lunch. They hadn't socialized much after graduation because their lives took different paths, but they got together for lunch every few months. Alexis had married well and owned a successful dress boutique in West LA.

After Carly told Alexis about Dylan's job and her feelings about that, she brought up her movie project.

"Oh, Carly. That's so exciting," Alexis exclaimed.

"I know. We never even thought about costume design in school."

"Carly, you've got a wonderful career. I love your blog, and apparently everyone else does, too. You should be very proud of yourself. I always knew you had a special spark in you to succeed."

When Carly left Alexis, she felt good about herself and her work—so much so, that she Face Timed Dylan later that night to tell him she loved and missed him.

A week later, Carly and Mateo sat in her apartment discussing his movie script.

"Carly," he said, "I've highlighted the costumes needed for each of the scenes."

"Oh, I've already made some sketches of each character's clothes for the first act," she said while spreading them out on the kitchen table. "What do you think?"

He took a long look. "Incredible. You've almost exactly captured my ideas. Now I know that my instincts were right about picking you for the job."

Carly smiled and poured him a cup of coffee. "Let's talk more about the second act."

They continued to meet every week, sometimes at her apartment, sometimes in restaurants, and even at picnic tables at the park. Costume design had been the farthest thing from her mind while in design school, but now it was what she woke up thinking about each morning.

A couple of months passed, and her projects kept her busy throughout the day, but her last thoughts at night were of Dylan. *What is he doing, and with whom is he doing it?* Face Timing was good, but it wasn't always possible with the time difference, and it didn't take the place of being next to each other.

So, when her phone rang out next to her bed in the middle of the night, she jumped to answer it.

"Oh, Carly, I'm glad I reached you," Dylan said.

"Dylan, it's so good to hear your voice," she said through a yawn.

"You too. I've missed you so much. How are you?"

Carly told him she was doing well and glad to be working with Mateo.

"Hey, I don't have anything to worry about with you and that guy, do I?" he asked, his tone sounding somewhere between joking and concerned.

"No, we're just friends. But what about you and those willing and able women over there?"

"I haven't met anyone as good as you, babe."

She was about to question if that meant he hadn't strayed when he changed the subject.

"Carly, I'm going on a special assignment, and I wanted to warn you that I may not be able to contact you for a while."

"Why? What does that mean? Are you going to be in danger?"

"Nah. But I can't tell you any more about it."

After they hung up, she lay there thinking that although he insisted he wouldn't be in danger, she didn't quite believe him.

———

Another two months went by without any word from Dylan. She missed him even more than she thought she would, especially in bed, and she really missed doing things as a couple. The one positive of his absence was that it gave her more time to spend on her blog, complete her other job for the sportswear company, and work with Mateo on the costumes. The two of them had gotten very close, spending more and more time together, shopping for ready-made costumes, working on script changes, and meetings with the producer.

He invited her to his apartment, promising her a real Peruvian dish: sea bass soaked in lime juice. He called it ceviche. All she had to bring was the wine. With little opportunities for a "date" night since Dylan had been gone, she looked forward to an opportunity to get dressed up, so she accepted.

When he opened the door that night his smile of welcome widened as he swept his glance over her from head to toe.

"Wow, you look terrific," he said.

"Thanks." She spun around to show off the dress. "I just finished making it."

After dinner, they relaxed in his living room and chatted about his life in Peru and his dream to make films.

"I can't remember a time when I didn't want to be a movie producer," he said, propping his legs up on the ottoman.

"I know. That's how it's been for me about designing clothes."

The longer they talked about their dreams, the more they drank. Carly hadn't felt so relaxed since she'd been with Dylan. She and Mateo became so laid back, in fact, that they found themselves on the floor, caressing each other. Suddenly Dylan's face flashed before her, and she sat up.

"I'd better go. I've, uh, got lots of work to do tomorrow."

The next morning, Carly awoke with a huge headache, but no regrets. It had been a close call with Mateo. She wished that she could talk to Dylan, or at least communicate with him. After last night, she wondered how much longer their relationship could survive this separation.

———◆———

Although Carly spoke with her mother once a week, she had grown weary of her mom's constant championing of her separation from Dylan. Amanda repeatedly told Carly that she needed to be free to pursue her own dreams. Carly learned not to argue with her and just let her talk.

This week, before her mother could mention Dylan, Carly said she had something else to discuss with her. "Mom, I've noticed some drop in followers on my blog."

"Yes, I've seen that when I go in there to check on it myself."

"I'm afraid that my revenue will drop, too."

Amanda chuckled. "Yes, that's the way it works, Carly."

"Any suggestions?"

"How much time are you devoting to it?"

"Well, I've been so busy with my other projects, I've been letting my assistant handle most of the day-to-day stuff."

"Well, that's OK, but I noticed that your engagement with your followers has waned, too. That's what kept everyone interested in the beginning."

"Maybe so."

"Well, with Dylan away, you should have more time for the blog, right?"

After their call ended, Carly sighed and shook her head. Her mother couldn't seem to resist saying something about her relationship with Dylan. She did have to admit that Mom was right about her blog, though. Carly didn't know how she'd do it, but she would try to devote more time to it.

During the next month, she blogged more. She posted some of the costumes she'd designed for Mateo's film, and her followers loved it.

After a few weeks, traffic had picked up a bit on her site. With that, and the date of Dylan's return approaching, Carly's future looked bright.

One early evening a few days later, Carly answered the door wiping her wet hands on a towel after washing out some dishes in the sink.

"Oh, Mateo." She let him in and pointed him to the sofa, but he didn't sit down, so she continued, "I was just going to call you. I think I figured out a way around that costume problem we've got. I think if we save the long gown for the third act it would make more of a statement. Don't you think—"

He dropped onto the sofa.

"What's the matter?" She smiled. "Don't like my fix?"

"Carly, I came to tell you that the executive producer dropped our project today."

"What? Why? Can he even do that this far into it?"

"He can and he did. He lost the financing from his backers."

Carly fell onto the sofa next to him. "Couldn't he look for the money somewhere else?"

"Believe me, I suggested he find some way to save it, but he'd already tried asking for money every place he could."

Carly saw that Mateo was on the verge of tears. She pulled him into her arms.

"I'm so sorry," she said. "I know how much this story meant to you, and how much time you've devoted to it."

She felt so bad for him that she put her own feelings aside to console him. It wasn't until after he'd left that she broke down for herself. There was so much about this movie project that was just right for her, and she felt sure they been on the verge of creating a work of art.

If she ever needed Dylan, it was now. She texted him to tell him that the film project was over. She tried to feel his comforting arms around her, imagining him soothing her the way only he could. Well, it wouldn't be long before he'd be back next to her in bed. She fell asleep holding onto that thought.

———

When she awoke and checked her messages, she was thrilled to see that Dylan had responded to her text, saying he would FaceTime her later in the morning her time. She blended a coffee drink for herself, went to her bedroom, and waited for his call.

When it came, she blurted out the whole story about Mateo's movie.

"I'm so sorry, babe. I know how much you wanted it."

"It was going to be my venture into costuming for films. I don't know if I'll ever get a chance like that again."

"Got any other jobs lined up?"

"No. I turned a couple down because of the movie."

"Well, you've still got your blog. That's a goldmine."

"Actually," she started, "it's been slowing down for a while now. I'm trying, but it's not bouncing back the way I'd hoped."

"You'll find something. Your creative mind is always working."

"I don't know about that," she said. "But at least you'll be here soon to comfort me. Your six months will be up in a week. Have you booked your return flight yet?"

Dylan didn't respond.

"Dylan? When will you get home?"

"Uh, Carly, that's one of the reasons I called. They've extended my assignment for another two months."

"What? Why?"

"They like what I've done, but there's more to do. They're figuring they'll need me at least that much longer."

Carly almost hung up on him, but gathered her composure and said, "Can't you even come home for a visit?"

"I'm working on that, but I'm not sure."

Carly knew if she stayed on with him any longer, she'd say something she'd be sorry for later. "I need to go now, Dylan. Let's talk tomorrow."

She didn't wait for his response and ended the call.

"Goddammit!" She stomped into the kitchen and flung the cold coffee cup into the sink, then whirled around and stomped back to the bedroom. She threw herself onto the bed, her mind racing through the last couple of months. She had gone from having a successful blog, a contract with a clothing manufacturer, the opportunity of a lifetime to design for a movie, and a loving man in her bed—to losing almost all of that.

She needed someone to cry to, someone to help soothe her wounds. She thought of the woman who had been there for her all her life.

She packed her overnight bag and headed toward Encinitas. Her mind darted from Dylan to Mateo, to the movie and her blog. Over the three-hour drive, she had lots of time to think about all her recent disappointments. Brushing her intermittent tears away, she barely noticed the bumper-to-bumper traffic of the crowded Friday freeways.

When she reached the freeway exit for Encinitas, she relaxed a bit at the thought of her mother's comforting arms around her. Even though Mom could sometimes put pressure on her to succeed and become her own person, Carly knew it was because she loved her. Growing up without a father was not easy for Carly, but it had to be even harder on her mom.

She pulled up in the driveway at the house about nine o'clock and saw the lights on upstairs.

Good. Mom is home.

She parked the car, grabbed her bags and hurried inside. She didn't see her mom, but she could hear the TV coming from her bedroom, so she climbed the stairs and hurried to the door.

"Mom, it's me." She pushed the door open. "I've had really bad day, and I want—"

Carly stopped short. Her nude mother was entangled on the bed with Lana, her mom's good friend.

"Mom?" Carly's hand shot to her mouth. "Oh my God! Mom!" she said and ran down the stairs.

In the kitchen, she stood with her head over the sink thinking she might vomit.

Amanda appeared in the kitchen door wearing a robe. "Carly, baby. I don't know what to say," she said as she reached out for Carly.

Carly took a deep breath and pounded the counter. "I just saw my mother in bed with a woman," she screamed. "I think that says it all."

Amanda stepped toward her daughter, but Carly walked to the other side of the room.

"I'm so sorry that you had to find out this way."

Carly paced. "Well, why didn't you tell me before?"

Amanda shrugged. "There never seemed to be a good time."

"A good time for who? Me, or you?"

Amanda stared down at her hands.

"Tell me something. If you're a lesbian, then why did you hook up with my father?"

"I was young, not really sure about my sexuality at the time, and he loved me so much."

Carly shook her head. "What a rotten thing to do to him. And to me, never letting me get to know him."

"I realize that now, but—"

"I really don't want to hear any more about it."

While Amanda pleaded for her to stay and talk it through, Carly grabbed her bag, slammed out of the house, jumped back into her car, and drove home to LA.

Because of lighter late-night traffic on the road, Carly got back to her apartment in record time. Though she rarely indulged while alone, she took a bottle of vodka out of her cupboard and mixed herself a drink. She sat up sipping it in bed, trying to make sense of the last twenty-four hours. Before she could, she dropped into a deep sleep.

The next morning, she woke up having to cope with the reality of her mother's affair with Lana, piled on top of Dylan's two-month extension in Europe, her canceled movie project, and her failing blog. Feeling she couldn't stand facing it all alone, she booked a reservation for the first flight she could find to Albany, New York.

———

Uncle John, Brooke's dad, met her at the airport with open arms. Summer in Kingsburg was lovely, as usual. As thy drove toward town, the rolling green hills on either side of the road seemed to embrace Carly and welcome her back. When they pulled into the driveway at Brooke's house, Grandma and Aunt Sandra hurried to meet her. They showered her with hugs and kisses and brought her up to date on the family.

"Oh, sweetheart," Grandma said, "it's so good to see you again, but you sounded so unhappy on the phone. Sit down and tell us what's happened."

Carly felt uncomfortable explaining the incident with her mother and Lana. But finally, she couldn't hold back her tears as she told them how hurt she was that her mother had deceived her.

"I feel like I've been living in the middle of a lie all my life."

"But it was your mother's lie. Not yours."

"True, but I feel betrayed. I mean I had a right to know about her and Lana."

"I'm sure your mom didn't think you needed to know while you were growing up," Aunt Sandra said.

"But I'm twenty-two now. She should've told me, not let me find out like that."

Grandma cleared her throat. "I think you should know that Amanda called me."

"She did? When?"

"A couple of days ago. She figured that you'd be in touch with us."

Carly dropped her head.

"She's distraught and wanted me to hear the story from her. She explained that that was why she couldn't have married your father.

I'm glad she did tell me. It made me feel better about his life with his woman friend in New York City. He never could've made your mother happy, and that would have broken his heart."

Carly nodded.

"She loves you so much, Carly. Try to forgive her for keeping her secret from you all these years."

Carly knew she had come to the right place. Grandma and Aunt Sandra said all the right things to comfort her. Before she knew it, they had changed the subject to her career. Carly brought them up do date on her successes and failures.

"Oh my gosh, Carly. Look at all the experience you've had at such a young age," Aunt Sandra said.

"How exciting to be part of making a movie," Grandma chimed in.

<hr>

A couple of days later, though still haunted by the image of her mother in bed with Lana, Carly's anger and vitriolic remarks had softened as she got more distance from the incident. It helped that Aunt Sandra drove the three of them to the lake house to take her mind off Amanda.

Just being lakeside again calmed Carly down. She looked out at the ripples and thought of Tina. So much had happened since she'd first heard about her. But learning what she had about her great-grandmother, she knew that she, too, could be strong through adversity. Sitting there deep in thought, she felt a tap on her shoulder.

"Hi, babe."

She turned to see Dylan smiling down at her.

She jumped up. "Oh my God. How did you get here?"

He threw his arms around her, and gave her a long, lingering kiss. "No matter. I'm here now, and I'm going to stay."

"How? Why?"

"They gave me a permanent assignment in New York City."

"That's wonderful for you."

"For both of us. I want you to come with me."

"Oh, I don't know—"

"Ever since we met, you've talked about being a fashion designer in New York. Now's your chance."

———

Carly and Dylan flew to California to pack their things, move out of their apartment, and take care of other moving chores. Carly bubbled with excitement about her new endeavor. *I'm finally going to get the chance to work in New York.*

That's when it occurred to her that she had never lived anywhere but California, and she panicked at the thought of living in a big metropolitan city. More importantly, she had never lived more than driving distance from her mother. Despite her recent feelings of betrayal about her, she couldn't go to New York without seeing Amanda.

Carly texted her mother to say that she would be by to pick up some things she wanted to take to New York. When she arrived, she saw her mother's car and braced herself for a confrontation. She didn't see her mother when she walked into the house, so she turned toward the stairs.

"Hello, Carly," Amanda said softly from the landing.

"Hi, Mom. I wasn't sure if you would be here."

"I couldn't let you move three thousand miles away without saying goodbye."

"I wouldn't do that," Carly said.

"But you've been so mad at me."

"Not mad. Disappointed."

"I know that finding out about my, you know—"

"It's not that. Oh, I was stunned and disgusted at first, but I've gotten past that. I have plenty of gay friends. It's the betrayal that I still feel."

"Betrayal?"

"Growing up, it's always been just you and me. I thought we were so close and had a special bond between us."

"We do."

"But you've lied to me all these years." Carly broke down in tears. "And I'm having trouble getting over that."

Amanda hurried down the stairs and pulled her into a hug. "Oh, baby. I'm sorry. I can't stand to see you so miserable. I'll never lie to you again."

After Carly had gathered the things she had come for, she and Amanda sat at the table and lunched on sandwiches.

Carly finished chewing a bite. "As much as I've always wanted to go to New York City, I'm scared. What if I bomb?"

"If you do, then you'll deal with that, too."

Carly smirked. "How can you be so sure?"

"Because I know you've not only got talent, but you have determination." She grinned. "You are my daughter, after all."

Carly beamed.

"That means that even if you don't reach the place you're aiming for, you'll find a way to accomplish something even better."

They finished their lunch, and Carly cleaned the table.

"Carly," Amanda said, "I'm sorry that I've given you so much grief over Dylan this past year. I've seen that he's really a good guy. I guess I just wanted you to reach your full potential before committing to a relationship."

"That's the great thing about Dylan, Mom. He understands how important my design work is. We support each other's goals."

Amanda nodded. "I'll miss you, baby."

"And I'll miss you. But you are the voice in my head, so you're always with me."

———◆———

A week later, Carly's plane began its slow descent into New York's JFK Airport, and Tina's face appeared in her mind's eye. Carly's heartbeat quickened as she thought about all the possibilities awaiting her. She now understood the anticipation and apprehension that Tina had felt in the 1930's as her train approached the City of Dreams. Peering out the window, she recalled Eva's fearless affinity for soaring above the clouds, and she was sure that both women were watching over her.

What a priceless legacy she'd received from the father she never knew.